UNDER LOCK AND KEY

FURY FALLS INN · BOOK 2

BETTY BOLTÉ

This is a work of fiction. Names, characters, places, and incidents are a product of the author's imagination. Locales and public names are sometimes used for atmospheric purposes. Any resemblance to actual people, living or dead, or to businesses, companies, events, institutions, or locales is completely coincidental.

www.MysticOwlPublishing.com

Dear Reader,

This story continues the series of six supernatural historical fiction stories set in 1821 northern Alabama. With each of these, I fully expect I'll discover more about the history of this state I call home.

I'd like to thank my beta readers—Leslie Scott, Rachel Capps, Anne Parent, Alicia Coleman, and daughter Danielle Bolté—who read a prepublication version of *Under Lock and Key* and provided invaluable feedback. I appreciate your time, observations, and suggestions for improving the story!

I'd also like to thank readers like you who continue to inspire me to write stories with joy and passion. I always enjoy hearing from my readers, so please drop me a line at betty@bettybolte.com any time.

If you enjoy this book, please subscribe to my newsletter via bettybolte.com be informed of the release of the rest of the books in the series. You can also learn more about me, my other books, and read excerpts of each book at my website.

Again, thanks for reading! I hope you enjoy *Under Lock and Key*.

Betty

Chapter One

What on earth was locked up in her mother's private attic? That one question nibbled at Cassie's patience. Whether she sliced carrots for Sheridan at the scarred table in the kitchen. Or ripped out weeds from around corn stalks in her abundant garden. Or sang ditties to entertain the Fury Falls Inn dining guests. No matter how she tried to occupy her time, she couldn't shake it.

She marched into the large kitchen where Sheridan and the Marple sisters bustled about preparing all manner of delicious foods. The savory aroma of simmering meat and onions met her nose, making her mouth water in response. She dithered inside, holding the smooth wood door open as she surveyed the table in the center of the room. The older sister flashed a wary look at her, one that hastily changed to welcoming.

The gray-haired woman had every right to be concerned. What if it had been Mercy who'd suddenly appeared? Working in a haunted roadside inn wasn't something most people would want to do. Even in such a progressive and seemingly enlightened area as north Alabama in 1821. Flint had convinced the sisters to return to work as scullery maids after her mother's death only because she'd been kind to them before and hoped her ghost wouldn't harm them. Not that Ma had been an easy person to work with by any account. But she'd never been physically threatening to them, so they'd somewhat reluctantly agreed to come back to earn their paycheck.

Meg, the younger of the two, grappled with a long paddle to stir the fragrant contents of an immense black cauldron hanging over the flickering cook fire. Leaning the paddle against the brick fireplace surround, she wiped her hands on a stained apron. "Hey, Cassie. How are you doing today? Feeling better?"

"The headache's finally gone. Thanks for asking." She'd suffered with a nagging pain at the front of her head for weeks after her mother died. Probably triggered by the grief and guilt swirling in her gut. Despite still feeling both emotions, the pain had finally gone away.

"You're looking like yourself again, too." A slight lift of Meg's mouth and brows accompanied the relief in her lilting voice.

"Good or bad?" Cassie chuckled and shook her head. "Just jesting with you, Meg. I'm fine."

"Glad to hear that." The tall dark-skinned cook, Sheridan, smiled at her, his golden eyes reflecting his pleasure at her presence. "Ready to help?"

Myrtle pursed her thin lips. "Are you sure you're up to it? It's only been a month since…"

"I'm fine. I promise." Cassie held up a hand to stop the flow of words that would only surge her grief over her mother's death. She inhaled, a long slow breath and then eased it out to quash the inner wave of sorrow. She met Sheridan's frown with a smile. Sheridan had become even more important to her since her ma had passed. An advisor. A calm and stable friend. She released the door she'd been holding open to swing slowly closed. Cassie strode over to peer into the cauldron hanging over the fire. "What are you making?"

"I'm expecting a crowd this afternoon for dinner, so we're all working on increasing the quantity of stew." Sheridan's eyes twinkled as crow's feet appeared at the corners. "Gotta keep folks fat and sassy."

"Smells wonderful." She smiled across the room to Sheridan, standing on the other side of the table. "Squirrel or rabbit?"

"Rabbit." Sheridan gestured at the brace of dead rabbits on a large flat tray on the table, already skinned and boned, ready to be cut up. "Flint thought it would be a good idea. Most folks seem to like it."

Warmth washed her cheeks at the mention of the handsome interim inn manager. Flint Hamilton. "I'm sure he thinks he knows what's best."

Sheridan arched a brow. "I thought you liked him."

"That depends on what you mean by 'like' now doesn't it." Her cheeks warmed more at the suggestive tone in his voice as she turned to peer into the cauldron again. Avoiding the mirth evident in her friend's expression.

"You know he's been a good thing for the inn, don't you?" Sheridan chuckled when Cassie refused to look at him. "Even if he can be bossy at times."

She harbored conflicting feelings about Flint. On one hand, the young man had come to the inn at her father's request so Pa could go take care of business in Georgia. An unwelcome surprise that became more welcome the longer Flint stayed. She liked his ways, his touch, his strong features. His steady management of the property led to improvements which increased business. Despite some rough patches at first, he'd proven to be a good addition. Attractive and kind, they'd grown fond of each other despite her mother's objections. Maybe because of them, if she were honest.

"And those rabbits are free for the hunting, which means more profit for the business." Sheridan eased his chin higher and then nodded once. "That's good management, in my book."

"The added benefit being fewer of the varmints to eat my garden." She needed any distraction from the uncomfortable conversation about her attraction to Flint. She pressed her palms on the wood surface piled with fresh beans and tomatoes, waiting for Myrtle's quick knife. "You can serve rabbit stew as often as you'd like."

She'd put a halt to any further developments to a relationship with Flint until her pa came home. Whenever that might be. She was confused. She needed to know whether he agreed with her ma that Flint wasn't the right man for her. Having only turned eighteen years of age, she wasn't certain of her own mind and heart. Marrying the wrong man could be devastating given the rarity of divorce. If she married the wrong kind of man, she might well die, emotionally or worse physically, from the decision. Better to be sure. If that meant delaying, then delay she would. Only, she had to find a way to distract herself from the sudden curiosity invading her thoughts. She gave up feigning interest in the stew and pivoted to face Sheridan.

Sheridan wiped his hands on his apron. "You wouldn't mind more venison either then?"

The suppressed humor in his voice brought a smile to her face. "That would be a resounding yes. Those hooved demons have no business invading my garden." She didn't need any more incidents like the last one.

The herd of deer living on their mountain had taken a fancy to the variety of plants she'd planted. All her hard work and attention was not for the benefit of the wild critters. The special fence kept them out as long as the gate remained closed. She grimaced at the memory of Flint inside, trying to shoo several deer out. His way of apology for the destruction of a third of her garden was to improve the gate so it swung shut and latched closed. Even that had been thwarted by young Teddy, an urchin who had been caught stealing vegetables.

"Where's Teddy?" Cassie glanced at each of the people working in the kitchen. "Shouldn't he be in here helping?"

"Fetching a bucket of water from the well." Sheridan sliced the rabbit into chunks with a butcher knife and placed the pieces back on the tray. "With all the additions we're preparing I needed more water, too."

Her heart sank as he deftly cubed the meat. "Looks like you don't need my help right now."

"No, we've got this under control." Sheridan waved the knife at her, shooing her out the door. "Run along and find something else to do."

Which left her at loose ends. Time on her hands. Intrigue swelling in her mind. Gramercy. Could she actually resist the temptation?

"Fine. Yell if you need me." She strolled out of the kitchen and paused in the large entrance hall of the inn.

The double doors stood open to allow the slight breeze into the building. The vase on the table beside the doorway held a mix of wilting pink and red roses. She should replace those soon. She squinted at the dining room. Perhaps she'd go play a few songs on the piano to entertain the few folks enjoying a cup of coffee or ale before heading on to their next destinations. But her thoughts strayed to the attic. Glancing about her, she didn't see anyone who would try to stop her. No one who could give her a reason to not attempt to gain access to the forbidden room.

Stealthily, she crossed the dog trot to the residence side of the inn, a strong wind blowing through the tunnel-like porch. Through the family parlor, past the troubling doll's house her father had sent for her eighteenth birthday, and up the stairs on the other side of the room. Perhaps when he returned she'd learn why on earth he'd sent her a child's toy. Her mother's hurtful explanation of him thinking of her as a child still rattled in her mind. Shaking her head, she eased down the short hall to her parents' bedroom.

Thunder rolled across the heavens, announcing the approach of a summer storm. Stopping at the closed door for a moment, she waited a beat and then slowly opened it. The scent of lavender wafted to her nostrils. She let out a relieved sigh. Everything had been put to rights after the attack on her mother.

She was grateful for the neighbor women lending a hand after the terrible way her mother had been killed. Now the silent bedroom her parents had shared for many years waited for Pa to finally come home. An event she longed for with her entire being. Everything would be fine once he was home and could hug her when she needed reassurance. She longed to have a heart-to-heart conversation with him about her mother's concerns regarding Flint. Then she'd find it easier to decide whether to follow her heart as she longed to do. She searched the silent space, noting the pretty quilt on the bed, the looking glass on the dressing table by the window. She stared at the tempting circular staircase leading up to the attic. She searched the room again with a sweep of her gaze. No sign of her mother's haint. Good.

She quickly crossed to the metal stairs and silently placed each foot as she ascended to the locked door. Grabbing the door knob she twisted, or tried. The knob didn't turn. Just like she'd feared.

She examined the door, searching for a way to gain entry. Any chink in the door. She ran her hand over the solid wood, no crevices or knots to exploit. She grabbed the door knob and shook it but it barely budged. Perhaps Sheridan could remove the barrier for her. The hinges were not visible, so the door would swing inward. Given the steep steps, that made perfect sense. But also the arrangement made it difficult to break it down. Blast. A cool breeze brushed her cheek as the heavens rumbled again.

"What do you think you're doing?"

"Oh!" Cassie whirled around, clutching the cold metal

railing with both hands to prevent her from tumbling down the steps. "Don't do that. You nearly caused me to have an apoplexy."

"Same to you." Mercy hovered at eye level, hands on her hips, on the outside of the circular staircase. "You have no business trying to open that door."

Cassie released the railing and stared at her mother's ghost wearing the blue flowered dress she'd been buried in, her ash blonde hair hanging in a queue down her back. But her aqua eyes studied her with fear lurking in the shadows. Cassie surprisingly sensed a hint of panic forming in her mother. Or was she merely detecting it in her expression? "Why? What's on the other side that you don't want me to see?"

Shifting her gaze sideways, Mercy crossed her arms over her chest. "Nothing for you to worry about."

"I think there is. I can't stop thinking about what is hidden in your private little attic." Indeed, the unusual and unbidden interest welling up inside consumed her thoughts day and night. A terrible need to see into the attic began a few weeks before, nibbling and gnawing at her until she thought she'd lose her mind.

Mercy speared her with a wide-eyed gaze, brows arched. "What do you mean? You can't stop thinking about it?"

"What have you tucked away in there?" Cassie hunched her shoulders and started down the steps. She'd have to try again some other time. Some other way. "You've shared everything with me. Or at least I thought we didn't have secrets from each other."

"Secrets?" Mercy averted her eyes but kept level with Cassie as she descended to the bedroom floor. "I don't have…any secrets."

Detecting the hesitancy in her mother's words along with surprise, Cassie stared at her until she blinked several times and glanced away again. "Are you sure, Ma?"

"I'm more intrigued by your sudden curiosity. You haven't seemed to worry about it until now. What's changed?"

Cassie pursed her lips. "You're changing the subject."

"I think it's interesting." Mercy drifted away to gaze out the window for a moment, rain lashing the pane while lightning flashed, before turning to face Cassie. "Why the sudden curiosity?"

"What do you mean?" Cassie hedged, detecting resistance and yet interest from her ma.

Mercy's voice quavered as she came closer to Cassie. "Tell me what's piqued your curiosity about my little attic after all these years."

She regarded her ma for a moment, a sense of concern flowing into her chest. "It's probably just because I know Giles is on his way and will demand answers as to whether those men stole anything out of the attic. Which I can't answer without going into the attic to see what's in there."

"Giles is coming? Good." She nodded to herself, her eyes distant for a moment. Then Ma peered closely at her. "I can tell you that they did not steal a thing from the attic. Only the keys to the door and to what's inside."

Her mother's words both assuaged her concern and made her curiosity flare brighter. A swarm of angry bees buzzed through her veins, propelling her toward discovery. "What's inside that needs keys to unlock?"

Mercy worried her bottom lip. "Nothing you need. It's just family heirlooms and old stuff. Don't worry about it so."

"Family heirlooms? From what family? My grandmama?" Cassie glared up the stairs. She longed to place a foot on the tread and climb up, but she stayed at the bottom. The door prevented her from seeing the hidden treasure she sensed lurking behind it. "And more importantly, exactly when did you get those heirlooms?"

"It's not important. Not yet. I've said too much already."

Mercy pressed her lips into a flat line with a flash of distress in her eyes and then vanished.

A crack of thunder shook the house as the wind whipped the rain against the window. She jumped at the sound and the sight and then exhaled her jumpiness.

"Ma, come back here." Cassie cast about hoping her mother's ghost would reappear and answer her questions. One second she was there and the next, poof. The empty room met her hopeful search. She started for the door, pausing before closing it behind her to address the room. "I will find out. Just you wait and watch me."

Giles urged his horse into a brisk trot, his long legs pressed firmly against the charcoal gray gelding. His companions rode close by, the darker skinned man's bass voice entertaining them as they journeyed together. They'd been riding for days and their destination grew closer by the minute.

"What's the hurry?" Zander Simmons stopped singing as he pulled up even with Giles, his brother Matt close behind on his chestnut horse.

His friends, once terribly abused slaves on a Louisiana plantation, had stuck with him through thick and thin. He'd first encountered them a couple of years before when delivering the planter's order of goods from Barbados. He'd seen the man whipping two black backs, punishment for something they hadn't done he later discovered. He couldn't in good conscience allow them to be beaten by the overseer one more day. So he'd traded the goods for the men, foregoing any cash payment, then immediately freed them. In exchange, they'd promised to help him with building and managing his import business in Mobile. Their varied talents and skills proved invaluable time and again.

"I have a feeling I need to get there. Soon." Giles glanced at Zander and then back at Matt.

Matt had managed to control his temper after he'd gained his freedom, but Zander still struggled to restrain the impulse to lash out, to fight back when challenged. By and large he succeeded but there were times when he could see revenge seething in his eyes. He'd become a strong and decent man despite the abuse. Pride and respect filled his chest as he met Zander's questioning gaze.

"My friend, I can tell you're anxious to see your sister." Zander dipped his wide-brimmed hat as he nodded. "Pay your respects to your mama, too."

"Very true." Swallowing the discomfort of confronting his mother's grave, he frowned as the sense of danger lurking at the edge of his consciousness increased. He inhaled the scent of Southern pine trees yet detected no apparent threats. Nonetheless, his unease remained high. An odd, disconcerting feeling. "I don't know whether any of my brothers are going to come. Cassie didn't say in her letter."

Zander adjusted his reins with a slight movement, his horse's head lifting from where it had dropped down. Saddle leather creaked as he settled his mount. "When was the last time you saw your family?"

"I was sixteen when I rode away from home for the last time." His papa had made it clear he would need to support himself as soon as he reached an age to earn a living. What wasn't so clear was the need behind his father's conviction. "Papa said I was old enough to strike out on my own."

"That's harsh." Zander's reply held a hint of anger in the deep voice.

"I did all right." What had happened that his mother wanted him to become self-sufficient at such an age? Maybe one day he would understand what it was or why she'd become so quick to anger. For the moment, his mission was to make sure his sister stayed safe and well provided for. "I'm a survivor."

Still the question echoed in his mind as he rode down the peaceful lane, the dust hot and dry in his nose and throat. Would he see his brothers at the inn? His father? A shudder racked his shoulders and he slowed his horse to a walk to calm the concern sloshing in his gut. Even his father had stifled his desires by denying Giles any attempt to become closer to him. Pushing him away firmly though with less urgency than his mother. Was it something he'd done but didn't realize that made his parents want nothing to do with him? He'd most likely never know, especially now that his mother had been killed. Not until his father arrived.

"I thought you were in a hurry." Zander slowed to match Giles' pace as Matt kept trotting for several more strides. He lifted a brow at him, his eyes searching Giles' expression.

"I'm sorry." Giles rested a hand on his thigh, the smooth leather reins gripped easily in his other hand. He stared ahead, down the gently winding dirt road snaking along the base of a series of low mountains. Matt dropped back to a walk and waited for them to catch up. "I feel like I must get there but at the same time I don't want to go."

"Why wouldn't you want to see your family?" Zander moved with the horse's long rhythmic stride, his shoulders thrown back and head held high. "I'd do anything to be able to see my parents again."

"I know. Since you were torn from them I can only imagine. And I have thought about coming home. For a visit only, of course. But not like this."

"I'll never see my parents again. Pop died in a carriage accident and Mama—"

"I wish I could do something about your mother's situation." Giles shook his head at Zander. "Seriously. If I could…"

"It's not your problem." Zander's eyes darkened as he looked at his brother riding in front of them. "It would do him a lot of good if we could have our family back together. But I don't see that happening."

"Do you know where your mother is?" At least he knew where his parents lived and worked. Or rather where his mother once lived. He imagined his papa would hurry back to the inn after hearing about her death. Surely he wouldn't ignore the events at home because of business. But then again, he was nothing if not a practical, and very stubborn, man. If the business wasn't completed to his satisfaction, he most likely wouldn't travel all the way home.

"Last I heard she was a seamstress to some plantation mistress outside of Charleston." Zander slowed his horse as Matt dropped back to join the conversation. He shrugged at Giles. "But that was when I was a little boy so who knows now where she is."

"Do you know how much farther we have to go?" Matt twisted in his saddle to look back at him as he rode closer. "I'm hungry. I keep picturing a juicy pork chop with brown gravy, and a nice fresh greens salad with a light dressing." He smacked his lips and grinned.

"Another few miles, I think. You may have to fight the inn's cook to prepare your meal, I'd wager. Cassie says he rules the kitchen." Giles smirked at his friend's crestfallen face. Matt's talent as a chef was well known in Mobile, and Giles enjoyed many a fine meal as a result. He spotted a ponderous coach-and-four listing at the side of the road ahead. "Looks like they've broken a wheel."

Zander followed the direction of Giles' gaze. "Guess we're going to help, right?"

"May as well. Come on." Giles urged his horse into a trot and soon they reached the broken down vehicle.

A man, wearing clothes much too fine for hard labor, struggled to wrest the shattered wheel from the carriage. A woman stood off to one side in a ruffled burgundy gown with black trim and matching bonnet, holding a frilly black parasol to protect her head from the strong summer sun. She leveled a surprised look at the three men halting behind the vehicle.

"Can we help, sir?" Giles rested his hands on the horn of his saddle. "Or can you manage?"

From the looks of things, the man didn't have a clue how to change let alone replace a wheel. The man's fancy trousers and suit coat declared him a gentleman. The beaver-felt top hat resting on the step of the carriage added to the impression. Zander knew how to work with carriages and wheels as he'd learned to make and repair the wooden wheels wrapped with metal among other skills. A spare wheel hung underneath the coach but would be difficult to reach with the right rear wheel in pieces. What a strange setup. He'd have put the spare on the top, but perhaps having it underneath kept it out of the way until needed. There must be a better place to put it. Something to ponder another time.

The sweaty man looked up at the sound of Giles' voice. "I'd greatly appreciate any help offered."

Giles glanced at Zander. "Do you mind?"

"No, sir." Zander swung out of the saddle and handed the reins to Matt. "This will take a while."

"I can help if you want." Matt prepared to dismount, hesitating for a split second as he waited for his brother's response.

"All right." Zander strode over to the man's side but didn't look him in the eyes. "I'm Zander, and this man is my brother, Matt."

"And I'm Giles Fairhope." Giles noticed the lack of last names as well as the reflexively averted eyes but kept his own peace. But he'd make one thing perfectly clear. He'd discovered it made a difference in how his dark-skinned friends were treated. "These two men are my friends and fellow workers. Not my servants."

The man blinked several times then nodded, understanding dawning in his narrowed eyes. "I'm John Baker."

"Nice to meet you, sir." Zander tipped his hat to the woman without meeting her gaze. "Mrs. Baker."

She angled her parasol to shade her face more as she addressed the group. "I'm glad you've come along. We almost made it home to Riverwood." She gestured toward a lane a little way down the road.

Zander grinned at her words. "That being the case, we can help you home and out of the heat."

Matt tied the reins in his hands to a tree alongside the road, then stalked back to stand beside his brother. Giles sat his horse, waiting for the two experienced men to assess the situation and solve the issue. He relied upon their skills and knowledge every single day in one way or another. He'd been very fortunate to find them and have them agree to work with him. Their abilities had made his business even more successful than he'd imagined. Combined, they had a wide array of skills and abilities they'd developed over the ensuing years the three men had worked together.

"First we need to get this spare one off the bottom." Zander bent down to peer at the hung wheel.

"Can you remove it?" Matt pushed his hat back on his head, rubbing his arm across his glistening brow.

"It's pinned by the coach. We're gonna have to lift the coach up and then drop this here wheel." Zander straightened and shook his head. "It's not gonna be easy."

"You two lift the coach and I'll get the wheel. Ready?" John positioned himself near the spare and waited for the other two to move to the other side of the vehicle.

Zander grabbed hold of the bottom of the coach, Matt lending a hand beside him. Muscles strained as the two men grappled with the coach. John fumbled with the dried leather straps holding the wheel in place. Matt tried to shift his hands on the heavy frame, one hand coming away and then grabbing for a handhold. Giles tensed as his pulse raced. He dropped the reins across his horse's withers.

"It's slipping…" Matt grunted as he struggled to keep a grip on the varnished wood.

John pulled the last of the straps off and dragged the wheel away from the coach just as Matt's hands slipped off and he fell backward, the full weight of the coach crashing down, pinning him beneath it.

Damn. Giles leapt from the saddle and sprinted to help, his horse shying to one side in a clatter of hooves and creaking leather. Zander scrambled to help but, strong as he was, could only lift the coach an inch off of Matt. Not far enough for the groaning man to pull his left leg out from under it. Giles raced to a sliding halt at Zander's side and grabbed hold of the coach and lifted with all his strength. The massive vehicle lurched two feet up off the ground.

"Get him out of there. Quick." Surprised relief flooded through Giles but he didn't know how long he could hold the vehicle. His muscles worked to steady the heavy coach, his lungs burning from the effort.

Zander quickly dragged Matt to safety while Giles held the coach by himself. Shocked at his ability to maintain his hold, he darted a glance at John's stunned gaze. With Matt safe, Giles lowered the coach to the ground and dusted off his hands.

"How'd you do that?" John cautiously approached Giles, a wary look in his narrowed eyes.

"I don't know, but I'm glad I could." He'd always been strong, but he'd never experienced anything like what had just happened. Perhaps the fear of his friend being permanently injured or even killed had spurred him to such strength. The buzz of energy flowed through his veins as he rotated his hands, inspecting them for any visual changes.

"Me, too." Matt slowly stood, favoring the leg with a gash seeping red. "It's not too bad, thank goodness. But man, that was incredible. Thank you."

Giles indicated the coach with a tilt of his head. "We still need to get the wheel on that thing."

Matt limped over to the wheel laying on the ground. He set it up on its edge to roll it around to hand off to Zander. He looked at Giles, brows arched over wide, twinkling eyes. With a sigh of combined relief and confusion, Giles walked over to appraise the situation. Rubbing his hands together, then flexing his fingers, he bent down to take hold of the thing again. With a grunt, he heaved and lifted the coach.

"That's incredible." John crossed his arms and shook his head slowly.

"Hurry up, Zan." Giles strained to steady the coach while the other man wiggled the hub onto the axle.

"Got it." Zander held onto the wheel while Matt secured it in place over the next several minutes.

Time enough for Giles to marvel at how strong he'd become in a moment of panic. But how? He hadn't changed his routines or tried to build more muscle. He'd never needed to worry about being able to handle whatever came his way. But this? This was new.

"Done." Matt stepped back, indicating to Giles he could release his grip.

He let go and rubbed his hands on his pant legs to wipe off the dirt from the underside of the coach. Zander led the gray over to Giles and handed him the reins. He nodded a thank you to his friend and then addressed the plantation owner. "There you go, Mr. Baker."

"That was indeed amazing. Thank you for fixing the wheel." John sauntered over to Giles. "Where you heading?"

"Fury Falls Inn." The mere name of the place sent a tremor through his shoulders. He squared them to still the unfamiliar sensation.

"You're nearly there." John motioned down the road, a dip of his brows hinting at his feelings about the place. "It's two miles from Riverwood to the inn."

"So you know it?" Just how neighborly were the Bakers to his family? Giles surreptitiously studied the couple, the silent communication flowing between them with each long look and tightened lips.

"Sure do. Reggie and I are business partners." John pulled a white handkerchief from his coat pocket and mopped his brow. "I've been keeping an eye on the young man he hired to run the inn in his absence."

"Why?" First his father decided to up and go so far from home without even waiting for his wife to return home. Then he hired someone to take his place but obviously didn't trust him. Otherwise, why have someone keeping watch over his performance? The sense of urgency ratcheted up in his gut. Could Cassie be in danger from the unknown manager? What kind of danger?

John folded his handkerchief and tucked it back into his pocket. "He's a real particular idea of what he wanted. He said Flint Hamilton would do a fine job since he's worked at his father's hotel downtown for years. And he wasn't wrong."

"So you've been in touch with my father?"

John raised his brows as he nodded. "You're one of Reggie's boys?"

"Yes, sir."

"Welcome home." John offered his hand to shake.

Giles accepted the handshake, surprised at the firm grip. "I'm just visiting. My sister asked me to come help out for a spell."

John flinched as his brows dipped into a concerned frown. "What do you mean?"

Strange reaction. Giles blinked as he peered at the man.

"Well, with Papa away and Mama murdered, she feels vulnerable. So I decided to come see the situation for myself and do whatever I can to make her feel more secure."

Mrs. Baker sauntered closer and caught Giles' attention with a slight wave of her fingers. "Did I hear correctly that you're Reggie and Mercy's son? Giles, is it?"

"Yes, ma'am." Giles tipped his simple felt hat to her.

"I'm Tabitha Baker, an acquaintance of Mercy's." Tabitha clutched the handle of her parasol with her gloved hands. She sounded friendly and yet a thread of something ran through the tone of her greeting. "I was so sorry about your mother's death. I did what I could to help your sister through it. Such a tragedy."

"Yes, ma'am." He still had his own reservations as to whether his mother's death was a tragedy or not, but Cassie loved her and had been devastated at her death. Why else would she have written to him pleading for him to come to her? His protective instincts flared with the memory of her entreaty. "Now that we have the carriage serviceable, we'll need to be on our way. Cassie is waiting for me."

"Surely you'd enjoy a rest and some refreshments before you continue?" Tabitha smiled up at him, inviting him to agree with her suggestion. "Your sister would understand."

"As tempting as that sounds, I must decline." Something in the woman's expression gave him pause. A particular glint of humor or insight reflected in their depths. As if she knew something about him he didn't. But how could that be when they'd never met before? "Shall I send your regards to Cassie?"

"Please. Let her know we'll come for dinner soon." Tabitha glanced at John. "Right, dear?"

"Yes. I make it a point to visit several times a week." John glanced at the two men preparing to remount their horses and then he looked up at Giles. "I like to keep an eye on the neighborhood, make sure everything and everyone is safe and sound. You know what I mean?"

John, too, had a hidden meaning lurking in his eyes as he studied Giles for several seconds. As Giles gathered his reins to mount, those protective instincts he'd first experienced earlier intensified the longer he looked into those shining eyes. "Yes, sir. I do."

Flint's shoulders burned through his cotton shirt under the brutal August sun. He dragged his shirtsleeve across his sweaty brow. Despite the heat, he must fix the roofing. With a sigh, he hammered the shingle into place. Rain threatened. He smelled its approach with each breath.

Pausing after the last tap of the hammer, he glanced at Teddy clinging to the ladder propped against the porch roof. "Hand me the next one."

"Yes, sir." Teddy reached into the bucket hanging from a hook on the side of the wooden ladder and pulled out another oak shake shingle. He held it up in a trembling hand.

"You won't fall as long as you keep a hand on the ladder." The scrawny boy was still in single digit years. His mop of dark brown hair and soulful brown eyes made him appear more urchin than child. Flint couldn't quite fathom what the child's home life must have been like before landing at the inn. From what he'd seen, the boy enjoyed the step up. "Trust me?"

"Y-yes, sir."

Flint took it quickly and then surveyed the remaining damage. Three shingles had come loose and fallen to the ground several days before during a sudden squall. Fortunately, nobody had been injured. Despite the clear blue skies above he knew within a day rain would arrive and a hole in the roof would threaten the interior of the inn. He couldn't have that. A leaky roof didn't make for a place people wanted to stay, which would lead to them not wanting to return and a decline in business. Thus, Flint had braved the heat of the midafternoon to fix it.

"Will that be all, sir?" Teddy clung to the two rails of the ladder, pleading with wide eyes.

"You sure you don't want to come on up here with me?" Flint gestured at the shimmering heat rising from the wood shingles and on to the surrounding hills. "You can see for miles."

Teddy's knuckles turned white as he shook his head. "I'm not one for high places."

Flint took pity on the kid. He didn't know he was afraid of heights. "Go on with you. But stay at the bottom until I come down, hear?"

Flint waited for the boy's nod and then resumed hammering the last shingle into place. Teddy demonstrated amazing bravery for a nine-year-old. He'd climbed up and down the ladder several times without verbal complaint, just the worry etched on his young face. He tapped the last fastener in place and then surveyed the activity below him. Late afternoon meant only a few customers coming and going. Give it another couple of hours and the supper rush and overnighters would arrive. Time enough to manage a few small tasks before then.

Grasping the hammer in one hand, he moved to climb down the ladder. Teddy stood looking up at him. "Hold the bottom."

The boy followed Flint's direction and then Flint started down the rungs. He'd almost reached the bottom when he heard forceful footsteps echo on the porch floor. Now what?

Dropping the last couple of feet to the crushed stone carriageway that circled in front of the building, he handed the hammer to Teddy. "Can you manage the tools, son? Looks like I've got another fire to put out."

"Fire?" Teddy glanced frantically around, eyes wide.

Flint chuckled at the shocked expression before patting the boy lightly on the head. "Just a saying. Go on."

"Yes, sir." Teddy snatched up the bucket of tools and lugged them across the drive to the tool shed to put them away.

Flint caught a whiff of cornbread baking, his mouth watering at the scent, as he greeted a pair of merchants on their way past him and up the steps to the inn. A couple of the dogs loped across the carriageway and disappeared into the barn. He glanced at the clear blue sky with traces of white clouds. Cassie hurried toward him. He climbed up the few steps to wait for her.

"Flint, I need your help." Cassie rushed up to him, her ankle-length calico skirts swirling to a halt.

He wiped his hands on his pants as he noted her flushed cheeks and fetching sparkling eyes. "What's wrong?"

"Can you break into Mother's attic?" She propped her fists on her slim hips, her eyes searching his.

"Maybe. Why?" Her tone suggested a resolve reflected in the tense stance she'd assumed.

"I can't stand not knowing." She hugged her waist as she chewed her bottom lip. "There is something important inside. I can feel it."

Her words quavered with intensity. "Can you be more specific?" He arched a brow and shifted his weight to stand squarely.

She huffed, letting out a long frustrated sigh. "I know with all my being that my mother is hiding something important in that room."

Mercy likely hid a lot of things from Cassie. From everyone. She was a very reserved woman when it came to sharing. In fact, he didn't know much about her at all. Other than the very clear fact of her dislike of his person. As far as she was concerned, he could do nothing right. But if she had mementoes filled with meaning and memories, he wouldn't blame her for locking them away. With so many people in and out, it was wise.

"I doubt she would have locked the door otherwise." He shrugged one shoulder. "When your father comes back, then he can open it."

"You don't understand." Cassie twirled away and flung her arms out as she turned back to face him. "I don't want to wait that long. Ma has been no help, either."

Although he'd encountered ghosts on more than one occasion, he still didn't enjoy the experience. He swallowed back the discomfort welling in his throat. "You spoke to her again?"

"Briefly. Long enough for her to tell me to stay out of the room and then disappear without answering any of my questions."

"Then that's what you should do. Stay out of the room." He shrugged lightly.

Her parents must have secreted personal belongings in the attic, away from prying eyes and hands. Most parents would keep their private belongings away from the little ones. Not that the attractive woman pleading with him was a child. Far from it. On the other hand, what if the supposed fictional treasure were in fact a reality, hidden behind a locked door?

Still, whatever was in the room really didn't belong to Cassie. "I'm certain your father will answer your questions when he gets back."

"That's months from now and you well know it." Cassie stomped a foot on the wooden floor, raising a puff of dust to settle back onto the boards.

Her petulance surprised him. Since she'd turned eighteen last month, she'd acted more mature, more grown up. The death of her mother must have undermined her new sense of confidence to some degree, but at least she had seen her mother's ghost and was able to speak with her. Whether that proved good or bad was left up for debate.

He peered at her with what he hoped was a supportive expression. "I understand your—"

"No, you don't. Don't even think you do!" She glared at him, folding her arms across her stomach. "I can't explain it but I have this feeling I must get into that attic and find out what's in there. I have to."

He couldn't agree to help her. He'd been hired to manage the inn, not break into his employer's private rooms. But the plea shining in those beautiful eyes melted his determination into a puddle of acceptance. "I'll see what I can do, but I still think you should wait."

"Thank you, Flint. I mean that." Cassie dropped her arms to her sides as she aimed her brightest smile at him. "I think it will help to solve the mystery as to who murdered my mother."

"How is that?"

"I don't know. Not until you open the door at least." She tugged on his arm, trying to pull him toward the open front doors. "Let's go."

"Now?" He pulled back, bringing them both to a halt. He glanced at the slowly setting sun, the trio of riders approaching, and then to the stack of boxes near the door, waiting to be carried inside and dispersed. "Surely it can wait until tomorrow."

"Please? I don't want to wait any longer." She pulled on his arm again, her eyes wide and hopeful.

"And I don't want to have to fix the door, too, so let me think about how we might get inside without having to break it off its hinges or whatever."

"But…" She pouted up at him, blinking rapidly.

The sound of hooves on the carriageway drew his attention from the anxious features of the girl he suspected he had fallen in love with despite the freeze she'd put on expressing his affection. As he stepped closer to the edge of the porch, he mused about their relationship.

He'd agreed to give her time and space for her benefit, not his. Though the fact that she'd hesitated gave him some doubts as well. He shaded his eyes with a hand as he walked down the steps. Three men on horseback rode toward the inn at a steady trot. He admired the horses, all sleek and fit, obviously well cared for.

"Who is that?" Flint didn't wait for an answer but strode farther away from the porch.

"Who…" Cassie caught up to him and raised a hand to shield her eyes from the sun. Then squealed before running across the open space to meet the white man on his charcoal gray horse. "You came!"

The burly man swung lithely from the saddle and grabbed Cassie up into a bear hug, holding her close. Flint strode out to join the group as the two black men dismounted from their chestnut horses, delight on their faces at the happy reunion. Given her shout, she'd been expecting whoever the man might prove to be. So, logically, it must be one of her brothers. He didn't know which one but he'd soon find out.

The man released Cassie to place her gently on the ground, as though he didn't want to break her. "I got here as soon as I could."

"I'm so glad you're here. Let me introduce you." She linked her arm in his and turned to face Flint. "Giles Fairhope, this is Flint Hamilton, the inn keeper while Pa is away."

Giles extended his hand and Flint clasped it. When he pulled his hand free, his fingers ached from the suppressed strength in the large man. He rubbed his hand down his thigh and surveyed the other two men.

"Nice to meet you. Who do you have with you?" Flint included the other men with his smile of welcome.

"Zander and Matt Simmons, my compatriots and friends." Giles tapped Cassie's hand where it rested on his arm. "Do you have room for us to stay here?"

"We'll make room, won't we?" She addressed Flint with her last question, glee plain on her face.

"Of course." He'd do anything to keep her smiling at him with such joy in her expression. "I'll have one of the girls freshen rooms for you. How many will you need?"

Giles glanced at his companions and a silent exchange passed between them. "One should suffice if you've some bunk beds. Two, if not. Now, Cassie, tell me what happened to Mama."

Teddy strolled across the carriageway to join the group. His shirt stretched across his chest and his pant legs didn't quite cover his bare ankles. Flint tapped a finger on his thigh, assessing the boy. Cassie might be capable of making him new clothes. He'd need new shoes before long, too, which would mean a trip to the cobbler. Flint welcomed him with a slight nod.

"It's a long story. But the short version is three men mistakenly thought she had a treasure in her room and when she couldn't give it to them they killed her." She shook her head as tears glistened in her eyes. "And took her special keys."

Giles stared at her for a beat and then frowned. "Keys? Why?"

"We're not sure why, but they open Mother's secret attic door for one thing." She swished her long skirts about her legs with jerky movements. "Can you help us find the men and keys? It's important."

"One of the reasons I came was to find those men and bring them to justice, one way or another. I'll stay long enough to do that much." Giles shot a frown at Flint who nodded in agreement. "But tell me first what's in the attic?"

"Possibly other family heirlooms, from what Ma told me earlier today." Cassie grabbed his arm, pulling him close. "You've got to help me."

Teddy opened his mouth, then snapped it shut as her words registered. His eyes widened. He shifted his weight, ready to spin around to go back from where he came.

Giles startled as the two black men took a step back in surprise. He peered at his sister, brows arched. "You spoke to our mother? Today?" He glanced at Flint for confirmation.

Flint didn't fault Giles for not believing his sister. Maybe even considered she'd lost her reason. "Let's talk about this inside." He pointed toward the steps leading onto the porch. "Cassie, why don't you show them into the parlor while I have someone take care of their horses."

"I'll do it." Teddy was quick to grasp the reins of the three horses and hurry them away toward the stable.

Flint huffed as the kid scurried away. He'd avoid the uncomfortable conversation, too, if at all possible. "Hey, Teddy! Bring in their saddlebags and stuff when you're done, you hear?"

"Yes, sir!" The boy practically ran with the three horses across the busy carriageway and into the shadowy barn.

Flint pivoted to follow the small group inside for a discussion he really didn't want to have.

Chapter Two

Memories of his childhood home outside of Montgomery resurfaced with a vengeance when Cassie led him into the large room. He stumbled, over nothing, as his swift perusal took in the contents of the family parlor and dining room. His mother had been so proud of the chairs surrounding the table for ten, with their fancy scrollwork and tapestry seats. Ones she'd obtained by trading her pastoral paintings. The painted floor boards wore her favorite colors of red and blue. Even the brocaded drapes brought to mind similar ones that had hung in the other home. His survey brought him to an immense doll's house, an anomaly if ever he'd seen one.

"What is that doing there?" Giles lifted a brow at his sister.

"Pa's birthday present to me." Cassie screwed her mouth into a disgusted smile. "Don't ask."

Giles stood in the center of the room for a moment, taking in the rest of the furniture and furnishings. A large fireplace graced the outside wall with comfortable chairs and side tables in a casual group in front.

"Go ahead, take a seat." Cassie motioned to the chairs with a wave of one hand. "It's better if you're not standing for this conversation."

"That bad?" He strode over to one and sat down. Gestured to his friends to do likewise. They took chairs opposite him as Cassie sank onto one beside him.

"I wouldn't say it's bad necessarily." She glanced around the group and then at Flint as he strode into the room. "Not really."

"All right, tell me what happened. Everything." Giles rested back, crossing his arms over his chest.

His little sister exhibited all the signs of nervous anxiety. Her mouth worked and her head slightly bowed, her hair half obscuring her slight frown. She drew in a shaky breath and glanced up at him, then away.

"I don't know how to say this." Cassie stared at her clasped hands in her lap, chewing on her lower lip. She sucked in another long breath and then raised her eyes to stare at him. "It's all my fault."

Flint grunted from where he stood. Giles understood the rough denial in the singular sound. Curious.

"No, it's not your fault at all." Flint moved to stand by Cassie's chair. "Don't think that way, Cassie."

"I can't help it. If I hadn't been a silly girl and let my mouth run away with nonsense, then those men wouldn't have had the impression there was something worthwhile hidden in her bedroom."

Giles leaned forward to rest his elbows on his knees, his chest tight and pulse beating in his ears. He frowned when he spotted tears on his sister's cheeks. "What did you say that gave them such an impression?"

"Ma had been showing me what she'd called her treasures, little stuff in her room that she brought with her from the south. Things with meaning to her but that have no real worth." Cassie picked at a fingernail. "I joked to Sheridan about that in the dining room and obviously some scoundrels overheard and misunderstood."

"So they went after Mama?" Giles jumped to his feet as

bile pushed up his throat. He paced the room like a caged bear, the urge to hit someone fisting his hands. "But Flint is right. You didn't kill Mama. Those men did. And for nothing." He marched around the room, grappling with the reality of his mother's senseless killing.

She'd once been kind and loving if a bit distant. But she'd taught him to swim and to play backgammon. The picture of simple yet loving Easter dinners she'd prepared for them to gather around the large table to eat floated in his memory. His childhood hadn't been perfect by any stretch of imagination, but she didn't deserve to die over trinkets. He'd find the villains and make them pay. He glanced at his fisted hands, surprised, quickly relaxing his fingers.

"There's not much to be done about it." Matt crossed an ankle over a knee, tapping his fingers on his leg. "There's not much law about these parts, is there?"

"A sheriff and deputy, but they're in Huntsville." Flint crossed over to the fireplace and leaned an elbow on the mantel as he addressed the group. "I have a working relationship with Deputy Barney Parker. I spoke with him and if we could identify the culprits then he'd do something. But we have no idea who the men are."

"But Ma said she could help us figure out who they are because she saw them." Cassie stared at Giles, hope in her eyes.

"But how could she…?" Giles didn't want to finish the thought let alone the sentence. He gripped the back of his chair, steeling himself for what he feared they believed. He didn't believe in ghosts. Pure and simple. They were made up stories to explain what was misunderstood. Yet something in their expressions forewarned him that they did believe in spirits haunting houses. "She's dead. Buried out back, you said. I don't see how…"

"Let me explain." Flint's Adam's apple raced up then down. "You may not believe us…I'm sure it will be hard to…

but your mother's spirit remained here. Haunting the inn."

"Are you trying to tell me she's a haint?" The man said it. Declared his mama a ghost. No. She couldn't be. What if she was? What would she do? Giles swallowed hard, quickly scanning the room as he clutched the back of the chair he'd vacated. His pulse roared in his ears and his stomach roiled. "I-I don't see her."

"She's not here right now. She comes and goes when it's convenient for her, not us." Cassie let out an exasperated huff. "She refused to answer my question about what she's actually got hidden in her attic. Simply vanished."

Giles drew in a delaying breath through his nose, willing his pulse to slow. They seemed serious but how could it be true? He looked at Zander and Matt, relaxed in their chairs. The idea of ghosts didn't bother them? He narrowed his eyes at them, then Flint. "You're convinced Mama is haunting the inn…seriously?"

"You can ask Sheridan or the Marple sisters if you don't believe us." Flint waggled his hand. "It took some strong persuasion to tempt the women to come back after they saw her in the kitchen. But I have done so by reassuring them Mercy won't harm them. And even more importantly to not let on to our guests because they won't come back."

"Which would mean they'd be out of work." A sound argument but still he had reservations about whether everyone had lost their minds. "Smart move on your part. Especially the keeping it quiet bit."

Zander chuckled. "Giles, man, don't you go on being scared."

He bristled at the insult. Even if were true. "I'm…I'm not."

"You're acting like you are." Matt tapped his crossed ankle. "Nothing to be scared of. Ghosts don't linger to harm, they linger to help."

"What's that supposed to mean?" He couldn't imagine

just how or why his mother would want to help when she'd never done so while alive. Not for him, anyway.

"I've heard tales of many ghosts who refused to cross over until they made sure their loved one was safe, or happy, or even sought revenge for their death." Zander spoke with reassurance echoing in every word. "You've nothing to worry about. Your mother is just trying to fix something left undone."

"I believe Zander's right." Cassie gripped the arm rests of her chair. "You'll see for yourself if you stay. I'm sure she'll want to see you. You've been away a long time."

He swallowed around the lump forming in his throat. He'd planned to pay his respects at her grave in due course, but he'd not expected to have a tête-à-tête with his dead mother. "Me?"

Cassie nodded at him, her eagerness lighting her features. "Certainly. Then she can describe the men to you and you can help Flint find them. Get the keys back so we can get into the attic." She glanced over at Flint. "Right?"

The excitement in her tone sent shockwaves through his gut. Giles also looked at the man standing by the fireplace, willing him to sense the outrage zinging through his every fiber. "Keys? We're after keys? I want the men. I don't care about any damn keys."

"We want both the men and what they stole." Flint pushed out of his casual stance to brace his feet and cross his arms. "You in?"

Cassie slid the knife under the apple skin and stripped it off, adding it to the slop bucket on the floor. The featured item on the dinner menu was Sheridan's famous pork pie. She'd volunteered to peel the pippins while Matt prepared the pastry for the crusts. Sheridan would grind the meat and seasonings together, then layer the mixture in large pie pans with sliced spiced apples and cider before topping it with a crust and baking it in the cooling bread oven. The resulting delectable pies brought customers from miles around.

The kitchen door swung open to allow Teddy inside, lugging in two full buckets of water. She greeted him with a smile. He seemed taller, more at ease since living at the inn for the last few weeks. He grinned back at her but then stumbled over a jutting floor board, sloshing the water before he set the wooden buckets down near the snapping fireplace. Matt, working at the other side of the table, grunted at the puddles on the floor.

"Careful, son." Sheridan paused with his butcher knife over the slab of pork on the table. "Now get a mop and clean up that mess."

"With what?" The boy stared at the older man, a slight frown on his face.

"There's a rag mop in the corner." Sheridan pointed to the mop with the knife. "You do know how to use it, don't ya?"

Teddy bobbed his head and then scurried to the corner to retrieve the mop.

Cassie peeled the apple in her hand with quick movements. She'd chosen to use the routine of food prep to settle the disquiet in her soul after the discussion with Giles about their mother's ghost. He seemed to have accepted the fact that the woman haunted the inn to suit her own whims, but some doubts lingered. Flint promised to talk to him, make him not only understand but to prepare him for when Ma first appeared to him. For a day now, she'd apparently been off pouting after Cassie rebuked her. She'd best recover her composure. Her son had arrived and they needed to make amends.

Meg bustled to the sideboard with an immense basket filled with greens for a salad. Cassie had picked them out of the garden earlier, a mix of parsley, sage, watercress, mint, leeks, and borage. A few onions and bulbs of garlic rested in a small bowl waiting to be chopped and added to the mix. Then dressed with olive oil and vinegar. Her mouth watered at the very idea of how fresh and delicious it would be alongside the savory pork pie.

Cassie darted a look at Matt and then kept her eyes on her work. "So, Matt, you like to cook, too?"

He shrugged lightly as he kneaded pie crust dough with confident hands. "I learned early how to make something outta practically nothing."

"Why is that?" Cassie cored the apple and then started slicing it into a large porcelain bowl. "I don't understand."

"No, miss, I don't suppose you do." He firmed his lips and then folded over the dough, forming it into a ball. "It's not your fault. It's just the way it is for folks like me. My master discovered I have a real talent for it, though, so he made sure I learned from the best in the area."

Cassie bit back any response she might try to make. She was out of her depth in this quicksand conversation. While her life was far from easy, she had had conversations with Sheridan about his experiences as a slave. Not all the details. Her friend didn't want to share those with her even if she pressed. Which she no longer did. She'd learned that lesson. Matt and Zander were freemen, like Sheridan, but she sensed reverberations of anger and despair suppressed within Matt though more so in the simmering Zander. Whatever Matt's experience had been on the Louisiana plantation, those memories would never be forgotten. Probably never forgiven either. Now how did she know that? She frowned to herself until she caught Matt watching her. Shaking off her ponderings, she flashed a small grin.

Teddy ambled by with the mop dangling in his hands.

"Hurry up there, boy." Sheridan cut into the meat, slicing it into chunks sized for the grinder. "Stop lolly-gagging around and get the job done."

Teddy shot him a defiant glare but picked up his pace and soon started swabbing up the water. Sheridan muttered to himself as he resumed chunking the pork.

Myrtle pushed slowly through the kitchen door, carrying a stack of freshly laundered aprons and towels. The scent of fresh air wafted into the room. She carried her bundle over to a side table and dropped the pile on top. The older woman pulled a chair closer to the table and then sat down and began folding a saffron yellow bib apron.

Cassie picked up an apple and looked across the table, trying to convey her desire for him to have a good life. "Giles gave you and your brother a new start." She picked up the corer to remove the center core from the apple and dropped it into the slop bucket. "I can only imagine what you've been through but if I know my brother, he'll always look out for you both. He's a good man."

Matt rubbed flour on the rolling pin, smoothing it over the barrel to completely coat it. "Giles and I are so close, Miss Cassie, you and I are practically related. That man has done a lot to help us out of a dangerous situation on that there Louisiana hell hole and I won't forget that. Zan and I had been trapped there since traded when we were little boys. Taken from our mother without even being able to say good-bye."

"Oh, Matt…" Words failed her for several beats of her thudding heart. She'd not been able to say good-bye to her own mother before she'd died, but at least she could still speak to her. But to be ripped from the family as he'd been had to leave emotional scars. "What on earth did they do to you?"

"It's not fitting for your tender ears. But I will say this." He cleaned his hands on the smudged waist apron while his eyes darkened. "If that beast of an overseer had beat on Zan one more time somebody would have died, and it wouldn't have been me or my brother."

Sheridan drew in a sharp breath. Cassie glanced at his serious expression. Sensed his curiosity and hope as clearly as if he'd spoken the words aloud. What was going on? She frowned.

"You were in Louisiana?" Sheridan stared at Matt, his eyes intensely watching every shift in the young man's expression. "Both of you are brothers and were taken there as boys?"

"Yes." Matt stilled his hands. "Why?"

"Where'd you come from?" Sheridan pressed his fists onto the table as he seemed to hold his breath, waiting for Matt's answer.

"I dunno exactly." Matt squared his shoulders, as if preparing for whatever the older man might do or say next. A defensive, reflexive movement. "I know we lived to the east but no idea how far. I was too young to think of such things while being dragged away from everything I knew."

"The east spans quite a bit of land." Sheridan narrowed his eyes, the fire lighting them dying out. "Probably nothing. Sorry."

The tension between the two men seemed to quiver in the air. An odd sensation zipped through her veins, a skirmish of worry and hope ending in defeat. She glanced at Meg and Myrtle, busily going about their tasks, oblivious to the emotionally charged exchange. Teddy finished mopping and carried the mop out of the kitchen to wring it out outside. She shifted her gaze back to Sheridan, her friend and confidante, now so sad. Confusion swirled inside her. Where had his fiery hope gone, died out like yesterday's embers? To try to smooth over the awkward pause, she smiled at Matt.

"Tell me more about my brother's life in Mobile." She resumed her chore, short efficient strokes shedding the red skin off the pippins. Forced herself to not keep looking at Sheridan as he hacked up the haunch into chunks to grind for the pie. Maybe he'd tell her later what his pointed question meant. "I feel like I barely know him anymore."

"He's a decent man. What more do you need to know?" Matt rolled the pin over the dough until it was the proper thickness. Then he rolled the dough onto the pin to center the circle of dough over the deep pie pan.

"What's his job like? I mean, what exactly does he do?" She didn't need a minute by minute description, but she had no idea what an exporter actually did to make a living.

"He trades goods with other men." Matt expertly pressed the dough into the shape of the pan. "Some of them here in the States, but most of them in other countries. France, England, China, West Indies, Barbados. All over."

"He knows people all around the world?" Shock rippled through her at the idea. She didn't know people outside of the state she lived in let alone in other countries.

Imagine having correspondence with people who spoke other languages. Surely they wrote in English. Or did Giles know other languages, too? She didn't know the answer to that question among many others. What about a girl? Was he seeing anyone? He didn't act as if he'd left a pretty woman in Mobile, anxious to return to her arms and kisses. Whoa. His personal life was none of her business. If he wanted her to know, he'd tell her himself.

Matt pushed the pie pan toward Sheridan's side of the table to wait to be filled. "I don't think he's met them, but he knows their names and the kinds of goods they need from him."

"They must trust him to do a good job then." Her brother worked with so many others, looking out for their needs and desires. A warm rush swept through her chest. "I'm proud of him."

"Yes, miss, you have cause to be. He's known for his honesty and integrity." Matt grabbed the mixing bowl and crossed to the sack of flour, scooping enough out to start another batch of pastry dough. He carried the bowl back to the table and added some salt, sifting it together. "Zan and me could have ended up dead if Giles hadn't taken a liking to our work."

"I'm glad he did or you wouldn't be here now making such delicious pastry." She finished the last apple and then wiped her hands on her apron. "I hope you'll save me a piece."

Matt revealed a gap-toothed grin when he laughed at her pleading. "If you say pretty-please."

Cassie snickered as she made praying hands and grinned at him. "Pretty please?"

"If you're sure?" Matt piled the flour on the table and made a well in the center, his grin mischievous. "Fine."

"You joker. Do you know where Giles is?" Cassie sprinkled cinnamon and nutmeg over the sliced apples. "I haven't seen him in a while now."

"I'm not his keeper." Matt added bits of butter to the well, hesitated as he tilted his head to one side for a moment, and then added a few more.

Cassie stirred the apples to coat them with the spices and then laid the spoon on the table. There was something Giles needed to do but hadn't even mentioned. "I didn't say you were, but I thought he might have said what his plan was for the day."

Sheridan huffed as he added meat and seasonings in the grinder and turned the crank, the ground meat oozing into a flat metal pan on the table. "Thanks for your help, Cassie."

She scanned the table and nodded with satisfaction then untied her apron and pulled it off. "If you don't need me to do anything else, Sheridan, I'm going to go find my brother."

Chapter Three

C assie had come looking for him and then insisted on him going with her to do the one thing he'd avoided. A chocolate Labrador retriever nosed his way ahead of Giles' reluctant feet. He ambled across the grassy expanse beside Cassie and a golden Cocker Spaniel toward the edge of the back yard where a lone mound of dirt marked his mother's burial site. Alone in death. He sighed as they approached the cemetery. Several tall maple trees framed the tract of land surrounded by a low picket fence with a closed gate. He'd put off visiting the grave, unnerved by the idea of paying his respects to a woman who'd treated him so unkindly in life. Until Cassie had snagged him and forced him into it.

"Is that a new fence?" The wood appeared raw and fresh, gleaming in the morning sunlight.

"Yes, Flint had it built after the funeral to keep the dogs and other critters out." Cassie lifted the latch and held the iron barred gate open. "After you."

He drew in a breath as he eased past her and into the enclosed area. "I wish I hadn't agreed to this."

"It's important for you to do this." Cassie closed the gate and stepped beside the rough rectangle of settling dirt, several stems of roses wilting on top. "To know where she's been laid to rest, even if she's not resting."

"So you say." He stared at the grave, his mother's frowning image front and center in his mind. He'd not seen any sign of his mother's ghost and he hoped to keep it that way. "I'm sorry, Mama, about everything."

The mound of dirt before him, heated by the harsh summer sun, covered the silent body in a casket made of pine wood. They'd been forced to bury her quickly due to the summer heat with the wood on hand. Nothing fancy for his mother's final resting place. Did she deserve better? She'd surely done the best she could. Even if fault could be found with her efforts. His mother's body lay in the ground and he didn't know how he felt about that fact. Inhaling, he smelled hot dirt mixed with the faint scent of roses and tears smarted his eyes.

If only Mama were content now that all her trials and worries had ended. "Are you certain she's haunting the inn and not resting in peace?"

"You'll see." Cassie clasped her hands together in front of her skirts.

"I hope not."

Cassie nodded. "Give it time and she'll find you."

A shiver swept his shoulders. "Did you write to Silas and Abram?"

"And Daniel."

"Any word?" It had been years since he'd spoken with his brothers. Once his best buddies. No longer.

"Not yet." She spoke with hope tinging her words. "Do you think they'll come?"

He shrugged. "Hard to say given the reason for leaving."

The Lab laid down on the other side of the fence but under the shady maple trees, tongue lolling as he watched the people inside. A hawk screamed high above, circling slowly in the clear blue sky. The spaniel trotted over to join the Lab.

Shade was a good idea. He strolled over to sit on a raised root under the tree, Cassie trailing behind him. He took off his hat and wiped his sleeve across his brow.

"That's better." Cassie joined him on a separate root, tucking her legs beside her and drawing a handkerchief from her pocket to mop her glistening forehead and cheeks. "I do hope they come. I've missed you all so much."

Her letters had been so upbeat he hadn't considered she was lonely. Hadn't thought about what her life might be like with their parents. "I'm sorry I didn't realize you felt alone."

She tore off a blade of grass to fiddle with in her fingers. "I didn't want to bother you with my feelings."

"How was it for you then?" He rested his hands on his knees, considering the softly spoken words hinting at suppressed pain. "With Mama in particular?"

She glanced at him and then studied the grass. "I survived. That's all that really matters."

She must have lived through hell to respond in such a vague manner. Guilt weighed on his heart the longer he regarded her bent head and averted eyes. "I'm sorry. I should have stayed closer to be a buffer of some kind for you."

With their mother dead and their father so far away, she'd had only Flint to protect her until Giles had arrived with Matt and Zander. No wonder she'd pleaded with him to come. He was pretty sure Flint was enthralled with Cassie, so his interest veered to the personal side. Which might or might not be what his sister desired. Good thing he'd chosen to journey north to be with her, to ensure she was provided for and ultimately safe. From any kind of threat to her person or emotions.

"We didn't have much contact with any of the family. I never understood why." The threat of tears washed her words.

"Speaking of which…" He swallowed the knot in his throat.

She'd suffered and longed for family, one broken and scattered to the winds. What little he remembered about his childhood years included an awful row between one aunt and his father. The day his cousin died. "Did you let Mama's sisters know of her death?"

"I don't know where they are. Like I said, we haven't heard from them in years." She aimed a half-hearted grin his way. "Ma didn't seem to care about them. She never talked about them even."

"Maybe there's some old letters in her room with an address?" He shook his head, thinking hard to remember everything about his two aunts. "I'm pretty sure they lived somewhere around Montgomery but I can't recall exactly where."

"I'll look but I doubt I'll find anything." Cassie sighed, then rose to her feet, and brushed off her skirt. "I need to get back to work."

Giles stood and replaced his hat, scanning the area set aside for the family cemetery. "There should be a marker of some kind. Don't you think?"

Cassie tied her bonnet strings with nimble fingers. "Yes, you're right. That's a good idea."

"I'll talk to Flint about it. See where I can get one made." He patted his hat firmly in place, aware of subtle currents beneath her gentle voice. "Let's go. We both have chores."

He struggled to grasp what Flint was telling him. He simply didn't believe his mother's ghost lingered at the Fury Falls Inn. She should be resting in peace, not haunting her home. He drummed his fingers on the wooden arm of the chair.

"I know it's hard to take in, Giles." Flint crossed his ankles, reclining in the matching chair opposite. "I've seen her several times. Cassie's spoken to her as many."

"But why?" His mother as a ghost could be a formidable thing to endure. It had been bad enough that she'd harassed him when he was a child. But to have her able to pop in and out whenever she'd like to watch, berate, harangue? A shudder rocked his shoulders.

"She wants her killers caught so they don't hurt anyone else." The conviction ringing in Flint's voice emphasized the sincerity of his statement.

"She told you that? That's how you know?" Could he accept what the man said? Giles gripped the armrest for a moment before dropping his hands onto his thighs.

Flint merely nodded as he studied Giles. He wished he could discount what everyone seemed to believe as utter nonsense, but how could they all be wrong? Zander and Matt hadn't flinched at the concept. Even the boy seemed to suspect they spoke the truth. Otherwise, he wouldn't have been so eager to avoid entering the inn. Which raised another concern. Exactly who was he?

"Talk to me about the boy. What's his name?"

"Teddy." Flint sat up straight. "We caught him stealing from the garden. Cassie put him to work instead of telling his father who appears to have abandoned the poor kid."

Zander shifted in his seat, resting his palms on his powerful thighs. "Lucky boy to be taken in rather than turned over to the sheriff."

Giles met Zander's haunted eyes. Wondered about the man's history yet again. Then addressed Flint once more. "You didn't try to find the father? Just sort of adopted the thief?"

"I rode over the ridge to his home once but the man wasn't at home. Cassie balked at the idea of leaving the boy to fend for himself. So we've let Teddy stay. He's been a big help, too."

"When did Mrs. Fairhope die?" Zander asked suddenly.

"A couple weeks ago." Flint glanced sharply between Zander and Giles. "Why?"

"And the boy showed up…when?" Zander's brows lifted slightly as he waited.

Flint tapped a finger on his chin. "Shortly after that." He pointed his finger at Zander. "In fact, we first saw him the day of Mercy's funeral. We caught him a few days later taking veggies."

Giles chuckled. "A thief who likes vegetables?"

Flint pushed to his feet to cross the short distance to the fireplace. "I know. He's a surprising kid. Says his pa goes up into the hills and is gone for weeks at a time."

"Long enough to cause some mischief." Zander crossed his arms over his chest. "What if his father is one of the men who killed Mrs. Fairhope?"

Flint propped his elbow on the mantel. "All the more reason to keep Teddy with us. He doesn't need to have such a bad person as his guide in life."

"What do you know about these men, Flint?" Surely somebody would have a clue. They needed some idea of who they were going after if they had any hope of finding them. "How many were there?"

"Three."

A woman's voice? Giles jerked back in his chair when his gaze landed on his mother. Suspended a foot off the floor on the other side of the fireplace from where Flint smirked at him. She wore a pale blue dress, her favorite color. The sight brought a rush of unwanted memories. Memories he'd shut away. Some he most definitely didn't want to remember.

"Mother?"

"Giles, I'm glad you've come." She pressed a hand to her chest. "You're needed."

Every fiber of his being clamored to jump up and dash away from the specter. But he was no coward. He'd face his fears without succumbing to the base desire to flee. He swallowed hard, hands gripping the chair's armrests, and blinked rapidly as he was forced to accept the truth.

His mother did indeed haunt the inn. She'd been murdered and needed his help to avenge her death. His protective instinct became a wildfire inside, consuming every shred of doubt as to his mission. "I'll find them. What did they look like?"

"Hard to see because they wore…hats and masks. Like Tradesmen." She lifted a finger to point at Flint. "He should have stopped them. He's useless."

Giles shot a frown at Flint. "What does she mean by that?"

"She doesn't like me much." Flint huffed a short mirthless laugh. "Everything is my fault, according to her."

Pity and empathy for the beleaguered surrogate innkeeper made Giles nod at Flint on his behalf. His mother could indeed hold a grudge longer than anyone else he'd known. On the other hand, Flint must have neglected something or caused some issue for his mother to have such a low opinion of the man. Best to keep an eye on Flint until he discovered the truth.

"Mama, don't be mean to Flint." Giles shook his head at the ghost. "He's can't be all bad."

"You'll see." Mercy glared at Flint for a moment and then gazed at Giles. "One man was called Joe. Bent nose. Brown eyes."

"Who else?" Giles leaned forward, anxious for the descriptions so they could get started hunting the murderers down. "What did the others look like?"

"No other names. But the one who shot me had green eyes." Her voice faltered, dying away for several beats before she continued. "The other man acted like he didn't want to be there. Like he'd been forced into joining the others. He was tall and thin, not as big as the others. Amber eyes."

"Fine. We'll find them." Giles carefully rose to his feet, propping his hands on his hips as he cast his eyes around the group and then back to his mother. "I won't let you down."

"Make sure you find the keys that Joe stole from me."

"The keys again?" He shook his head and frowned at his mother. "Why are they so important?"

Mercy shifted and shimmered, fading as she spoke. "You need them most of all."

"But why?" Giles stepped toward her vanishing form. "Mother? Come back."

"Infuriating, isn't it?" Flint pushed away from the mantel to walk over to Giles.

"Very." Giles stared at the empty space where his mother had been. Was that guilt on her fading features? Why should she feel guilty? Questions swirled in his mind but one thing was perfectly clear. "At least now we have something to work with."

"All right. Anything else?" Flint picked up his hat from the table and dusted it off.

"One thing more." Giles met Flint's quizzical gaze. "Where can I get a grave marker for my mother's grave?"

"There's a stone carver in town. You want to get one?" Flint tapped his hat into place.

Giles nodded. "Yeah. Can you arrange for it?"

Flint shrugged. "Write down what you want put on it, and I'll put in the order."

"Good. I'll let you know." Giles turned and headed for the door.

"Where you going?" Flint called after him.

"To find Cassie."

Later that afternoon, Giles finally convinced Cassie to sit down with him to figure out what to put on the stone. She'd been insistent that she had to finish the sewing for a few guests who'd hired her to mend their garments. Since when had she taken in odd jobs to make money? She was full of surprises. He strode into the parlor where they'd agreed to meet before dinner.

"There you are." Giles pulled out a chair at the large dining table. "Let's get this done quickly. I'm tired of thinking about what to say."

"You only raised the question a few hours ago." She searched his eyes for several moments. "What's wrong?"

He raked his fingers through his hair and then dropped the hand to the table. "What can we possibly say about her?"

"I've been toying with some ideas." She tapped a pencil against her cheek, a sheet of paper with several lines scrawled on it in front of her. "It doesn't need to be long or overly sentimental."

"Such as?" He leaned closer from his seat to peer at what she'd written.

She pushed the paper toward him and pointed with the pencil at the first line. "Obviously her name and date of death. But how about something like this…

Our Mother

Mercy

Wife of

Reginald Fairhope

Died July 14, 1821

"Do you really need that first line?" He scrunched his brow. Finding the balance between honoring his dearly departed mother and reflecting their honest relationship caused the beginning of a headache.

"Not really, but I thought it was a nice touch since we're doing this. If you don't want it, we can remove it." She glanced at him and then crossed out the offending line. "Do we want to add her age as well?"

"Do you know her date of birth?" He scratched his head. "I know her birthday was on Christmas, but what year?"

"She would have been forty years old this Christmas." She wrote down the current year and subtracted forty from it. "So, that makes it 1781."

"I don't know if we need to figure out the exact age…" Would anyone really care about her time spent on earth? A fierce roar threatened to erupt at the thought. He cared even if he'd avoided being around her. She was his mama and he'd always love and defend her no matter what she may have done in life. "We should put it down. How should it be done? Do you know?"

"Most stones include the years, months, and days of a person's age." She tapped the pencil on the page for several moments. "I think we should do the same."

"Fine. Figure it out then." He sat back in his chair, wrestling with his own emotions over the inscription. Over the need for a grave marker for his mother. Revenge sizzled in his gut. He needed to bring those men to justice, true, but he'd like to take a few satisfying swipes at them before he turned them over to the sheriff.

"All right." She scratched on the page the number of years, months, and days. Adding a new line to the inscription they'd decided on.

Aged 39 years, 6 months, 19 days

"There. How's that?" Cassie pointed to the new line with the pencil.

He shook his head as he counted the letters. "Too long, but the carver can abbreviate when he gets to work."

"I can do that now." She crossed out the line and rewrote it as

Aged 39 Y's, 6 Mo. & 19 D.

"Good, that's enough." Giles reached for the paper but she swatted his hand. "What?"

"What about a saying or poem at the bottom?" She frowned lightly at him. "Say something about how much we'll miss her, or that we loved her. Something?"

Hell, no. What could they possibly add honestly about their relationship with Mercy? "No, that's enough. Let's keep it simple. How we cared for our mother is our business and nobody else's."

"That's fine." She peered at the paper for a moment. "But let me rewrite it before you give it to Flint, just to be clear what we've agreed to."

"Good idea." He settled back in the chair, watching her make a fair copy of the agreed-upon inscription. "I'm glad I came to help you through this."

She paused in her writing. "I'm glad you thought of a marker. Something permanent instead of a wood cross or nothing."

"I wanted to be sure you're able to manage until Papa comes home." Giles drummed his fingers on the table. "I can't stay long, but I will confer with Flint regarding the financial situation before we leave."

Cassie pressed her lips together and nodded once before resuming writing. "I see."

Probably not. She couldn't understand how difficult being in his parents' home proved for him. Not only the memories that had been unleashed upon his arrival but the grief and guilt he felt upon learning just how mistaken he'd been about Cassie's mental well-being. For years she'd written to him occasionally to let him know about the comings and goings, about her garden, and learning to cook at Sheridan's side. Without a word of complaint or hint of feeling isolated and alone. Part of him wanted to stay and insure she never felt that way again.

On the other hand, he needed to get back to work or the persistent man who had been pestering him about buying his business would insinuate himself into the operation.

Giles couldn't let that happen. He fisted his large hands. Damn his father for abandoning his responsibilities on some scheme or another. He'd worked hard to build his import/export business. He let out the breath he'd been holding as he watched his sister finish the last line. No way. He simply couldn't walk away from his business to babysit his little sister for months. No matter how much he might worry about her.

Chapter Four

Climbing the stairs to confront her parents' empty bedroom always quailed her heart. But she needed to see if they had any correspondence with her aunts and touch up the room. Surely, her aunts would want to know their sister had died. Her pa should be the one to tell them, but while he was away the chore fell to her. Oh dear. What if something happened to him and he couldn't come home? She hesitated, a short gasp of concern escaping her mouth. She braced to open the door, keeping her hope of soon seeing her pa snug inside her heart. He simply had to find his way back to the inn. Nonetheless, she couldn't remain standing outside the room until he did.

Pushing the door open, she hesitated. Nothing had moved since her last cleaning visit. Not that she had expected it to. But she wasn't sure of her ma's abilities. Pulling the dust rag from her skirt pocket, she went first to the wardrobe that stood guard near the bottom of the circular staircase. She glanced up the stairs to the locked door, wishing yet again she could enter the forbidden room. What lurked in the shadows up there? She felt the familiar urge to place a foot on a tread and climb up, break down the door, pound it to pieces so she could satisfy the desire to know.

Instead, she concentrated on the task at hand. She ran the piece of old shirt over the aged wood of the wardrobe, wiping away the layer of dust that had settled on the deep red surface. She walked to the window and shook out the rag, careful to hold it below the windowsill. Then she strode over to the dressing table. Lovingly wiped down the rich mahogany wood frame of the elegant looking glass. Abram had gifted the lovely mirror to Ma years ago. One of her treasures that ultimately got her killed. She inhaled sharply as she clung to the wooden frame.

Her ma had forgiven her, as had Flint. Everyone but her. The pain of her guilt and stupidity flashed through her again, never far from her thoughts. If only she'd kept her mouth shut and not teased Sheridan about her ma's treasure in front of strangers. She knew it was dangerous living in the northern wilderness of Alabama, but she'd not realized it was dangerous inside her very home. Her eyes stung for several beats of her heart as she pressed her lids closed.

Dogs barked outside. Carriages and wagons rattled past the open window bringing a steadily increasing flow of customers. The distant cry of a hawk, high and plaintive, floated into the room. She let the held breath ease from her lungs as she opened her eyes. She saw the familiar collection of boxes, the empty silver filigreed bowl that once held the precious set of keys, the figurine of a fairy reading her book on a red dotted toadstool.

Lifting the wooden box with the engraved dove on the top, she opened it to reveal a stack of letters inside. She flipped through them, searching for any from her aunts. Nothing. But she frowned when she noticed a recent one from her pa. She slipped the paper out of the box and unfolded it. Her pa's bold script marched across the page, flourishes and loops carefully made. She glanced around, nervously searching for any hint of her ma's presence.

She shouldn't read it. But it was right in front of her. She bit her lip, holding the trembling paper in both hands. She'd just take a peek.

He talked first about the reason for his delay in coming home. And about Flint's worth as a replacement innkeeper. But her jaw fell open at his next words.

I hope that Cassandra received the fine doll's house I sent for her birthday. I couldn't be there but I wanted her to know I was thinking of her. I thought it would give her the opportunity to begin contemplating what her own future home would be like. Now that she's reached eighteen years, we'll need to find her a husband ere long. So she might as well begin with a little playful yet helpful way to plan for her own home. What kinds of furniture and furnishings she'd like to collect. That sort of thing. What did she think of it? Please write and tell me.

Her ma had not told her the real reason behind the seemingly juvenile gift. No, she left her to think her pa still thought of her as a child. A girl still playing with dolls. Hurt nearly doubled her over.

"Ma!" Cassie spun around, searching desperately for her ma's ghost to appear. "Where are you? I need to talk to you."

She stared down at the page for a minute as tears pressed her eyes. She swallowed hard. No tears. Anger replaced the wave of sorrow at the misunderstanding. Yet another one.

"Ma?"

Mercy materialized in front of the wardrobe, shimmering into a solid form. Until she spied the letter in Cassie's fingers. Then with wide eyes, she vanished again.

"Come back here. We're not through."

Why hadn't she and her mother been able to talk to one another? To share their confidences rather than keep secrets from each other. Why wouldn't her ma talk to her now? She balled the letter and threw it across the room to bounce off the wardrobe.

"Ma, I can't believe you wouldn't tell me the truth." Pressure built in her breast the longer she thought about how her mother hadn't said the words necessary to relieve the embarrassment and disappointment she'd felt upon receiving the doll's house. In front of the man whom she had come to cherish and hoped to have a future with as his wife. If her mother didn't think she deserved to know the truth of how things stood, then she'd have to decide matters for herself. Flint had been understanding about her desire to consult with her pa before proceeding with their relationship, but it could have all been avoided if only Mercy hadn't concealed the real reason her pa had sent the toy. A beautiful and elaborate toy, but still a child's plaything.

No, not a toy in fact. Her pa had actually considered it a way to transition into married life and having a family of her own. To think to the future as someone's wife. Someone's mother. He would probably agree with her choice of Flint as a husband, given his trust in the young man. She could imagine the kind of home she'd create. The pretty and functional furniture. The knitted rugs, pieced quilts, sewn drapes at the windows, maybe painted wood floors or, if her husband's wealth allowed, carpets to cushion their feet. She needed to decide for herself what path to follow with regard to marriage. Her ma needed to understand Cassie's decision to follow her own guidance going forward.

"Mother, stop hiding and come out here and talk to me."

She swiped at the collection of boxes on the table, but kept an eye open for her mother. Though she had little hope she'd comply with the command appearance. Her ma only did what she wanted. Apparently, that included keeping secrets. What else did she know that she didn't let on about?

Exasperated with the silence from her ma, she propped her fists on her hips to survey the room. She'd touched on most everything. Exposed the beauty beneath the layer of dust from the open window. Good enough for now. She turned her attention to the room at large. "For the last time, Ma, why didn't you tell me the truth?"

Only bird song and the sound of traffic outside met her ears. With a sigh, she shook her head and went out the door, shutting it firmly behind her.

"Flint, we have a problem."

Giles stopped at the bottom of the steps in the entrance hall of the inn. Sheridan hurried past him from the kitchen to stand by Flint on the front porch. Teddy traipsed along with him, a frown etching the young boy's face as he carried a sloshing bucket of water. But more than the boy's concern, the tone in the man's voice raised Giles' instincts. Which gave him pause. Ever since he'd arrived at the inn he'd been on edge, aware of currents of anxiety and tension but unable to pinpoint the cause. At first he'd assumed it stemmed from his mother's violent death. But more seemed to be stirring the pot than that one act.

"What sort of problem?" Flint glanced between Teddy and Sheridan.

"You tell him." Sheridan motioned to the boy. "You discovered the issue."

"The water I pulled from the well…" Teddy looked uneasy, pointing at the bucket even as his gaze drifted to a group of men striding toward the inn's front steps. He blinked up at Flint. "It smells awful."

Flint straightened to glare down at the boy. "What do you mean?"

Teddy muttered something Giles couldn't hear and then

fell silent. Giles crossed the room to stand by the group, intent on learning more.

"He means it's fouled. Just smell it if you don't believe us." Sheridan crossed his arms over his strong chest as he welcomed Giles with a lift of his chin. "I can't make stew or soup or much of anything without water."

"Fouled? With what?" Flint glanced at Giles then back to Sheridan.

Deep inside, Giles sensed the problem was no accident. Like a newly discovered sixth sense working within. How he could sense it he didn't fathom, but the certainty remained. "Or by who?"

The trio gaped at him. He shrugged at their surprised expressions.

"You think someone did it intentionally?" Flint studied Giles, his sharp question echoing in the quiet. "Based on what?"

Good question. He had never experienced the sensation before that moment. Somewhere deep inside him a knowledge of impending threat squirmed and wiggled, causing him great unease and yet certainty. Somehow he didn't think Flint would accept his gut feeling as evidence of wrong doing by anyone. Hell, he couldn't explain why he was certain the well had been deliberately fouled. But he knew it in his bones.

"I just know we need to take measures to find out if someone messed with it or if there's some other cause." He gestured to the bucket reeking with a stench he couldn't quite place, probably because of the dilution in water. "What is that odor?"

Sheridan grimaced with a huff. "I believe it's caused by a dead skunk discarded into the well."

"Nobody wants to use that then." Giles couldn't imagine getting closer to the bucket let alone wanting to consume the water in any way. "Get rid of it."

"We'll need to dig a new well, but that takes time." Flint shook his head as he looked at Sheridan and then Teddy. "I guess you'll need to fetch water from the spring for now."

"All the way up there?" Teddy hunched his shoulders under the new direction. "That's a long way."

"I know, son, and I'm sorry." Flint dropped his hands to his sides. "You best get busy."

Teddy lifted the bucket at his feet. "I'll grab the other bucket and go." With a beleaguered sigh, the boy started to turn back toward the inn.

"Make sure you scrub that bucket out with sand before using it again." Sheridan scowled at the boy.

Teddy glared over his shoulder at the cook and then trudged outside.

A surge of warning flashed through Giles. Something felt off, dangerous. He scanned the area until he spotted the bowed shoulders of the boy lugging the bucket across the carriageway toward the stable. The danger centered on Teddy. He frantically looked about, trying to understand the form of peril but saw nothing untoward. The feeling inside him swelled until he thought he'd be sick. He had to protect the boy. Every instinct screamed at him.

"Wait." Giles raised a hand toward Flint to stop him from leaving. "He'll need somebody to protect him while he's up there so far from the house."

Sheridan halted on his way inside to turn back, a creased brow revealing his concern. "You think the boy needs a guard?"

"I do. If someone deliberately messed up the well water, they must have a reason." Giles cut a look at Flint as his own conviction swelled in his chest. "Until we know what that might be, then you need to take precautions. Everyone needs to be careful."

Flint's hand went to the flintlock pistol hanging from his belt.

His eyes glittered as he met Giles' gaze. "I will protect this place and everyone in it."

"The threat may not be in the building but up in the woods." He glanced toward the forest starting at the edge of the clearing and blanketing the mountain beyond. Sensed a hidden threat lurking in the shadows. "I think someone should go with him."

"I'll have Marshall keep an eye on the boy." Flint left his hand on the butt of the pistol as he turned toward the stable. "He's a strapping young man."

Giles nodded as he recalled the stable hand. Tall, strong, long blond hair pulled back in a queue, with steady hazel eyes. Perhaps his stubborn streak would also serve well to look after Teddy. "He'll do fine."

"I don't know how much good he'd do in protecting the boy though." Sheridan shook his head as he started inside. "We don't even know what kind of danger we're facing."

"Then we need to be ready for anything, don't we?" Flint met Giles' frown with one of his own. "Unless you know something more about who's behind this?"

"I wish I did. I know only one thing about them." Giles' instincts flared brighter as he scanned the undulating cloud shadows flowing over the mountain.

Flint hesitated before going down the steps to the carriageway. "What's that?"

"They're watching us."

The next afternoon, Giles curried his gray with firm circular motions. He needed to do something. Not just sit around and wait for trouble to come to him. A disturbance lingered in his gut. Was he imagining it? Maybe. Ever since he'd arrived at the inn, though, he'd become aware of so much more than he'd ever experienced before. Perhaps the result of walking into a place where a crime had been committed set him on edge. More to the point, he stayed on alert. He rubbed the horse's haunch harder. Dust floated off the gelding's hide and he sneezed.

"Bless you." Zander popped up from where he'd been picking out his horse's hooves with a curved metal tool. "Try not to blow the roof off, all right?"

"I'll do my best." Giles turned away from the gray horse to clap the curry comb against his other hand, releasing small chunks of dirt to fall to the floor of the barn. He frowned at the wooden oval in his hand, picking at the rows of serrated teeth with a dirty finger.

"Something botherin' you, boss?" Zander propped his elbows on the chestnut's back, peering at Giles with concern in his dark eyes.

"Nothing I can explain." Giles resumed currying, careful to not breathe in too deeply. He glanced yet again toward the sunlight illuminating the end of the aisle at the carriageway. Trouble was coming but what kind? "Just a feeling."

The sound of someone whistling floated to his ears as he worked. Somebody was certainly in a good mood. He glanced over to Zander's quizzical expression then back to the doorway. Flint strode into the barn, whistling the tune of "Brown-eyed Belle."

Interesting song choice, given that was one of Cassie's original songs, one she often sang when she entertained in the dining room of an evening. The ballad about a young woman's beguiling a young man into falling in love with her, only to find she was not a beauty but a hag in disguise. The mischievous story delighted her audience nearly as much as her lyrical voice enchanted her listeners no matter which songs she sang. Apparently, Flint enjoyed that one the most.

"Quit that racket, will ya?" Giles paused in his task to grin at the man. "What's up?"

Flint swaggered to a halt near the stall where Giles worked. "Just got word that the esteemed senator has confirmed his intended visit this fall. And..." Flint waggled his brows as a grin broke onto his face. "He's bringing several influential friends with him. Do we have room? Why yes, yes we do."

"This is good?" He tapped out the curry comb and laid it on top of the stall wall.

"Very good news for the inn. It means more business and thus ongoing employment for everyone."

"Doesn't hurt your reputation either." Zander eased out of the stall he'd been working in to stand in the aisle beside Flint. "Entertaining government officials."

Flint looked sheepishly away and then met Giles' gaze. "True, but not the main point."

Giles peered closer at Flint. Strange reaction to his comment about the man's reputation. What was the main point if not the improvement of his stance in his chosen profession? Perhaps he harbored some other concerns beside his reputation, but what? Wracking his brain, he finally landed on a possibility.

"Does the good senator know about the ghost in residence?" Giles patted his gelding's silky rump as he sidled into the aisle to join the other men.

"Keep your voice down." Flint skimmed the other stalls then relaxed when nobody else was in the barn. "He's not going to know either. If word gets out the inn's haunted, we'll not have any business let alone the senator's."

"Or you could make it known and attract gawkers and curiosity seekers." Giles chortled at the horrified expression on Flint's features. "You don't think that would work?"

"That's a profoundly terrible idea." Flint shook his head, eyes narrowed. "Don't you dare even suggest such a thing again, you hear me?"

"I was joking with you. Calm down." He met Zander's amused gaze. "Zander gets my humor."

Zander smiled broadly at Flint. "He pulled your leg but good."

"Don't start." Flint shook a finger at Zander. "You should know better than to agree with such advice."

"I'll have you know my opinion is highly regarded among my peers." Giles puffed up his massive chest and crossed his arms. "Show some respect."

Flint lifted a brow as he stared at him. "You're not among your peers here. This is my territory."

So now they were getting into a spitting contest. He smirked at Flint, darting a glance to Zander's grin. "We'll see about that."

Pounding footsteps approached from outside, drawing the three men's attention away from their good-natured banter. Marshall raced inside and skidded to a halt when he reached the group, his long queue whipping around to rest on his shoulder. He bent over, panting as he braced his hands on his knees.

"What's wrong?" Flint moved closer to the younger man.

Giles cast a worried glance to the doorway, instincts on full alert. "Where's Teddy?"

Marshall breathed heavily for another moment and then straightened to aim wide eyes at Giles. "Gone."

"What?" Flint grabbed the man's upper arms to stare into his distraught expression. "Tell us what happened."

"Some man took him away."

"What do you mean?" Giles stepped forward, prepared to shake the information out of him if he didn't spit it out first.

"This man appeared out of the bushes and told Teddy to go with him and he did." Marshall glanced at Flint and then back to Giles. "He didn't want to, but he went."

"Did he put up a fight?" Zander balanced his weight on both feet.

Marshall shrugged. "He resisted and argued but the man insisted."

"Where did all this happen?" Flint turned to face the distraught younger man.

"I'll show you. Up by the spring. Hurry." Marshall spun around and ran outside.

The four men raced out of the barn and up the winding trail to the sight of the abduction. However, when Giles stopped his uphill sprint, breathing hard, his frantic search found no sign of a struggle.

"I don't see anything." He scanned the area, looking for anything amiss but finding everything as it should be. "Where did it happen?"

"I was sitting over there on the rocks while Teddy dipped the buckets." Marshall waved in the general direction of the springs nearby. "I heard a man arguing with Teddy and when I looked up I saw Teddy following the man into the forest. I went after them, but they disappeared into the trees. I followed them until I lost the trail. I didn't know what to do so came to tell you."

Simmering worry erupted in Giles' chest as he stared at the faint trail vanishing into the dense underbrush. Could he follow them? Perhaps if he hurried, he could catch up to them. He took a step but Flint grabbed his arm, preventing him from following through on his plan.

"No, wait." Flint held up his other hand to emphasize his command. "I don't think that's a good idea."

Glaring at him, Giles pulled back until Flint's hold broke away. "Why?"

"I imagine it was his father come to get him." Flint shrugged as he gazed up the mountain. "These mountain folks are a mysterious and violent lot. You don't want to cross them."

"You think he's safe?" The worry continued to squirm inside, urging him to go despite Flint's explanation.

He peered at Flint's calm expression and slowly the tension inside eased. Maybe Flint was right about the situation. Maybe he had overreacted after the unusual feelings he'd been experiencing. He was the stranger to these parts. Flint had more experience with the people and their ways. Even if it made no sense to him. Like Flint had said, he wasn't among his peers or on his own turf. He forced his shoulders to relax along with his stance.

"I hope so." Flint bumped his fist into Giles' shoulder. "Come on, let's go."

Without a word, Giles followed the others back down the trail. Everything inside him wanted to turn back and go after the boy, to make sure he was safe. He didn't like the uncertainty and concern on the kid's behalf that still roiled his gut. Another unknown. Another disturbance to his senses. Conflicting emotions warred in his chest as he made his way back to the stable. But one question lurked in his mind. How much longer could he stay with so much wrong surrounding him?

Chapter Five

Cassie's melodic voice moved Flint as she played the square piano in the dining room. The sedate hymn cast a somber mood over the people eating their suppers. A fitting frame of mind for a Sunday evening. Her hands moved gracefully over the keys as she poured her heart into the song. Although they hadn't been able to spend much if any time alone, she'd frequently sent longing looks his way. If only they could talk without others nearby, then maybe he could gauge her feelings toward him. Toward them.

The front door opened and John Baker strode into the dining room. Flint crossed the crowded room to greet his neighbor and his boss's representative. Ever since Flint had been made aware of John's true purpose in frequenting the inn, he'd ensured the man was welcomed. After all, the reports he sent to Reggie Fairhope would prove important later. When Flint went looking for a different situation.

"Mr. Baker, nice to see you." Flint stopped in front of the man.

John skimmed the room with a proprietary perusal. "You've got a good crowd this evening. I'm very glad to see you're doing a fine job. Sadly, I only have a little while before my wife expects me home."

"I have a seat over here, where you can listen to Cassie sing." Flint shook off the impression that his guest was beginning to feel like part owner and led John to a small table near the piano. "How's this?"

"Fine, fine. Bring me a tankard of ale, won't you?" John dragged out a chair and sat down. "'The Old Rugged Cross.' Interesting choice."

Flint studied the older man for a beat. "Why is that?"

"I associate it with Easter, not late summer." John laid his top hat on the table and relaxed back in the chair. He surveyed the murmuring crowd. "Looks like she's put everyone to sleep."

Flint rested his hands on the back of a chair across from John. "They're showing their appreciation. Let me get your drink."

"Indeed." John folded his arms as Flint crossed the room to the bar.

He glanced over his shoulder at John, pondering his meaning. He stepped behind the bar and grabbed a tankard, stuck it under the tap and filled it with the foamy beverage. Cassie's singing had lulled everyone into a gentle daze as they listened. Shutting off the tap, Flint scraped the foam off the top of the tankard. Cassie finished the hymn and switched to singing the more upbeat and patriotic "My Country Tis of Thee" as he moved out from behind the bar and carried the drink to John.

"My country tis of thee, sweet land of liberty, of thee I sing…"

Liberty brought to mind the unfortunate incident with Teddy. Was he free or held captive by his father? Officially, it wasn't any of his business. If the boy's father came and took him home, even if in such a rude fashion, then what could he do about it? Like Giles, he hoped the boy was safe at home. Still, a sliver of worry stuck in his heart as he set the tankard on the table in front of John.

"That's a good song." John hummed along before lifting the tankard to quaff some ale. "They really react to her song choices, don't they?"

"Do they?" Flint hadn't noticed the connection but after John had brought it to his attention, he could see the livelier tune had indeed brightened the faces and the volume of sound in the room. "Music always has an effect on people."

John set the tankard on the table, pinning Flint with a curious look. He motioned to the surrounding guests. "Looks like things are going pretty good for you."

"Yes, sir. Only two guest rooms are vacant, the dining room is bustling with guests, and everyone is safe."

"Good to hear, son. Any problems I can help with?" John took another drink, wiping foam from his upper lip with the back of his hand.

"Just one at the moment. I need to dig a new well."

"Why?"

"Somehow a dead skunk ended up in the only one we had." He hesitated to voice Giles' opinion about how the animal had found its way into the well. Better to keep it an apparent mystery. "I've started to figure out where to dig one, but in the meantime we're lugging water from up the hill."

"That's inconvenient, isn't it?" John kept his attention on the girl at the piano, a slight frown weighing down his eyebrows.

"It's a temporary solution. It will take a while to dig a new well and have it ready to use." Why was John staring at Cassie so intently? A worm of unease wriggled up his spine at the unwarranted attention the man paid to his girl. "We'll need to start on it first thing in the morning."

"I'd be happy to send over some of my field hands to take care of that. Just say the word." John turned to address Flint directly. "Two of my blacks will get it done in half the time."

Cassie glanced at him from her seat on the stool in front of the piano. The frown she aimed at him spoke volumes of her opinion about the offer of slave labor, but what choice did he have? While he agreed abolition couldn't arrive fast enough, he knew those who owned slaves had no intention of giving them up. And they needed a new well as quickly as possible. If help was close at hand, he'd be a fool to dismiss it.

Sheridan had continued to make it very clear how much he relied upon the fresh water being available for his food preparations. Likewise, the overnight guests needed water to refresh themselves after their arduous journeys over the uncomfortable roads. Teddy grumbled his way through retrieving water as needed though Flint worried he'd quit if something wasn't done and soon. Then he'd be down two more employees and the maintenance of the property would suffer. Having some strong men take over the manual labor would achieve the desired results much quicker than he and his staff could do.

Suppressing a sigh, he nodded. "I'd appreciate that, sir. If you're sure you won't miss them."

"They'll only be here a few days. It will be fine."

Cassie started singing a ballad, a slight frown marring her beautiful face. He wanted to please her, to honor the resistance she had to slave labor, but he needed the help.

"Thank you. I—" A whisper of movement caught his attention.

Mercy. Floating near the fireplace behind John. She pointed toward John with a frown on her brows. What did that mean? She knew who John was and why he visited so frequently. What possible problem could she have with his presence? At the moment, it didn't matter. She posed a far greater risk to the success of the inn than anyone or anything else. She must leave before someone noticed and realized the inn was haunted. Frantic, Flint shooed her away.

"What's the matter, boy?" John peered up at him and then started to turn to look behind him.

"Nothing." He needed to distract him. Keep him from spotting the ghost. Flint pointed to the tankard. "Want another? As a thank you for your help."

John settled back in his chair with a big smile. "That's mighty nice of you."

Flint grabbed the tankard with one hand while waving Mercy away with the other. She gave him a sad shake of her head while glaring at him and then vanished. What was the matter with her?

He hurried to refill the tankard and return it to John's table. Cassie continued singing, moving through several happy tunes while John sipped his beverage. Flint stood guard nearby, arms crossed, observing everyone enjoying the simple entertainment. Cassie seemed more like herself than she had for some time. Although she kept her distance from him, she also seemed to be more confident in herself. Since Giles' arrival come to think on it. Was she avoiding Flint or preoccupied with her brother's presence after so long a time? Or worse, losing interest in continuing their paused relationship?

He really must find a way to get her alone. He had questions only she could answer. He cared for her and could only hope she still cared for him. He needed to know. If she'd talk to him.

She should let it go. Seriously. But she couldn't. Her ma had ruined her birthday with her snide comments. Then never corrected the false impression by sharing her pa's real reason for sending the doll's house. Why? The question rattled around in her brain and soured her stomach. She'd ask her ma if only she'd come when called. But of course Ma wasn't a trained dog and had never listened to Cassie when she was alive. Why would she deign to do so as a ghost with the ability to pop in and out at will? Especially when she obviously knew she'd wronged her only daughter.

Cassie swung the broom harder, creating a cloud of dust and flicking dirt off the front porch onto the ground. All the muddy boots of the men as they tromped in had left the boards littered with dirt clods. At least the chipped stone carriageway reduced the amount of dirt and mud around the inn itself. Dusting the furniture in the guest rooms had become much easier as a result. Still the working men dragged the stuff in on their boots. At least sweeping the mess away gave her a way to vent the confused anger warring in her chest.

Flint strode through the open doorway onto the porch beside her. "Will you walk with me, Cassie?"

Lord, he was a handsome man. She wanted to be with him, but her emotions at the moment cavorted in all directions. She barely knew her own mind let alone her feelings for him. She wanted time to consider all avenues forward before committing to any of them. She forced herself to resist his allure with difficulty.

"I'm busy." She shook her head as she turned her back to him and kept sweeping.

"That can wait a while." He stilled her efforts by moving up beside her and laying a hand on her wrist. "Please?"

She shook off his hand. "I really want to finish this."

"Are you mad at me?" He dropped his hand away but stayed near. Too near for her peace of mind.

"No." The swish of the straw broom on the wood boards steadied her with each stroke. Helped her contain the irritation inside.

Flint sidled in front of her. Taking her hand, he forced her to look into his eyes. "Then come take a walk with me. Just up to the falls and back."

His eyes enthralled her, begged her to accept his request.

Dropping her gaze to their joined hands, she sighed. "You're not going to let me finish?" She didn't want to peer into his captivating eyes. She'd lose herself in his kindness, his understanding, and worst of all his caring.

Gently he pried the broom handle from her trembling fingers and propped it against the wall. "We won't be gone long. It will be good for you to get some air."

She folded her arms around her waist rather than let them reach out to touch him. "I'm really not in the mood."

He clasped her hand in his and tugged until she stepped closer. "For me?"

His soft question shattered her resolve. Her heart called out to his, clamoring to be with him. She'd do most anything for him. How could she refuse? She peered up at him. "Fine."

"Thank you." He squeezed her hand and silently led the way down the steps, past the clusters of customers arriving for midafternoon dinner, and across the yard to the narrow trail snaking up the mountainside. "You've been acting differently ever since your brother arrived."

"Have I?" Her emotions had swung back and forth and all around so much she barely knew herself. The anger toward her ma made her ill. Which only fueled her irritation. The whole situation upset her normal easy-going manner. What was wrong with her? Finding an emotional balance to maintain any sense of comportment had become nigh impossible.

"Are you upset, sweetheart?" He pulled her to a halt, taking both her hands to hold her close. "Is it having your brother here?"

"No." Giles had nothing to do with it. She was relieved to have him home. She needed him to help her sort out what to do about everything. To find the men, the keys, some peace of mind.

Birds twittered and chirped from the surrounding forest.

The distant mooing of the cows crawled up the hillside. The scent of hot dirt and pine trees invaded her nostrils. Standing with him so far from the inn helped her emotions calm down, settle like dust during a rain shower. Or was it merely the fact he was holding her hands and looking at her with his concerned eyes?

"Is it something I said?" He wrapped his fingers around her hands. "Did I hurt your feelings?"

"No." Why did he think he was at fault? She looked away, staring into the distance at nothing in particular. Echoes of confusion and anger filled her core.

"Cassie, talk to me." He used a finger to bring her chin around so she could see his serious countenance. "What is wrong?"

She couldn't explain a situation she didn't understand. She felt joyous one moment and angry the next, coupled with worry and manipulation woven into the mix. The result made her emotions careen about like a handful of thrown pebbles. The more she tried to calm down the more agitated she became.

"I don't know." Confusion swirled inside her as she tried to sort out the mix of emotions that had been clashing inside up until moments before.

"Do you…still care for me?"

She dragged in a long breath and looked away again. Did she? She had at one point in time, but after her ma's death she'd given up pursuing a relationship because she needed to sort out how things changed. Her role had shifted to taking care of the inn like her mother once had. So much responsibility had suddenly landed on Cassie's shoulders she didn't know how her ma had managed. She was responsible for all the people who lived and worked at the inn. Her garden had to be weeded, planted, watered. The entire place had to be clean and welcoming despite the endless dust and dirt, the stinking sloppy spittoons and bits of trash left behind by the guests. Simples and purges needed brewing and concocting to have on hand in case of illness or injury.

The list of tasks seemed endless. Even entertaining the people each evening meant additional work to keep the piano in tune and learn new songs they'd enjoy. She didn't mind writing some ballads of her own to perform, but seeking out new ditties and tunes wasn't easy living so far from town. The mending she did when she had time, but mostly in the evening after everyone had gone to bed, gave her a little money to set aside for her hoped-for future. A future that now lay in tatters because of her ma's death. All while wearing a pretty dress and a smile. She was exhausted.

"Cassie?" Flint's eyes darkened as he waited for her reply. "My feelings for you haven't changed. Have yours?"

He deserved the truth but could he handle it? Would he understand this time if she put him off yet again? He'd more than likely throw up his hands and walk away if she asked him to wait any longer. Especially when her own feelings were so mixed up and confused. She sucked in a fortifying breath as she searched his compelling eyes. She didn't think she could handle his rejection.

"I don't know."

"What's that supposed to mean?" His eyes narrowed, hiding their depths and his feelings.

"Just what I said. Are we done?" Her heart ached as she watched him shut down even as he asked about their future. She stepped back and crossed her arms over her chest. "I have a lot of work to do."

He hauled her hands back into his as he tried to bring her closer to him. "Cassandra, listen to me."

"Haven't you said enough?"

"No, I haven't." Flint dipped his head, pressing a feather-light kiss on her lips. "I need to know if you're still my girl."

Oh yes, she wanted to be. Could she? With all the conflicting emotions and uncertainty swirling inside and around her, she should not. She didn't want to hurt him, but she must be honest with herself and with him.

"I need to finish the sweeping." She pulled her hands free, preparing to head back down the trail when Flint lifted his head up in surprise. She jerked her chin up to stare at the smile slowly spreading across his face. "What?"

"Well, hey." He stepped around Cassie, grinning at someone behind her.

The flash of annoyance at his sudden desertion vanished at the sound of running footsteps. She spun around in time for Teddy to wrap her in a hug. Relief and shock ripped through her as he pulled her into a desperate embrace. When he'd left so precipitously the other day she'd feared for his safety along with her brother. But she'd agreed with Flint that they couldn't interfere between father and son. She'd longed to hike right on over the hill to see for herself, but stayed home and prayed for his well-being.

Now, his fear tingled her tongue and made her grip him harder. She sensed his relief and joy wrapping the worry inside. What caused him to shake so? "Are you all right? Where have you been?"

"Pa made me go with him but as soon as I could, I slipped out." Teddy gnawed on his lip as he aimed wide eyes at her. "You don't mind, do ya?"

Chapter Six

Giles carried the guitar out to the front porch and sat on a cushioned seat near the open doors. He needed air. With luck, strumming the instrument would ease the knot in his gut. Release the worry consuming him. Cassie wasn't the same carefree little girl he'd left years ago when he'd fled from his mother's dominance. Back when she was so easy to be around, smiling and laughing with joy. She seemed stressed and worried much of the time. Something must be bothering her but she hadn't shared with him the cause.

She'd often invited him to come visit, but he'd found one reason after another to avoid doing so. He saw no point in venturing to face his mother's attempts to put him down. Or his papa's, for that matter. He worked hard to forget the things they'd done. But being around Cassie, and seeing his mother's ghost, was awakening memories he'd buried deep. Almost as if a door in his mind had been unlocked and flung open, scattering its contents throughout his mind. The more he remembered, though, the more he wished he'd forget.

"Hey, boss." Zander strolled across the carriageway to trot up the steps and claim the other chair. He motioned to the guitar. "You all right?"

"Fine." His friend knew him well. When he played, it was to give himself time to think, to process what was happening in his life. At the moment, he had much to ponder. "Where've you been?"

"Went for a walk along the river."

"Looking for something?"

"Nah. Just wanted to get the lay of the land." Zander stretched his legs out in front of him, crossing his ankles. "Found some interesting tracks."

"Like?" Giles strummed the strings, wincing as he adjusted the tuning. Strummed again. Better.

"Lots of folks like to walk along the river." He tapped the table with a finger. "It's quite trampled in places."

"I doubt that's unusual." He played a ballad, one filled with sentiment and longing for a girl who had left. He didn't sing though, nobody wanted to hear him mangle the tune.

He surveyed the bustling scene before him as he sang and strummed. Men of business and merchandising talking earnestly as they came and went. Ladies escorted by their gentlemen out of carriages and into the dining room for a late afternoon repast. Dogs sniffing about, laying under a tree. The pigs snuffling and foraging. A typical scene on a hot summer's day.

He kept strumming even when he spotted his sister leading Flint and young Teddy rapidly toward the inn. Teddy? Relief swept through him at the sight of the boy, smiling in Cassie's wake. She marched quickly across the space, avoiding the clusters of people and the flock of chickens pecking the grass on the edge of the carriageway. She marched up the steps and inside without more than a sharp glance in his direction.

Flint ambled up the few steps into the shade of the porch, Teddy right beside him. Giles rested the instrument against the small table separating him from Zander. "What's got her all het up?"

"I don't know exactly." Flint hooked his thumbs into his waistband. "We didn't get to talk much before this whippersnapper showed up."

Teddy frowned up at Flint. "Did I interrupt somethin'?"

Flint tousled the boy's hair with a smirk. "Just Cassie being upset about something I'd asked her."

Cassie definitely had been annoyed about whatever their conversation had entailed. Hopefully, his sister would find a way to shake off the irritation. Then with luck she'd settle down enough to be able to speak to him about it later. He'd find out and eradicate the issue on her behalf. Whatever, or whoever, the irritant might be.

Giles rose to his feet, arms crossed. "I've not seen her so mad in many a year. What did you say?"

"That's between us." Flint frowned and eased back a step. "Besides, it's not like you've been around to see how she's been lately."

A low blow to raise the matter of his staying far from his parents for the past several years. The man gloating at him had no right to pass judgement on his actions. He'd done what he had to do in order to make a life for himself, to survive in a harsh and often cruel world. He'd do it again if put in the same position.

"I'm here now to protect my family in this time of crisis." He inspected Flint from head to boots and back, pinning him with his steady regard. "From every threat."

Zander shifted in his chair, poised to stand and join the argument. Giles stilled him with a look. Grateful for the backup but he could deal with a light-weight man like Flint.

Flint rested his hand on the butt of the pistol hanging at his right thigh. "We're in agreement on that."

Giles stared the other man down. "Don't be part of the problem then."

"I'm not trying to be, believe me." Flint nodded once and then addressed the boy. "So your pa came for you?"

Teddy swallowed hard. "He wasn't none too happy to come back and find me gone. Said he tramped all over the mountain until he found me working here."

"So he made you go home." Giles studied the nervous boy. "Does he know you're here?"

The boy shook his head, wide eyed. "No, I sneaked out while he was sleeping."

"Teddy…" Flint grasped the boy's shoulder. "It's not right for you to defy your pa. He obviously wants you home with him."

"But I feel safer here." Teddy glanced between the two tall men. "You all take care of me. Besides, you need my help."

"Do we?" Giles crossed his arms again. Surely there were enough other hands around to manage running a farm and inn.

"To haul the water. And help Miss Cassie in the garden. And pick out the horse stalls." The boy pleaded earnestly with his eyes. "I'm helpful to ya…."

Flint released the boy's shoulder. "Yes, but if your pa's returned and wants you home, then that's where you should be."

Oh, to be wanted at home by your father. Giles swallowed the lump in his throat. With luck, his own father won't object to his presence when the man eventually decides to return to the inn and Cassie. Not that he'd come to see his son. No chance of such an event coming to pass. But he'd surely wish to comfort his only daughter.

"Don't send me home." Teddy's eyes glistened with hope and unshed tears. "He don't want me. Not really. Not since my ma died."

Giles started to shake his head but stopped himself. The boy belonged with his family, especially since his mother had passed. The thought gave him pause. He'd walked away from his own family until notified of his mother's passing.

What right did he have to insist the boy go home to a father who didn't want him? Like Giles' parents hadn't wanted him around. He understood how the boy felt.

"Well…" Flint glanced at Zander and then Giles. "While I understand, I don't want your father to be angry with you or us."

"Let the boy stay, Flint." Giles picked up the guitar and rested it on his lap. "He's better off here than with an absent father no matter how much the man protests."

"If'n he comes again, then I'll talk to him." Teddy bobbed his head emphatically. "I'll take care of it. I promise."

Flint stared at the eager boy for several long moments then finally shrugged. "You can stay. But if your pa raises a fuss, then you'll have to go home. Is that clear?"

Teddy threw his arms around Flint's waist. "Thank you. I won't let you down."

Giles' heart swelled with happiness on the boy's behalf. Teddy grinned, eyes closed, as he hugged Flint with all his little boy strength. Giles pictured himself hugging his own father as a boy, way back before everything fell apart. How he missed the closeness of those years.

Prying the boy off himself, Flint shooed him away. "Go find Marshall and get back to work."

"Yes, sir!" Teddy raced down the steps and ran for the stable.

"You've a soft heart." Giles rolled his eyes at the smirk on Flint's face. "You may have just bought trouble."

An angry father, especially one of the mountain folks, may indeed pose a direct threat to the inn and its people. He'd keep his eyes open, looking for the trouble to come to him. Ready to defend the property with all his might against any danger the delinquent father may pose.

"Afraid?" Flint drew in a breath as he glanced between Zander and Giles. "I think we can deal with a father who neglects his son most of the time."

"There's a bigger question." Teddy dodged around a fast-moving wagon pulled by nervous horses and dashed into the shadowy barn. Giles returned his gaze to encompass the other two men. "What's the man up to?"

Cassie fought her way out of the tangled sheet before the sun could light the bedroom. She'd tossed and turned through the wee hours, stewing over the hurt from her mother's attitude toward her. Her bare feet landed on the wool carpet as she quickly changed into a tan calico day dress and braided her hair into a long chain down her back. Shoved her feet into leather shoes. Snatched a black ribbon from the holder on her dresser and tied it roughly at the end of the braid. Good enough for working in the kitchen and garden. She dared her ma to tell her otherwise.

Tiptoeing but longing to stomp, she made her way downstairs and pushed into the kitchen. Bacon sizzled on the griddle. The mouthwatering aroma of baking bread filled her nostrils. Meg glanced up with a smile as she worked with a large bowl of flour, cutting in the lard and butter. Myrtle sliced a haunch of ham and piled the slices on a platter. In the midst of pouring a cup of steaming coffee, Sheridan lifted a brow at Cassie's sudden appearance.

"Good morning." Cassie stopped at the edge of the large table. "I need to keep busy today. What can I do?"

Anything would suffice. Keep her hands occupied, preferably hitting something. She eyed the food preparations before her. Her eyes landed on a sharp, shiny knife on the table.

"You're up early." Sheridan hefted the coffee pot with one hand. "Want some?"

"Thanks." The table held a variety of items awaiting chopping. The knife tempted her fingers. "Making stew again?"

"It's popular." Sheridan handed her a cup of coffee and studied her for a moment. "What's the matter?"

"I should plant some okra, then you could make it a gumbo instead of plain stew." She swallowed a mouthful of hot coffee.

"If you did, I could make some Limping Susan for a change." He hefted his mug in a mock salute. "Just for you."

She huffed at his defensive tone. Her friend had taken umbrage with her questioning his menu. But why did he have to fix the same things day after day? Would a touch of variety kill him? But she couldn't say that to him. "What on earth is Limping Susan?"

"It's popular back on the coast. A stew made with bacon, rice, okra, and spicy seasonings."

"Bacon and rice?" She shuddered. "I can't imagine such a combination."

He peered more closely at her. "You seem off this morning. What's really wrong?"

"Nothing." Or everything. Feeling out of control and moody mixed together. And the ever-present anger simmering in her chest.

"If you say so." He swallowed a gulp of coffee and set the cup on the table. "But I don't believe you."

She sipped the strong brew and held the cup between her hands as she considered how to respond to his doubtful expression. She needed to vent the anger simmering inside at her mother's deceit. The sharp knife gleamed beside piles of onions, carrots, potatoes. The temptation proved irresistible. Plunking her cup on the table, coffee sloshing over the side, she grabbed up the blade.

"I don't think that's a good idea this morning." Sheridan stared at her while she examined the sharpness of the blade. "Not in the mood you're in, I mean."

"What kind of mood do you think I'm in?" The anger inside scared her. She'd never felt such a prolonged intense feeling before. Especially not directed at her ma. What was wrong with her?

"What are you mad about?" Sheridan put his hand out, palm up and wiggling the tips of his fingers.

She inspected the blade again, angling it one way and another. When Sheridan cleared his throat and wiggled his fingers again, she slowly laid the knife handle in his hand. He set the knife down on the table on his other side, far away from Cassie's reach.

Absurd. Her anger surged at the insult. "Gramercy, Sheridan, I wasn't going to use it on anyone." Not really. Maybe in her imagination but never in fact.

"I want to be sure." He studied her, a slight lift to his lips. "Do you want to talk about it?"

The scullery maids perked up, their movements halting, eager for gossip or family secrets. Being the butt of servants' jokes or gossip wasn't going to happen. Cassie drew in a breath and let it out to a count of five. Somehow she needed to let the anger go. But she couldn't. She'd tried all night to rid herself of the seething snake writhing inside. She always came back to the fact her mother had misled her about her father's intentions behind her birthday gift. As if her mother didn't want her to grow up, become a wife and mother. Instead wanted to keep her at her side, under her heavy thumb. Ultimately, to deny her the right to be a woman. But why?

"Only one person can help me and she isn't talking to me." She pressed her palms to the table, leaning on them.

His brows dipped in a frown for a second then he nodded. "That's a problem all right."

"I just don't understand…" She shrugged and splayed her hands. "What did I do to make her so protective and defensive at the same time?"

"I don't know." Sheridan sidled around the table to stand beside her. "Sometimes parents don't have the answers or even understand the questions. But we do the best we can."

Only Sheridan hadn't been allowed to raise his family. He must resent not having the opportunity to teach his boys about being a good man like him. About not having his wife to love. He'd been denied so much. She sensed a shadow of sorrow as her anger softened into irritation.

"Even when you have no control?" Knowing his family had been split up so many years ago saddened her. The irritation dissolved into regret on his behalf. Perhaps her pa would succeed in finding Sheridan's wife, but what about his sons? Finding the boys was nigh impossible after so many years had passed. "I sure don't have any control over my ma."

Meg hummed softly as she poured a quantity of milk into the bowl and stirred it. Myrtle piled the slices of ham in a cast iron pot, adding some ale and herbs before hanging the heavy pot near the cooking fire. Both women peeked at her as they worked. Meg made the dough into a ball and then placed it on the sturdy table. Lifting a large rolling pin, she hesitated, peering at Cassie.

"Family is important, Cassie. Your mother loved you. You know that." Sheridan rested his big hands on the table, his fingers curling into fists. "Look at me, Cassie. Listen. She had her reasons for everything she did, even if she didn't share them with you."

"That's the point. She kept secrets from me. Ones that changed the way I saw my own life. Made me feel like my father still thought of me as a child."

He flattened his hands on the hard surface. "Did you consider maybe she didn't know at the time? Only found out later and then it was too late."

"Too late?"

"She was killed. Perhaps she didn't have chance to tell you."

"She's talked to me since…" Heat flushed her cheeks as she regarded her dearest friend. "She could have told me at any time she wanted. But did she? No. It's very frustrating."

Myrtle crossed the room to snare a cast iron baking dish and carry it back to the table. Meg grinned at Cassie and motioned to her.

"What, Meg?" Cassie shifted her weight to rest on one foot.

"If you want to work off some frustration, come beat this dough." Meg flourished the rolling pin and laughed. "It works wonders."

"There's a good idea." Sheridan straightened and moved back to his work station. "Beaten biscuits. Without a sharp knife in your hand."

"You act as if you think I'd hurt someone with it." She pouted at him. "I thought you knew me better than that."

Sheridan guffawed. "Of course I do, but let's not dance with the devil, all right?"

She huffed a sigh. "Fine."

"Go on with you." Sheridan gestured to the rolling pin in Meg's hand.

"What do I do?" Cassie took the offered rolling pin, hefting the weight of the heavy wood.

Meg pointed to the ball of dough hunkered on the floured table. "Start whacking and keep it up until your arm gives out. Then I'll take over."

Cassie pictured her mother's face on the dough. No, not her face, but her secrets and deceits. Then she did as instructed. Pounding on the white mass with strong strokes. Meg occasionally turned the dough, flipping it over so Cassie could continue. The thud of the wood hitting the soft dough satisfied her need to hit something. And made further conversation impossible so she didn't have to say any more in front of the women. She'd said too much already.

She struck the dough again and again, always with one question simmering in her mind. What else had her mother kept secret from her?

Chapter Seven

S nippets of arguments and chidings interspersed with scenes of punishment and fights. Giles didn't recall experiencing any of it and yet they felt like suppressed memories reawakened. He'd lain in bed the previous night recalling everything he could about his childhood. The time he'd spent in the sprawling manor outside of Montgomery with his parents and brothers and sister. He'd been happy back then, young and free to run and play in the woods surrounding their home. Free to swim and dive into the large lake down the road a piece. Up until his cousin had drowned and then everything changed.

His parents had changed most of all. He could barely remember them before the incident, but he could hear his mother singing as she tended her garden or humming while she stirred bubbling soup in the cauldron over the cooking fire. Then his cousin's drowning and the subsequent falling out with his aunt triggered a gradual divide in the family that ultimately couldn't be overcome after the passing of his grandmother. Without a word of explanation, they'd moved and sent their sons out into the world to fend for themselves. Find work and build a life all without the love and support he craved. As much as he remembered, though, he still had questions.

He hurried to the family residence part of the sprawling building. He needed answers.

He strode into the parlor and paused at the open door to take stock of the contents of the room. Merely standing in the room swept unease through his chest. Surrounded by memories of his former life in the furniture and pictures on the wall. Not all of those memories were welcome. He shoved the door closed and moved farther into the room.

"Mama, come here." Giles paced the painted floor boards, past the doll's house and back around the dining room table. Then back to where he started. Searching for his mother's ghost. "We need to talk."

He slowly scanned the four walls of the room. Glanced up at the ceiling. Swept his gaze another time through the room. He huffed in frustration. Nothing. What did he expect to happen? For her to pop up beside him like a rabbit out of its warren?

He cleared his throat and tried again. "Mama, I assume you can hear me so show yourself. I have questions only you can answer."

Feeling foolish, he flopped into one of the chairs by the cold fireplace to wait. A pile of ashes on the brick floor spoke of a recent fire but none burned during the searing heat of the day. While a little cooler than Mobile, northern Alabama still experienced hot summers. A group of framed oil miniatures graced the mantel along with a bouquet of red and yellow roses in a glass vase.

The pretty doll's house between the front windows drew his attention. Cassie had every right to be upset with Mercy for misleading her about why their father had sent the gift. Without his papa's explanation he'd have assumed Mercy spoke the truth, which would hurt a girl's feelings as she worked on becoming a young woman. He didn't blame Cassie for holding a grudge and wanting to know why she'd not revealed his reason once she became aware of it. Another question for his mother.

"Mother!" He raised his voice to try to compel her to appear. "I need to speak with you. Please?"

Maybe if he used his manners she'd condescend to show herself. He surveyed the room, searching for any changes for several moments. Then, he saw a shimmer and her ghost emerged.

Ignoring the demanding underlying instinct to flee the ghost, Giles blinked several times and swallowed hard as he gripped the armrests. He'd asked for the chance to ask her questions but suddenly wasn't sure he wanted to know. Who was he fooling? Of course he did. "Thanks for coming."

"Are you enjoying your visit?" Mercy hovered inches from the floor in the center of the room.

"So far. But Mama, I've so many questions." Seeing her gentle smile helped him release his grip on the chair. She wouldn't hurt him. She loved him. Once.

The smile faded as she stared at him. "Questions?"

"Yes." He sat back in his chair, studying her. "Why do you stay here?"

She splayed her hands in front of her. "I don't know. I don't seem to have a place to go yet."

"Maybe finding your killers will help set you on your way." He vowed to locate the rogues and bring them to justice. But the descriptions such as they were provided little to work with. "Is there anything else you remember about them?"

"They said they were looking for my treasure and stole the keys to the attic door. Joe pocketed them. But, Giles, listen to me. You have to get them back."

"Why? I could just break down the door." Despite the thickness of the wood door, his increased strength should make short work of taking it down. "It's replaceable, after all."

"That's not the problem. The keys open more than the door. Your sister and brothers, all of you..." She drew in a deep breath and blew it out, her eyes narrowing. "Never mind. When your father comes home, he'll settle the matter."

"What matter?" He leaned forward to grip his hands between his knees. "What will Papa have to take care of when he gets home?"

Mercy shifted her eyes to look away at anything but him. "It's nothing. I shouldn't have said anything." She stood and floated away, pacing without touching the floor. "It's for your pa to tell you."

The same father who had forced him and his brothers to leave home. "I've always wondered why Papa sent us away when you moved here." There, he'd forced the words into existence. "Why did he?"

Mercy looked away and then back to meet his gaze. "He said it was time for you to be a man." She swallowed nervously, glancing away briefly.

"I could have been a man living up here with you instead of being sent away by my own father."

"But look at how you've turned out. He was right."

"Maybe. It just seemed odd that he'd break up the family, starting with the death of my cousin and then finishing the work practically right after we buried our grandmamma. What was that about?"

"Your cousin's death couldn't be helped." Mercy lifted another few inches from the floor and moved farther away. "After my mother died, we felt it best to leave."

"I tried to save George, you know. But Papa made me get out of the water and wouldn't let me go back to pull him out. The one time I failed."

The accident haunted him as surely as his mother's ghost haunted the inn. He stared at his mother as the scene replayed in his mind. The bigger and older teenager had dived in from the high bank and took a while to surface. He floated on his stomach, silent in the water. Giles thought he was playing around and left him alone for a time.

But after too many minutes went by and the boy didn't move, Giles splashed his way into the water. Tried to drag him out of the lake but he seemed to be hung up on something under the surface. Not moving. He'd pulled as hard as he dared and had started to budge the inert body when his father had appeared suddenly at his side and forced him to let go and retreat to the shore. Telling him the boy was already dead and they had to leave. No other explanation and Giles, though he'd struggled and fought to go back in, had been dragged by the arm all the way home.

At the funeral a few days later, Reggie and Mercy kept the family apart from their aunts and uncles and other cousins. They had little contact with the extended family for several years. Then the sudden death of his grandmamma caused more inexplicable tension. A few months later, they'd packed up and moved away, exhorting the boys to go make their own ways but keeping Cassie close at hand. It was all very odd and confusing.

The memories were stark and painful. He met his mother's fearful gaze and frowned. "What really happened? Why did you become so angry and mean toward us?"

The side door opened and Cassie sauntered inside, stopping when she spied Giles and Mercy. After a moment, she softly closed the door and stood there, arms crossed. Mercy turned at the sound of the door closing and then drifted closer to the fireplace, away from Cassie's glare.

Cassie huffed and walked closer to Giles. "Ma, I'm so mad at you right now I could spit."

Mercy shimmered and shifted away, her gaze flashing to Giles and then back to Cassie. "I'm sorry."

"For not telling me the truth? I saw Pa's note. You told me he thought of me as a child! Not that he was trying to help me prepare to be wife." Her voice shook as she confronted their mother. "Why?"

"I didn't know his purpose until after our spat over the

silly house." A flash of annoyance swept through her eyes. "The same day you dared to suggest having relations with Flint. I'd do anything to prevent such a union."

"That's not your decision." Cassie lifted her chin, fire in her eyes. "I'm not a child and I will make the choice of who I will or won't marry. Not you."

"Your father and I—"

"I will seek your advice and your blessing, but you will not choose for me." Cassie strode closer to Mercy. "Understood?"

Mercy folded her arms across her chest and nodded slowly. "I don't like it though."

"Now that's settled, tell me, Mama, what is Papa going to deal with when he gets here?" Giles stood and eased closer to his mother. "I really need to know what you're worried about telling us."

A flush of fear bathed Mercy's face before she shimmered completely and vanished.

"Again? I don't believe this." Cassie huffed and shook her head. "Ma! Come back here. We're not done." She sighed out her frustration as she threw Giles a glare and then flounced across the room and up the steps.

A door slammed and Giles was left alone with more questions. The biggest one being, what was his mother afraid to tell him?

Cocoa trotted beside Cassie as she strolled toward the shady gazebo. A cool burst of wind carried the scent of rain. She frowned at the letter in her hand. Pa had finally written to her and she wanted privacy to read what he had to say. She longed for news of Sheridan's wife and sons as well as a date when she could expect his arrival. She hurried up the few steps into the relative coolness and settled on her favorite seat on the center metal bench. Cocoa sniffed around the outside of the small building before joining her, crouching at her feet to keep watch on the customer traffic in the distance.

Cassie opened the letter, unfolding it to hold between her hands.

July 31, 1821
Savannah, GA

Dear Cassie,

First, let me say how much I wish I could be there with you. I know you're grieving your mother's death and trust that Sheridan and Flint are looking out for you in my stead. You know I love you and wish you well.

When I arrived in Savannah, I was not expecting the welcome I received. I have not been in close contact with my brothers and sisters in years. I had not realized that my oldest brother had taken over the carpentry shop I've been working with to build the furniture for the inn. Imagine my surprise when Beck greeted me with a bear hug! I've been staying with him as he's unmarried and has a spare room. He's being a bit difficult to work with and not doing what I want so much as what he wants. As a result, I must stay and make sure he listens to my demands.

That concern aside, I've been treated like the Prodigal Son by the rest of the family. My other brother Wesley introduced me to his wife and children. My sister, Cordelia, is also married, although my other sister, Scarlett, is not. Scarlett is living with Cordelia to help her with the children.

It's been wonderful to see everyone, let me tell you. Scarlett has been hinting at me moving here, but I don't want to do that. I will be coming home in another two months. Which seems like a long time but isn't from the perspective of the fine quality work needed for this job.

Write me back and tell me how you're doing.

Love,
Your father
Reggie Fairhope

"Well, how do you like that, Cocoa?" She read the letter again, then dropped it onto her lap and stared ahead. "More aunts and uncles."

People went about their business, arriving by coach or on horseback or on foot. Talking and laughing as though her entire world hadn't just been overturned like a top-heavy coach-and-four. Beau and Pickles spotted her and came loping toward her, their tongues hanging out of their mouths. A flock of chickens scratched in the yard beside the inn. Cattle lowed in their field beyond the stable. Flint strode from the stable toward the inn, talking with another gentleman in business attire. Normal, everyday scenes which suddenly became surreal.

She had family in Georgia whom she'd never heard of before. How could that be? A huge secret kept from her all of her life. Aunts and uncles and some number of cousins. What about grandparents? She skimmed the letter but her pa had made no mention of them. Perhaps they weren't alive. Maybe he hadn't seen them yet. But who knew…she surely did not.

He made no mention of searching for Sheridan's wife. Didn't ask about his own sons and whether they were coming to the inn. So much left unsaid. She hadn't ventured to tell him that Ma haunted the inn, fearing he wouldn't believe her. Or think she'd lost her mind. Or both. But to never reveal he even had brothers and sisters in Georgia choked her, making it hard to swallow around the knot in her throat.

Her parents the expert secret keepers.

She balled up the letter in a tight fist, bouncing her hand on her thigh. "How could they?"

Jumping to her feet, she paced the small confines of the gazebo. She clutched the revelatory paper in her fist. The earlier anger returned the more she considered how much she'd been deprived of by her parents refusing to let her know about the rest of the family. Was she the only one who was kept in the dark? Did Giles know? If so, she'd be even more upset. If not, then her parents were hiding something. Something bigger than the secret of her father's side of the family's mere existence.

She stopped pacing as an idea swiftly formed. "Come on, girl. I have a letter to write."

Cocoa rose to her feet and followed her down the steps to the grassy yard. Beau and Pickles turned and followed them to the residence, staying outside when Cassie yanked open the front door and stormed into the parlor. Marching to the stairs, she ran up to her bedroom and soon was seated at her writing desk. She snared a piece of paper and a quill pen and tapped the feather against her cheek, considering her words.

Tues., Aug. 7, 1821

Dear Pa,

Thank you for your recent letter. It's good to hear that you are well.

We are doing fairly well here with only a few minor challenges that Flint has taken care of. It is a godsend that you found him to manage in your extended absence. I do wish you'd come home soon, though. I need you here, not hundreds of miles away. Please don't delay any longer than necessary. Giles is here and I hope to hear from my other brothers soon. I don't know how long he'll stay, so you may want to cut short your business and come home. I need you.

Have you had any luck finding leads to Sheridan's wife and sons? I'm anxious to know.

What a surprise to find your brother running the carpentry business! But to be honest, it was a far greater surprise to me to learn I have aunts and uncles and even cousins in Savannah. Do I have grandparents there too? Why didn't you and Ma ever mention any of them? Did you have some kind of falling out with them like you did with Ma's sisters?

Write back and tell me more about them, please. I'm curious!

And come home soon, Pa. I think Ma might like to have a word or two with you.

Love,

Cassie

Chapter Eight

*E*arly the next afternoon, Cassie strolled out to her garden. The one place where she could relax and forget her cares. She swung a bucket of gardening tools at her side as she hummed a tune. She'd kill some weeds and prune some bushes and try to not be angry at her mother and father. Holding onto being upset had made her slightly ill for too many days. What did it matter? She knew the truth now about the gift and her family and would just have to move on. Or try.

She continued humming, absorbing the humor from the happy ballad as she opened the gate to the large garden and propped it open. Setting the bucket inside, she pulled on her work gloves as she surveyed what plants needed tending. The corn stalks rustled in the cool morning breeze, the tassels golden against the green ears. Red and green tomatoes hung on the bushy plants in the next row. Beans climbed up the poles in their row and cabbages nestled among leaves in another. Neat and orderly, tended with love.

She knelt down by the cabbages and began pulling the few weeds that dared to invade her garden. Singing "Brown-eyed Belle," she moved on to the next row and worked her way down to the end. The idea of adding okra to the mix wiggled through her brain. Not a bad idea.

"Hey, sis."

Rocking onto her heels, she rested her hands on her thighs. Giles strode into the garden. From her position on the ground, looking up at his height and the breadth of his shoulders, she felt small indeed. She scrambled to her feet, brushing dirt and bits of grass from her long skirt.

"Good morning. Did you sleep well?" He looked rested but tense. As if on alert.

"Fairly well. The bunk beds are not all that comfortable, but it's better than the floor." Giles smirked at her. "If Zander would quit snoring it would be even better."

"Pa's gone all the way to Georgia to have special furniture made so our guests are more comfortable. You'll just have to wait until he gets back to try out the new ones."

"We'll be fine for our visit." He scanned the garden's bounty and smiled. "Did you do all this? By yourself?"

She bristled at the surprise in his tone. "Of course."

"You've always had a way with plants. Even as a baby, you crawled out to the flower beds Mama used to have."

"Wow, I'd forgotten about Ma's gardens."

"She spent hours working with the flowers. Roses mostly. And her magnolia trees were amazing." Giles strode over to the row of corn stalks, fingering the silky tassel on the nearest ear. "Why on God's green earth did Papa decide to move all the way up here? So far from the rest of the family."

"He wanted to start new is what he said. Have his own place and livelihood." Giles stared at the tassel for a moment, long enough for Cassie to realize how much she'd pushed aside in her own memories of her childhood. "Why do you ask?"

"Doesn't it seem strange to you that they felt they had to move hundreds of miles away in order to start a business?"

He dropped the tassel as he turned to face her. "The broken ties with the family. Do you ever hear from them?"

"Rarely. I think Ma might have received a letter a few years ago, but no, not really." Cassie walked over to her brother, sensing the deep hurt and confusion inside him. "I just had a letter from Pa about his family in Savannah. Did you know about them?"

He gaped at her for a moment and then snapped his mouth shut, running his fingers through his hair. "Not an inkling. That's incredible."

"Yeah, he said he ran into his brother Beck and then was treated well by the rest of his brothers and sisters, and their children." She bit her bottom lip, struggling with chaotic emotions tumbling in her chest. "I feel so cheated."

"I had no idea we had family in Georgia." He raked his fingers through his hair again and then crossed his arms over his chest. "Why didn't he ever say anything?"

She laid a hand on his crossed arms, his shock mirroring her own. "I figured they must have had an argument or something. Ma never talks about her sisters or parents. I don't even know if they're alive."

"I have no contact with them. Only with you, to be honest."

"I'm glad you came home, Giles." She squeezed his steely forearm. "I always feel safe with you around."

"I'll look out for you as best I can. Which is why…" He dropped his arms to lay his large hands on her slim shoulders. "Which is why I told Flint to stay away from you if you're not interested in his affections."

A flush of annoyance warmed her cheeks. Not him, too. First Ma and now her brother interfering with her love life. "I can handle him. That's none of your business."

"You asked me to come to help you sort things out. I came because I need to protect my family. To do that, I need to find those men who dared to rob and murder our mother."

"Well, that's fine but leave my relationship with Flint out of that vow." She took a step away from her brother. "I'm sure Pa would like to see you, too. So will you stay until he gets home?"

"I sincerely doubt our loving father wants to see me. He's the one who sent me away in the first place." Sarcasm dripped from the word *loving*.

"You can't leave me here alone without family. Please." She studied his stoic expression, feeling his wavering like a leaf in a gentle breeze. "That's why I wanted you to come."

"Once those men are behind bars, I have to go back to my home in Mobile. I've got a business to run." He crossed his arms again. "Let's be clear on that point. I can't stay here. Not in Papa's house."

She huffed out her frustration with the stubborn man. She stepped toward him, moving close enough to lay a hand on his arm again. "I want you to stay. I *need* you to stay. You don't know what it's been like. And now I feel adrift. I don't know what to do. Please?"

"I—" He shook his head, dropped his arms to his sides. "I can't."

How could he be so infuriating? He'd come all this way to help her. He had to stay to help her figure out what to do with the inn, with everything. She didn't know how to supervise a business and a household. Ma had been teaching her but she hadn't taken the reins into her own hands before. She made a fist and hit his shoulder. "You can. You just won't."

"Stop that." He grabbed her upper arms and shook her gently. "You're asking me to do something I don't think I can."

She wriggled in his grasp but he held onto her, his grip tightening. "You're a grown man and can do anything you put your mind to. Let me go."

"No. You're wrong." He held onto her, pulled her closer to peer into her eyes. "You're too young and naïve to understand the way of the world."

His fingers dug into her arms, lifting her off the ground as pain ripped through her. "Ouch!"

He startled and set her down, then released her. Eyes wide and hands open, he gaped at her. "I'm so very sorry. I don't know what just happened."

She rubbed her arms with her hands to erase the pain and the impression of just how strong her brother had become. "How are you so strong when you're a merchant?"

He shrugged and shook his head, his eyes worried. "I've always been stronger than other men. It's the way I'm built, I guess."

Teddy ran up to the garden gate and paused, concern on his young face. "Are you all right, Miss Cassie?"

She nodded to him and then speared Giles with her gaze. "You need to temper how you use your strength so you don't hurt people." She stopped rubbing her arms and left them folded across her waist. "Please stay with me. At least until Pa gets home. I don't know if the others will come home, but I need you here."

He balled his hands into fists at his sides as he stared at her for several silent moments. "I'll think about it." He held up a hand when she smiled up at him. "I'm not making any promises, though."

Her joy dimmed but at least he'd agreed to think about it. Given enough time, she could convince him to do as she'd asked. "You need to find those men and the keys. Where are you going to start?"

Giles rubbed a hand over his jaw. "Do you know anybody named Joe with dark eyes?"

She searched her brain for any clues as to who this mysterious man might be but she had no recollection of him. "No. Why?"

"He was the man who shot Mama."

Teddy jerked as if poked in the chest.

Cassie shot him a look. "Do you know this man, Teddy?"

"I'm not sure." He chewed on his lips. "My pa has mentioned a man named Joe but I haven't met him so I don't know what color his eyes are."

Cassie sensed in the boy the beginnings of worry sprouting like crocus through snow. He returned her silent regard with narrowed eyes and a flat line across his lips.

"There are probably many men named Joe." Giles strode to the gate and tousled the boy's hair. "Don't worry about it, son. I'll go see what Flint knows."

"I'll go with you." Cassie pulled her gloves off and shoved them into her skirt pocket. "I've got to get to work waiting on customers." She picked up her bucket and followed Giles and Teddy through the gate. The weight of the tasks resting on her shoulders made her stumble. Something had to change and she knew what it must be. "I need to speak to Flint, too."

The clanging of pots from the kitchen punctuated the steady hum of conversation in the dining room. Cassie hesitated at the open doorway as Giles brushed past her. She surveyed the crowd of hungry people occupying nearly every table and chair. Flint smiled over an elderly gentleman at the far side of the room, gesturing to the steaming plate of ham and cabbage in front of him. A quick pat on the shoulder and Flint straightened, his gaze meeting hers from across the room. A shiver swept down her back as she clutched her fingers together. A mere look could cause her to tremble. Best she kept her distance from him. Keep the barrier raised between her needs and desires as long as possible.

Giles moved to block her view of Flint, exchanged a few

words and then with a nod spun and left the room. Either he'd been very succinct in his questions as to what Flint knew about the trio of bandits or he'd arranged to talk with him later. She'd guess the latter so they could talk in private. If only she could delay contact with him as well. But she had work to do. Too much work to do, to be blunt. Flint made an impatient gesture with his hand.

Stiffening, she inhaled and started toward him. He strode closer until they met in the middle of the room. His cologne tempted her to draw in a deeper breath but she ignored the impulse. His height and wide shoulders declared his strength and capability. The gentle light in his eyes reflected his kindness and understanding despite the slight frown pulling on his brows. All qualities she admired. If only she could let her guard down and be with him as they once planned. Before her mother's murder, when all she desired was to flee and marriage her only option.

Things had definitely changed.

"You've made great strides in improving the business." Cassie cast her gaze around the room and then looked up at him again. "Pa will be pleased."

"Where have you been?" Flint splayed his hands, palms up. "The place is packed and I can't do your job as well as my own."

She squinted her eyes at his tone. "I've been ensuring we have the food to feed them with. I'm here now to wait on everyone." She shook her head at him. "But I need you to think about finding more servers because I can't be everywhere. Maybe Hannah will come back?"

"No, she was adamant on that count." He propped his palms on his hips. "I tried to convince her but she'd have nothing to do with a…"—he lowered his voice as he glanced quickly around him—"a haunted inn."

"Then you'll need to find someone else. Several someones for that matter. Oh, and a maid to help with the rooms. Meg and Myrtle are needed in the kitchen, not making beds and emptying chamber pots."

He stared at her, his mouth falling open. "I'm not made of money."

She lifted a brow at him as she smiled. "Since we have more people coming, I'm assuming you've managed to increase the income as well. Use that to pay a few folks to help out. Or service will falter and we'll lose that extra business you're so proud of."

He huffed before quickly donning a smile as a group pushed back from their table and each lifted a hand in farewell as they left the inn. "You've a point."

"I can't manage what I've always taken care of as well as what Hannah and Ma did by myself, Flint." She folded her arms across her chest as she peered at him. "You need to put the word out that you're hiring additional help. Oh, and one other thing. Make the women buxom and attractive and you'll draw in even more hungry men."

She suppressed her delight when he glanced sharply at her, searching her eyes for any hidden meanings. She may be young but Hannah had taught her about flirting with men. Keeping her distance but encouraging their attention and thus their business.

He cleared his throat. "I'll think about it."

"Think fast because there are a lot of hungry, hungry men. Most even care about the food." She waggled her brows at him. "Some of them will want a comfortable bed to lie in, too."

His hands fisted as he dropped his arms to his sides. "I'll take care of finding you some help so you can keep up with your gardening and assist Sheridan in the kitchen."

She grinned wider at him. The unspoken assumption being she wouldn't need to be around the men at all. "In the meantime, let me get busy in here to take care of these folks."

"For now. But I'll be around in case you need help with anything." Flint relaxed his hands as a familiar group appeared in the open doors to the dining room. He shot a last warning look at Cassie before pasting a smile in place and marching across the room to greet the newcomers. "Mr. Baker. Mrs. Baker. And Miss Haley. Welcome."

"Do you have a table for three?" John doffed his top hat and held it in one hand at his side.

The way he perused the room, slowly dragging his gaze over every individual, gave Cassie chills. Tabitha Baker held herself rigidly upright, a tense smile on her lips. She'd confined her lustrous red hair beneath a becoming nut brown bonnet but her bright green eyes swept the room. Her daughter, Haley, stood at her side, fidgeting with her long pale blue skirts. She radiated curiosity as she scanned the unfamiliar domain. A tremor of unease washed through the young woman who rarely ventured off the plantation let alone to visit Fury Falls Inn.

Cassie's own curiosity made her stare at the girl, looking for similarities and differences. Brown hair with flashes of red glinted in the lamplight. Soft brown eyes gazed back at her across the space, slowly shifting from defensive to friendly. Haley was an enigma and yet Cassie somehow could feel her trepidation and deep interest in her surroundings. Could sense it on a physical level in her core. The odd and unusual sensation sent a current of disquiet through Cassie's gut. She blinked and looked at Flint, breaking the connection.

"Right this way." Flint ushered the family over to the recently vacated table. "Cassie will take care of you."

A brief irritable wave flashed through her core. Naturally, she'd be the one to wait on them. So many others sat at tables, waiting for their food and drinks, too. But Flint obviously wanted her to give priority to the Bakers. The feeling of inquisitiveness flowing from Haley combined with

Tabitha's deep concern and John's curiosity swirled through her gut, leaving behind a slight queasiness. On the surface, they appeared cool and calm, belying their underlying emotions. An interesting and intriguing disparity between appearance and reality on display right before her eyes. Her own opinions notwithstanding, she must do as requested. John's report to her pa on Flint's managerial skills proved important to both him and her. If she had any hope of having a relationship with him, then she needed him to stick around, not be let go. She pasted a smile on her face.

"Of course." She scurried to clear the remaining dishes from the table, placing them on another table to take to the kitchen to be cleaned. "What can I get you to drink?"

She took their orders, all the while aware that Haley surreptitiously observed her as closely as she returned the favor. She sensed the other girl's approval and openness as she efficiently handled their requests. She smiled to herself as she went to the bar and fixed their beverages and hurried back to the table, carrying their drinks on a large tray. Dodging between the tables of guests, she offered quick grins to regular customers. As she approached the Bakers' table, a movement off to the side of the fireplace drew her attention.

Her ma hovered nearby, a frown on her face as she observed the family settling in for their meal. Wary fear flowed from the ghost to smack into Cassie's core, wiping the smile from her face. She bit her lip as she stared at her mother's spirit, trying to sift through the conflicting emotions assaulting her. Flint glanced at Cassie with raised brows and a tip of his head. A silent demand that she do something about the ghost. Anything. She nodded, though uncertain what she could do about her ma's presence.

Moving to the opposite side of the table, she handed out the tankards and cups before placing the tray against her leg. She rested her hands on the cloth-covered surface. Good.

All eyes aimed at her as she smiled. "Sheridan has fixed a delicious dinner of ham and cabbage with carrots and parsnips. Or you can have some rabbit stew and corn bread. What would you like?"

Flint sidled around behind John to confront Mercy's ghost, making a quick shooing motion with his hand. Cassie tried to keep her eyes on the Bakers but couldn't help noticing the heated yet silent conversation in hand motions between her ma and Flint. Mercy seemed to be trying to warn him of something but what remained a mystery. The very fact she deemed something enough of a threat that she'd set aside her animosity to try to warn him, set her teeth on edge. But what was she worried about? Finally, Mercy tossed her long ash blonde hair back from her frown and vanished.

Cassie relaxed shoulders she didn't realize she'd tensed. "I'm sorry, Miss Haley. What did you want?"

A wave of surprise flowed over Cassie as the girl tilted her head with a lift of a brow. "I'd enjoy the ham, please."

Cassie struggled to ignore the emotions roiling through her as she met Haley's smile. Wrestled with feelings not her own. She needed distance to put her own feelings to rights. She inhaled sharply and gave a brief nod. "Wonderful. I'll go get your meals and be right back."

Somehow she could detect what others felt and experienced. Cassie had many questions without easy answers. Something had changed deep inside in a place she'd been unaware existed. But what? And how?

Chapter Nine

The buzz of many voices amidst the clink of metal forks on glazed plates brought Flint back to the moment. Every time the haint appeared all of his hopes and plans for his future verged on disintegrating. People didn't want to be around the wandering spirits of the unfriendly dead. He assumed she wouldn't harm anyone, but how could he know how vengeful her soul was? She'd shown her disgust for him in life. He couldn't predict what she might do to him after death. Especially if she somehow blamed him for her demise. For not being there to protect her as he'd promised. Another broken vow. His hand trembled as he tried to resume a normal conversation with John Baker, despite the man's alert demeanor. Had he seen Mercy? His heart raced as he smoothed his vest into place.

"While we wait for Cassie to bring your meals, please let me know if there is anything else I can get for you." Flint tried to assess how much the man had witnessed during the silent debate Flint had with the ghost.

He could tell she was trying to convey an urgent message to him but he didn't want to have any communication with her in full view of the customers. If word spread he was talking to ghosts, again, then his reputation would suffer.

Worse, business would fall off and then he'd have to answer to Reggie Fairhope. After John reported the decimation of the clientele and thus prosperity of the inn. Then what would happen to Flint's plans of finding a better position with more prestige and importance than running the rugged inn on the edge of the woods?

John peered at him for several seconds, toying with the serrated knife on the table. "Looks like you're managing well. Any problems I should know about?"

He shook his head. "The well is coming along thanks to your men."

"Glad to hear it." John tilted his head as he looked up at Flint. "Something else seems to be bothering you."

If John could tell there was more that kept Flint up at night, then it wasn't good for his worries to be so evident. He struggled to wrestle any lingering concerns or doubts behind a façade of confidence. He didn't want the man's report to Reggie to include any hints of incompetence or mismanagement. Better to act as if all was well under control. Business was booming after all. The remarks he heard from the guests confirmed they were pleased with the place and the food. More people had visited the springs in the last month than all of the previous summer months combined. He'd underscore the positives and not the concerns.

"Only that we need more help." Flint chuckled as he straightened. "Cassie is overworked trying to take care of everything left undone by Mercy's death and Hannah's quitting."

"Hannah was quite an asset. I'm sure you must miss her." John nodded sagely. "I can imagine there is much to do."

"We'll find someone to take her place." Flint glanced at Tabitha and Haley and then back to John. "I'd appreciate it if you'd put out the word that I'm hiring servers and maids. They just need come talk to me."

"Do you plan to put an advertisement in the paper, too?" John fingered the back of the knife blade.

Flint shrugged even as he pondered why John played with the knife as if he had intent to use it when his meal had not yet arrived. "Cassie just reminded me of the need so I haven't gotten that far." He ran a hand over his stubbly jaw. "I suppose that would be the most effective way to invite girls to apply."

Tabitha folded her hands on the edge of the cloth-covered table. "If I hear of anyone in need of a position, I'll be sure to send them your way."

Flint nodded once in acknowledgement of her offer. "Thank you, ma'am."

Haley started to speak, but Tabitha laid her hand on her daughter's wrist with a slight shake of her head. Interesting. He regarded her abashed expression and then met Tabitha's steady gaze. She angled her head to one side with a slight smile on her lips. Unsure what her silent request meant, he kept quiet and addressed John instead.

"Probably an advertisement is a prudent step to take." For some reason, when John released the knife, Flint relaxed.

"If you write it out, I'd be happy to take the announcement with me when I ride in to town tomorrow."

Cassie sashayed across the room toward Flint, a large tray held above the heads of the seated guests. He admired the sway of her hips. Her trim figure looked mighty fine in a pastel dress with a white apron tied around her waist. Her long, wavy hair was pulled back into a braid down her back. She smiled at him and his world rocked for a moment. He adored her with all of his being. If only he could let the world know the depth of his feelings. If he could tell her that would be a fine start. He returned her smile, trying to let her know how he felt. The tray slipped in her hands, tilted. She grabbed for it as he moved without thinking to her aid.

She caught the tray with both hands, lowering it to waist height as she closed the few feet between them. He helped her steady it by grasping the front edge.

"You all right?" He pulled his hands away, aware of their close proximity to her person. Not close enough for his liking, but propriety must be maintained.

"Yes." She gazed at him, eyes twinkling as if she understood exactly what he'd rather be doing with his hands. "What did Giles say to you?"

Her question veered in a different direction than he thought she'd go, so it took a beat for him to respond. "He invited me to go hunting tomorrow."

"Hunting? I didn't know you hunt." She braced the tray on one hip.

"I don't usually but if your brother wants me to, then I will. Need a hand?"

She raised a shoulder, dismissing the exchange with an easy shrug. "Will you place these round, please?"

Her eyes glinted with humor and something else he couldn't define. As if she shielded any hint of her thoughts and feelings from him. Keeping her apart. When all he wanted was to grow closer.

Without a word, he lifted a steaming bowl of smoked ham and buttery cabbage and placed it on the table in front of Haley. Cassie sucked in a breath when his arm brushed the girl's shoulder as he pulled back. He cut her a look but her composure remained a mask of polite observation. In fact, of late she'd been acting far more removed from the events surrounding her than ever before. A significant change in her mannerisms he couldn't fathom. She'd always been so friendly and welcoming.

Perhaps she'd elected to resist his affections while Giles remained at the inn. Not wanting to reveal how much they cared for each other until her father returned home. Giles may have told her about warning Flint away. Or had her feelings for him waned? He flashed a look at her trying to understand her motives. Her reasoning. Maybe she simply wanted to keep their budding relationship private. He finished setting the other plates and bowls on the table.

"Smells delicious." Haley lifted her fork to pick through the piping hot meat and vegetables.

Flint grinned at the girl. "I'm sure you'll enjoy. Sheridan is the best cook in these parts."

"You're lucky to have him." John sampled a bite of ham and moaned in pleasure. "The inn would not be as popular without him."

The smirk on the other man's face startled Flint. A ripple of uncertainty wiggled down his spine. Sheridan drew people from all around with his tempting meals and desserts. What if he left? Flint would have a real problem replacing the cook. Reggie had ensured the man would stay for several years after giving him his freedom. Years ago. Still, the cook had only recently agreed to stay despite the haunting of the inn.

Flint relaxed his tense shoulders with an effort. "It's a good thing he has no intention of leaving."

"Yes, it is." John hefted his forkful of cabbage. "I'm very glad to hear that. After all, the senator's visit in a few months will require this caliber of cuisine or better to make the requisite impression to earn his approval and recommendation to others. Your job depends on it."

Cassie lifted the tray with both hands, holding it in front of her like a shield. "Thanks for the reminder, Mr. Baker, but we've got everything under control. Flint is working hard to make sure the senator has a wonderful time. Sheridan has been trying some new recipes. And now we have Matt to help him as well." She smiled brightly at the group. "You can tell my father that we'll be ready."

John stared at her before pursing his lips. "I do hope so, Miss Fairhope."

Tension between the two simmered in the air for a time. Finally Cassie lifted her brows and the tray and whirled away, marching toward the kitchen. His girl had changed over the last few days—more forthright and confident—and he wasn't sure the change was a good thing.

Crouched in the underbrush, Giles listened to the stable boy—Linus? Lemuel? No, Liam—work the hunting dogs. A short whistle followed by a long, and the silky Cocker Spaniel, Cocoa, led the retrievers up the hillside above the springs in search of wild turkeys to shoot. Giles could almost taste the roasted birds as he waited beside Flint and Zander. They'd been hiking up and down the mountain for more than an hour with no luck. On the lookout for the gobblers with long multi-brown wings folded against their sides. Hiding in the woods as surely as the men who killed his mother.

"Why don't we try for elk instead of turkeys?" Flint shifted noisily, fumbling the flintlock fowling piece to the pine needle covered ground. "Or even deer. They'd yield more meat for the effort."

Zander grunted from where he stood behind Giles. "Venison is fine roasted in a pit like a hog. Never had elk, though."

Flint smiled over his shoulder at the tall black man. "I haven't either. Could be interesting to try."

Giles glanced sideways at Flint, his grip tightening on the barrel of his gun, and then stared at Liam's slow movements. The point of the hunting expedition was not to bring down the biggest game. He needed to ascertain Flint's ability with a gun and so he'd devised the test to see for himself whether the mild-mannered innkeeper could hit what he targeted.

"Quiet, both of you." Good thing the damn gun loaded with bird shot didn't fire as the other man grappled it back across his legs. "The more noise you make the less likely you'll be able to shoot anything."

"I can shoot. Don't you worry." Flint flashed a grin at him. "I was taught by the best."

Looking at him out of the corner of his eye, Giles couldn't imagine a shooting expert living out in the wilds of north Alabama. Who could Flint have found to instruct him on the finer points of marksmanship? Images of a gunslinger passing through or worse some sharpshooting squirrel hunter pretending to know how to handle a pistol or rifle with precision floated in his mind. He turned his head to look at Flint's bright-eyed smirk.

"Just how often do you use your flintlock pistol let alone a fowling piece?" Giles kept his voice low as Liam turned the dogs to cast in the other direction.

Flint huffed. "It's not a matter of frequency but intention. Deputy Parker showed me how to aim to kill, not merely injure."

Giles kept his doubts to himself about whether a mere deputy could teach anyone how to properly handle a firearm. He needed proof that Flint was capable of protecting his sister after Giles left for the south. He wouldn't stay at the inn any longer than to fulfill his promise to find his mother's killers. He'd left his business shuttered and therefore losing money during his absence. He had to go back ere long. An inner voice whispered he didn't want to see his papa. He brushed the thought aside, wrestling with the wary curiosity he felt about confronting his father after the many years of silence. But before he left his sister's safety in the hands of strangers, he must prove to himself he wasn't abandoning them to insecurity and danger. Flint was his first concern on that front.

"I was talking with my mother—her ghost, anyway." He swallowed and shook his head. Still hard to believe he could see any ghost let alone his own mother.

"She probably had something unkind to say about me, huh?" Flint flicked a glance at him and then stared straight ahead. "She's damn hard to please."

The animosity between the innkeeper and his mother worried him. What had she seen in the man that made her so resentful toward him? His mama had spent far more time observing Flint than the few days Giles had been on the property. He'd not found any fault with what he'd seen of his actions and interactions with his sister and the customers. Not yet. But he'd keep his eyes and instincts open for the nuances his mama would have picked up on that he may have overlooked.

"What did she have against you anyway?" His mother's harsh side could be downright unpleasant to deal with. He had first-hand experience with her when she didn't like something or someone. "What did you do?"

Flint snorted softly, mindful of the need for quiet. "Simply that I am living and working on her property."

"What do you mean?"

"She came home from a shopping excursion to find me in charge after your father had left to deal with business in Georgia without telling her." Flint shifted the fowling piece to balance across his legs. "She didn't take to the idea of not being trusted by him to be the boss, to supervise the inn's guests and residents."

"She wouldn't." Giles fingered the gun propped against his leg. He was ready to shoot as a backup to Flint but he wanted to see how well the man handled a weapon. Something in Flint's tone gave him pause. "Was there anything else she objected to?"

Flint peered at him out of the corner of his eyes for several moments. "Did she say something?"

"No." Flint's expression had turned wary, setting off inner alarm bells the longer Giles waited for an explanation. "Why?"

Flint studied him, tapping a finger on the long double barrel of the gun. "Well, she probably hopes it will pass. And maybe she's right."

"Meaning?"

Shrugging, Flint sighed. "I thought Cassie liked me, but I guess I was wrong."

"So you do have feelings for her?" He'd suspected as much and cautioned Flint from pursuing Cassie if she didn't want his attentions. Giles could only hope he'd listened.

"I do. She wanted to wait until your father comes home before engaging any further in a relationship. Now…" Flint shrugged again, staring ahead.

"She called it off?"

"Not exactly. More like she's avoiding being alone with me. I get the feeling she's changing her mind about us. As if there ever really was an *us*."

"She's still a kid at heart. She doesn't know her own mind." Giles regarded the silent man beside him. "Thank you for respecting my sister's feelings, Flint. You're a real gentlemen for understanding."

Flint chuckled and then sighed. "I appreciate the vote of confidence."

Zander shifted his weight from one foot to the other, the rustle of fallen leaves crackling behind Giles. "If the girl isn't interested, then it's best you keep your distance."

Flint glanced over his shoulder at Zander. "I'm trying, but we do work together."

Zander grimaced as he rested the butt of his gun on the ground beside his leg. "That makes it harder but you're respecting her by doing so."

Flint firmed his lips and turned back to observing the dogs and Liam.

The set of his jaw spoke volumes about the effort it took for Flint to honor Cassie's wishes. The fact he did respect his sister wasn't lost on Giles. He could see from Flint's attitude and actions the deference he held toward her desires and demands. Not every man had the self-restraint or confidence to wait, be patient and willing to listen to her preferences. In time, she'd come around to his way of thinking as long as he continued to not press his suit before she was ready.

"You're a good man, Flint. Not everyone can say that." Giles tapped his knee with his palm. "Speaking of not good men. What do you know about a man named Joe with dark eyes?"

"Not a thing, but I haven't had chance to meet everybody around these parts." Flint gripped the gun as Liam paused in his slow movements.

"My mother said a man named Joe was the man who shot her. Young Teddy said his father has mentioned a man named Joe but he's never seen him. He may or may not be connected."

Flint frowned as he slowly turned to stare at Giles. "And Teddy's father disappears for weeks at a time. Maybe to ride with two other men doing mischief and mayhem?"

"It's possible." Zander grunted as he dropped to sit cross-legged behind Giles. "But how do we figure out who those men are?"

Flint rose from his knees to a squatting position, stretching out first one leg then the other. "Introduce ourselves to Teddy's father, I guess. See what he has to say."

Zander nodded, shifting the gun to hold across his knees. "We'll need backup in case he's one of the murderers, or at least an accomplice."

"Wait… Cocoa found something." Giles craned his neck to peer at the dog.

Liam raised a hand as the spaniel darted into a copse of birch trees. The long caramel and white hair disappeared into the brush.

Zander scrabbled to his feet as Giles motioned for Flint to take the lead. "You take the first one."

Flint rose and eased forward. He raised the gun to his shoulder and tilted his head at Liam. The gangly young man acknowledged Flint's sign of readiness and gave a sharp whistle to Cocoa. A commotion erupted out of sight and then a flock of turkeys burst into the air, flapping their wings furiously, while Liam ducked down in place. Flint fired into the center of the fluttering feathers, striking three turkeys which fell to the ground.

Beau leapt toward a downed bird and carefully brought it back to Liam, Cocoa trotting up a moment later with a smaller bird in her mouth. The young man praised the dogs and accepted the good-sized birds, shoving them one by one into a burlap sack to carry back to the inn. Pickles hurried to retrieve the last bird to bring for his own praise and reward.

Impressed, Giles stood and sauntered over to Flint. "Nice shooting."

"I told you I can shoot." Flint shouldered the weapon as the hunting party started walking down the hill toward the springs and then on to home.

Giles was fairly pleased with Flint's performance and the reassurance it gave him regarding the man's ability to defend the property and the people on it. "Deputy Parker taught you well. Guess I should thank him for looking out for my family's interests." He chuckled as he stepped over a protruding rock in the path. "I won't be around forever to…"

"Wait." Zander cut him off with an outstretched arm. "What's that?"

He followed Zan's pointing finger to spy a trampled area behind some bushes off the path about ten yards. Charred tobacco lay on the ground, emptied from a pipe no doubt. Several small branches on the bushes hung as testimony to a man's presence. The sight made his skin crawl with concern. Giles hurried over to stand on the spot and look down the hill. To see what the man would have seen. A clear, straight view of the back side of the inn. The entire area, from stable yard by the river on the right all the way left to the far end of the clearing and Cassie's garden. The perfect place to spy on the comings and goings of the residents and guests of the Fury Falls Inn.

Chapter Ten

The rhythmic motion of rubbing down Buck after their ride into town gave Flint time to think without being disturbed. The letter burning in his vest pocket weighted his movements. Rubbing the soft bristled brush over the tan-and-white paint kept his hands busy as his mind whirled with conflicting desires. He brushed away dried sweat with his right hand as he smoothed down the hair with his left.

All the way into town he'd hoped to find a reply from any of the inquiries he'd sent out a month ago. Visions floated through his mind of what his next step would be regarding his dream of owning a hotel. Saving his money was the first step. Gaining more experience with handling various crises and issues was another. Convincing a larger hotel owner to hire him dovetailed with the need for more experience and would also build his reputation for providing comfortable and clean accommodations for travelers.

When he picked up the mail for the inn, one of the letters was addressed to him. He recognized the return address on the stationery of the high-class establishment in New York. A busy and thriving place where people from all walks of life converged. He'd seen sketches of the city but had never dreamed of actually having the opportunity to work in such a metropolis. After he finished taking care of his horse, he'd mosey into the office and read the letter. But his priority was his horse's care.

He shifted to work on Buck's neck, lifting the mane out of the way to make long strokes down the muscular expanse. Buck nickered and then shook his head, sending dust flying into the air. Flint coughed and waved the cloud away then resumed his brushing and his musing.

No matter what offer he received, he first had to complete the obligation he'd made with Mr. Fairhope. He'd committed to staying through November, another three months. If an offer came in too soon, he'd have to try to negotiate a later start date. He needed the referral from Mr. Fairhope before he moved to a bigger opportunity as well as the promised bonus of five hundred dollars. With those two pieces of the plan secured, he would have a solid chance of fulfilling his dreams.

He lifted the forelock and gently brushed Buck's face. Snorting, Buck raised his head, nose in the air until Flint grasped his poll and convinced the horse to lower his head. "Behave yourself."

He tentatively stroked the brush down the long nose, braced for the gelding to react. Buck started to lift his nose again, but Flint pressed down on the bridge with his hand. When the horse relaxed, he tried again, this time without the horse rebelling. "Good boy." He moved to work on the off side of the horse.

But New York? Such a long way from everyone he knew and cared about. His parents and grandparents surely would not make the arduous journey to visit so he wouldn't see them nearly as often as he currently enjoyed. His sisters would be growing up and marrying in a few more years and he'd not be part of their lives if he took the position. He'd be alone among strangers, but surely he'd make friends among the others who worked with him.

He also needed to ensure the inn was managed properly before he would feel comfortable leaving. That it was ready for their important guest, Senator Percy Graham, when he arrived the first week of November. Flint had listed the improvements he planned to make over the next few months to meet the higher standard necessary to impress the senator. Not a long list, but some of the changes would take time so he'd laid out a schedule.

One important consideration came in the pretty form of Cassie and his hopes for a future with her. If she'd have him. Her wavering on how she seemed to feel about them concerned him. Perhaps he shouldn't consider her in the equation. After all, she was the one who kept pushing him away. Keeping a cold shoulder between them while she waited for her father to come home. Months from now, if then. What if something detained the man even longer? How long could Flint bide his time and put all of his plans, as well as all of his hopes and dreams, on hold?

Buck shifted to cock his right-hind fetlock, enjoying the grooming. The steady clip-clop of hooves drew Flint's attention away from his horse to look down the barn aisle. Marshall led in two new horses, trailed by Teddy. Ever since Marshall had been assigned to guard Teddy the two had become inseparable. Everywhere Marshall went, Teddy went, too. Marshall put the horses into two separate straight-in stalls, tying their bridles to the rings on the wall.

Flint held his pride over the innovation close to his chest. He had converted two box stalls into six temporary stalls for in-and-out guests' horses. Typically, the guests would arrive late morning, have their midday meal and then take the waters for several hours before departing for their next destination. No reason to allocate a large box stall to horses only staying a few hours. He reserved the nicer stalls for overnight guests, a perquisite which might encourage repeat customers.

Teddy lingered in the aisle, watching Marshall's expert handling of the horses. He glanced at Flint, a question in his eyes. Gnawing his lower lip, the boy stared at him with wide eyes filled with trepidation. He was a cute fella, intelligent eyes, straight nose, and strong jaw. When Flint left, he'd miss the lad. Teddy acted like a younger brother, willing to please and aware of the older man's authority over him. But also rebellious and dismissive at times. Just like a brother.

"Something on your mind?" Flint stepped back to survey Buck's coat for any last vestiges of dried sweat. Brushed off an invisible speck or two.

Shrugging, the boy continued to look at Flint. Something about his hunched shoulders and furtive glances at Marshall made Flint suspicious. He strode to the shelf along the outside wall of the stalls. Dropping the brush in its place, he pivoted to address Teddy.

"What's eating at you?" He started to fold his arms but the boy jerked as if he'd run away. Instead, Flint shoved his hands into his front pockets. "You know you can talk to me."

Marshall finished giving the horses hay and joined Teddy and Flint in the aisle. He nodded to Teddy. "Go on. You know you should."

Teddy trembled where he stood, swallowing repeatedly. "I dunno."

Marshall pressed his fists onto his hips. "Tell him what you told me."

Flint arched a brow at the older boy before turning his full attention on the kid. "Tell me what?"

The boy's Adam's apple sped up and down in his throat. "I—" He glanced at Marshall and then met Flint's gaze. He swallowed again and drew in a bracing breath. "I know where the missing keys are."

Carrying a large, flat basket over her arm, Cassie sauntered out of the summer heat into the inn's cooler entrance hall. She set the basket of cut flowers down by the table and fingered the pathetic darkened petals and drooping leaves of wilted rose stems standing in a vase. With a sigh, she lifted the vase with both hands and carried it out back to her compost pile, dumping the contents on top. She examined the layers of rotting kitchen scraps, dead flower stems, and other matter. She nodded once to herself. The soil from the bottom of the pile made a perfect fertilizer for the vegetables and flowers she'd planted. She shook the last drops from the vase and then filled it at the well before going back to her abandoned basket. She paused beside Giles and Flint standing just inside the door, deep in earnest conversation over Teddy's tousled head.

"I don't know who has been spying on the inn, but it's obvious somebody stayed in one place long enough to flatten the vegetation." Giles shook his head, concern etched into his furrowed brow and dark eyes.

"But why? What could they want?" Flint stood near the open doors leading out to the front porch. "It's not like we're hiding anything."

Giles tensed his shoulders. "I don't know. But I don't like it."

"I think I might know." Flint's firm hand on Teddy's shoulder kept the boy close at his side. "It was most likely this boy's father, waiting for the right time to grab him and take him home."

"That's when I saw the keys I told you about." Teddy grimaced at the look of surprise on Giles' face. "When he dragged me home, I mean. They were on the wall. They weren't there before."

Cassie eased past the group and set the vase in place on the table. She sensed the turmoil inside each of them until finally she sorted out who was feeling what. But how was she sensing their emotions? She couldn't explain it so kept it to herself. What if they thought she was a witch or something? What might happen to her? The people in the surrounding area were good Christians so they may not cotton to having anyone with unusual abilities in their midst. If indeed she had somehow developed a unique capability. Until she understood what was happening to her, she'd best keep her suspicions to herself. Look at how they'd whispered and pointed at Flint for being able to talk to ghosts when he first arrived to work at the inn. Then he'd not only proven he could but others could as well. Not everyone, though, seemed to notice Mercy's ghost. She frowned at the realization, listening to the guys' discussion.

"So it's likely that Teddy's father is involved if he has the missing keys."

Flint's words brought Cassie's retrieval of the golden yellow sunflowers from her basket to an abrupt halt. She dropped the stem back into the basket before striding over to join them.

She peered at the distressed expression on Teddy's face. Sensed the fear he felt inside as keenly as if it were her own.

Giles crossed his arms and peered down at the boy. "What does your father look like, boy?"

Teddy shrugged defensively, his fear increasing the longer Giles scowled at him. Cassie moved closer to him, lending him her silent encouragement and support. He flicked a glance at her, relief flowing from him to her core, then aimed his wary gaze at the two men. Why could she suddenly feel what others were experiencing? Sometimes the emotions of the guests overwhelmed her and she had to leave the room. Not that she'd always had that reaction. Only since her mother had passed had her own emotions cavorted uncontrollably inside of her. The small group before her had strong mixed feelings of fear, determination, and hope.

"You know your father. Just tell us what he looks like, son." Flint briefly squeezed the boy's shoulder. "Hair color, height, whatever you can think of."

"He's tall, like you, Mr. Flint. Muddy brown hair. Yellow eyes like a cat." Teddy shrugged lightly. "Not much else."

Flint let go of Teddy as he met Giles' gaze. "Sound like any of those rogues?"

"Mama said one had golden eyes, so possibly." Giles dropped his arms to his side, hands fisted. "What about the keys, boy? What do they look like?"

"They look like keys." Teddy's eyes widened as Giles leaned forward to glower at the boy, annoyed by his vague answer. A fine shiver raced through Teddy. "I don't know. Silver? Different sizes."

Her ma had explained the various keys to Cassie. A long, rounded one that opened the attic door. A shiny silver one to open a chest of papers, and another one with some kind of strange symbol on the head that opened her ma's chest containing her wedding dress. Family heirlooms her ma had insisted she didn't need to see then. Suddenly her ma's reluctance to share what was in those trunks floated into Cassie's mind. If they'd found the keys, then the mystery of the attic's treasure would finally be solved.

Cassie bobbed her head with hope and excitement. "That could be Ma's set."

"There's only one way to find out." Giles pointed to the trembling boy. "Take us to meet your father."

"Now?" Teddy darted his gaze around the group, his fear increasing with each breath. "I-I doubt he's home." He gulped and tensed as if to run away but Flint gripped his shoulder again.

"How do you know that?" Flint gave the boy a little shake. "What do you know?"

Teddy whimpered and tried to pull away from the strong grasp on his shoulder. "He's usually out all afternoon, until after the sun sets."

"What's he doing all that time?" Giles glared at the boy as if he were somehow at fault.

Cassie considered the boy's statement. How could the man leave his young son alone for such long periods? It wasn't right. Teddy was a bright child but hampered by a negligent father, no mother ever mentioned, no family for that matter. In the short time Teddy had stayed at the inn he'd proven to be a hard-working lad. Ire welled inside her the more she considered the life the negligent father forced his son to live.

Teddy twisted under Flint's grip. "I dunno."

"Since he's not home in the afternoons, we'll go tomorrow morning at first light. Wake the man up if need be. Agreed?" Giles glanced at Flint who nodded. "We'll take Matt and Zander as backup."

"Do you think we'll need so many men?" Flint released his grip on the boy. "He's only one man. We can manage."

Teddy took two steps away from Flint, rubbing his shoulder. Cassie sensed Teddy's startled reaction to the calm assurance in Flint's voice. The misplaced certainty of overpowering the boy's father. Dread washed through her, a stream of concern emanating from the boy. She stared at the lad until he squirmed under her regard. His worry for the men's safety crystallized in her core.

"Take them." Cassie rested her hand on Giles' upper arm. "Please."

"Why?"

"Trust me, Giles. I can't explain but you will need them." She shook her head in frustration. "I can feel it."

"You can feel it?" He frowned at her for a second and

then cleared his expression. "Don't worry, sis, if you think it's necessary I will take them."

"Thank you." For everything. For coming home. For seeking their mother's killers. For trusting her without any evidence.

"He may be the key to finding the other men as well." Giles spoke directly to Flint. "Be prepared for anything, you hear?"

"I'll be ready." Flint's sober expression showed how seriously he was taking Giles' words of caution.

"Be careful. If Teddy's father has the keys, he's one of the murderers." Cassie shivered, the skirts of her day dress swishing in agitation.

Teddy inhaled sharply, eyes wide in his astonished face. "No, that ain't true. Is it?"

"Sorry, son, but Miss Fairhope is right." Flint rested his right hand on the butt of his pistol strapped to his thigh. "We're going to find those men and get justice for Mrs. Fairhope one way or another."

"But he's my father." Teddy splayed his hands out in distress. "You're gonna kill him?"

"Not if we can help it." Giles considered the boy's screwed up features with a somber expression. "I'll do my best to take him in alive."

Would they kill the man? Cassie suppressed a gasp. If they captured him, what would they do with him? If he fought, they may well end up killing him. Not the outcome anyone wanted. But the man may force their hand. Especially if his friends showed up and stood with him.

Flint addressed the frightened boy with a gentler tone than he'd used before. "You've only to introduce us to your father and we'll take care of everything."

"Including you." Cassie wrapped an arm around the boy's shoulders and squeezed. "You don't need to worry about what will happen to you. You have a home here for as long as you need one."

The boy nodded as tears swam in his eyes. "I thank you for that, Miss Cassie." He darted his gaze to Flint and then Giles. "Please don't kill him. He's not all bad."

Giles firmed his lips with a nod. "It'll be up to him."

If things went well, the men would simply apprehend Teddy's father, retrieve the keys, and turn him over to the authorities.

If things didn't go well, someone would get hurt or killed, most likely Teddy's father. The murderers would still be on the loose. The keys lost forever.

Teddy would lose his father either way and need to stay at the inn. No matter how she looked at the potential outcomes, one thing remained constant.

Tomorrow would change everything for everyone.

Chapter Eleven

$\mathcal{A}$ thin column of smoke drifted from the stone chimney of the lonesome log cabin toward the low-hanging clouds. Giles grimaced at the rundown condition of Teddy's pitiful home. Shingles missing from the roof. Warped floorboards on the front porch curving upwards like pine wood shavings. The white chinking between the logs unevenly applied, leaving slits and holes for the air and bugs to pass inside unimpeded. Not even a mangy dog to warn the inhabitants of their approach. Living so far out in the wilderness he'd have definitely kept a dog or two on the property to protect those who lived there. The curs would provide a warning let alone company for the boy while his father was away from home.

"Go on in, Teddy." Giles motioned for the lad to go up the single step to the porch.

Without a word, the boy hunched his shoulders and stepped onto the porch to open the door. Giles followed with Zander at his side, while Flint and Matt stayed outside to guard against any surprise visitors. Zander would defend him with all force necessary, but having the others as additional backup ensured they'd come back out in one piece. He hoped.

"Where you been, boy?" A gruff voice rang out inside the dim interior before a chair scraped harshly across the wood floor. "Who the hell are you?"

As his eyes adjusted, Giles could make out the owner of the voice. The tall and lean man stood braced to repel an attack. His eyes darted between the men and his son, finally landing on Giles.

"What do you men want with my son?" He motioned to the boy with one hand. "He troubling you?"

"No, sir. You his father?" Giles waited for the man's short nod. "I'm Giles Fairhope. What's your name?"

"Adam Jacobs." Adam relaxed slightly, but kept a wary eye on the men.

Giles took his time surveying the sparsely furnished room. Certainly the home hadn't seen the benefit of a woman's touch. A table and two chairs stood in front of the fireplace. A rumpled bed along one wall. Dirty dishes piled on a sideboard. Bare walls. No wonder Teddy didn't want to stay in the cabin when his father was away. Then his gaze lit upon a key ring hanging on a nail on the wall.

He turned to Teddy and pointed at the set of shiny keys. "Is that the ones you told us about?"

"Yeah." The single word reluctantly emerged from Teddy's tense mouth.

"Where'd you get those keys?" Giles infused as much menace as possible in his voice as he slid his gaze back to Adam.

Adam narrowed his amber eyes. "They're mine."

"You sure about that?" No surprise the man doubled down on his claim by lifting his chin in silent challenge. "Hey, Flint. Get in here."

Footsteps on the rickety porch preceded Flint hurrying into the cabin to stand by Giles. "What?"

Giles indicated the ring on the wall. "Are those the keys you've been looking for?"

Flint strode toward them as Adam started to cross the small room to prevent Flint from inspecting the set of keys. Zander stopped Adam in his tracks, a flintlock pistol pointed to his chest. Flint picked the ring off the nail and laid the keys across one palm. After a moment he looked at Giles with the hint of a grin.

"Cassie will be happy to see these." Flint jingled the keys and then pocketed them.

"That tells me, Adam…" Giles ambled over to the man, aware of his son's witnessing of the unfolding events. The man should die for his part in Mercy's murder. Giles' fingers itched to pull his gun, but then he'd end up in trouble and not able to do his duty toward his family. But no way would the other man get away with what he'd done. "I believe you were involved in the cold-blooded murder of my mother."

Adam's face blanched then flushed dark red. "You dare barge in here and accuse me of a crime I had nothin' to do with?" Adam shook his head but didn't otherwise move since Zander kept the weapon trained on him.

"That's right, I am. Why did you take the keys?" The trembling man's explanation might prove enlightening or a lie.

"Who says I took them? I could've found them." A wary smirk spread on Adam's face.

Giles lifted a doubtful brow at the other man's shifty eyes. "You found them? Sure you did. In my mother's bedroom when you and your pals went there to steal from her. Why'd you take them?"

Trapped into admitting his presence at the scene of the woman's murder, Adam quaked in his boots as he glared at the big man. "No reason."

"I don't believe you, Adam. What did you plan to do?"

He lifted a shoulder in a half shrug. "She was so sure she had nothing but she wanted those keys pretty bad."

"So?"

"I was waiting for the right time to sneak in and see what she was hiding."

"You planned to go back?" Anger swept through Giles at the idea of this man prowling around in his sister's home. What would happen if the thief had encountered his sister or any of the staff? Someone would get hurt or worse. Cassie was right to be worried for her safety. Good thing he'd come home so he could ensure the villains were caught and punished. "You're not very bright, are you?"

"Smart enough to know when that arrogant wench was lyin'." A sick grin widened Adam's mouth. "She's got more treasure than she let on."

Cassie apparently agreed with him. She'd expressed more than once how eager she was to find the keys in order to gain access to their mother's private attic. What hid in the shadows of the small room? Mama had her mementoes and gewgaws but he didn't know of anything of any true value. Then again he hadn't visited in years. Things may have changed significantly in the span of time since he last spoke with her. Nonetheless, the criminal standing in front of him would never know. Giles intended to make certain of that fact.

He pulled his weapon and aimed it at the man. "So now you have a choice to make. Go with Flint and Matt to see Sheriff Neal or stay here to face my vengeance. Choose."

"No!" Teddy lunged forward to stand in front of his father, his arms wide and eyes frightened. "Don't hurt my pa."

"Move, boy." Giles motioned to Zander to take it easy but kept his gun trained on Adam. He didn't want the boy harmed but the man had to be brought to justice one way or another. "It's up to your father, not you."

"He's not a bad man, Mr. Giles. Honest." Teddy's wide eyes shimmered in the dull light of the room. "Please… don't shoot him."

"No, son." Adam gripped the boy's shoulders and

pushed him aside. Teddy stumbled against the table, slapping his hands on its surface to stop from falling. "Don't be foolish. This man ain't gonna shoot me."

"I'm not?" Giles stood with legs braced, gun leveled on the man who had the nerve to push his son away. Still, relief at not having the boy in the line of fire flickered inside. "Don't be so sure."

Adam held his hands wide apart at his thighs. "I'll go with them, no problem. You ain't got any proof I did anything. I'll be back home in time for supper."

"Fine. Flint, give me the keys and you and Matt take this varmint to jail." Flint handed over the keys and Giles slipped them into his front pocket. "The three of us will go back to the inn and make sure things are secure there."

"You're taking my boy?" Adam groused. "He ain't done nothing."

"I'm taking him so he's safe and cared for while you're gone." Giles shook his head at the man. "It's not right to leave a young boy to fend for himself like you've done."

"He's smart and quick." Adam grinned. "I've taught him how to be resourceful."

"By stealing? Not such a good lesson." Flint took hold of Adam's arm and started toward the door. "Let's go."

Matt pulled a length of rope out to tie the man's hands together. Then they hustled him to the waiting horses and soon were mounted and cantering away. Giles turned to Teddy with a fond smile. "You're a good son, Teddy, just don't go following in your father's footsteps."

Zander put his gun away. "Yeah, you don't want to end up in jail. It's not a good place to be."

Teddy swallowed hard and nodded. "Thanks for not hurting him, Mr. Giles. He don't know no better."

Giles tousled the boy's hair, pleased the situation went as smoothly as it had. It had been a good morning. "Come on. Cassie is waiting for us."

Finally. Excitement bubbled and fizzed inside as Cassie trotted up the circular stairs to the foreboding attic door. Giles snickered behind her as he climbed more sedately, carrying a glowing oil lantern in one hand. She cast a quick glance over her shoulder at him with a big smile plastered on her face. No matter how silly he may think her, the time had arrived to discover the mysterious contents of the locked room.

"I can't tell you how eager I am to find out what has been hiding up here." She held out her hand, wiggling her fingers. "Keys, please."

"Are you sure you want to do this now?" His eyes sparkled as he dipped one hand into his pocket, hesitating as he regarded her for several beats. "We could wait until——"

"Give me the keys, Giles." She thrust her hand closer to him as she turned her smile into a scowl. "I've waited long enough, thank you very much."

In fact, the compulsion to enter the room had increased with each passing day. A living, breathing beast unfurling in her, stretching and clawing its way through her entire body. Seldom did the idea of breaking through the door leave her in peace. She had nearly fetched an axe to chop her way through the wood, but Flint had made it clear she wasn't to harm the door. He didn't want to have to replace it. But something called to her from behind the door. She could almost hear it whispering her name.

Giles dropped the key ring onto her palm. "Be my guest."

Clutching the keys tightly, she felt the beast tense, poised to spring from its hiding place. She drew in a long breath and let it out slowly, turning to face the door. She chose the largest of the set and tried to push it into the slot but it was too big. With a huff, she tried the next one, a shiny silver key, and it slid inside but was so small it had no effect. "Blast!"

"Want me to try?" Giles leaned against the railing, one step down from the landing where Cassie fumbled with the keys. "Maybe it takes a man to open it."

"No." What an inane comment. She'd ignore his play on manhood as the answer to everything. She fingered the rest of the keys, debating which of the several to try next.

She finally settled on a copper key with an intricate scroll design with a flying owl, wings outspread and talons extended as if to catch some kind of prey, in the center on the head. She stuck it into the lock and twisted her wrist, a click following. She paused, pondering the set of metal on her palm. She didn't want to ever lose them again. She thrust the keys back to Giles and then turned the knob.

She pushed the door open into the shadowy space. Blinking to help her eyes adjust, she stepped through the doorway. A window provided enough light to outline the contents of the room but nothing specific in the lumps and squares scattered around. She detected the lingering feeling of regret and unease tangled into a mire of uncertainty. Yet the layout appeared comfortable and welcoming. If only she could see better.

"I need more light." She dawdled just inside the doorway, perusing the room. Soaking in the echoes of emotion.

"Here, let me by." Giles surged past her, casting the bright light of the lamp into the dark recesses. "Looks like Mama had her own private study."

"Indeed?" Cassie followed him farther into the fair sized room. She gasped and clapped her hands together as she slowly spun in a circle. "Oh, my."

The beast inside curled up and purred with pleasure at what Cassie saw. Several trunks of varying sizes and designs were positioned around the room. Shelves of leather- and cloth-bound books lined one wall. A fancy wooden chair and matching table stood by the window, a small oil lamp waiting on its polished surface. A thick, cream-colored crocheted blanket draped over the chair back. A fine carpet with a floral pattern woven into the wool covered the floor with a Franklin stove nearby. Her mother's private space, where she must have spent a good deal of time alone. Reading, sewing, going through what was in the fancy trunks.

"Let's see inside those." Cassie strode to the nearest trunk, to her mind the prettiest of the lot.

The largest of the bunch, it stood on four squat legs near the door. She smoothed a hand over the rich walnut wood of the flat top, leaving finger trails in the fine layer of dust. The front wall featured carved flowers and arches reminding her of the windows of a cathedral. A decorative lock with a metal shield graced the front. She tugged on the lid and it slowly opened without much resistance. Inside were layers of clothing, including the promised wedding gown and veil. Hadn't her mother said she'd locked the gown away? Then why was it unlocked? Another curiosity. She fingered the silk, fine lace edging the bodice and trimming the veil. Giles came to stand beside her as she pawed gently through the dresses and blouses and skirts lovingly folded inside.

"Ma said one day I might want to wear her wedding dress." Cassie sighed as she lowered the lid. "Someday."

Her childhood dream of finding a strong, responsible man to care for and raise a family together had changed since meeting Flint. She wanted more than just a pleasant life with a prosperous husband. She wanted someone to love her, to look at her with affection and respect. To laugh with her and comfort her when she felt sorrow or pain. She once wanted only Flint. Now she wasn't certain if he was indeed the right man for her. She needed to confer with her father, if only he'd return home.

"You'll find a husband, Cassie." Giles touched her arm,

smiling gently at her. "You're too pretty and smart to not land a good man."

She may already have but the timing for them seemed off. Flint was patient. She hoped he'd wait for her to figure out her own mind. Ever since her mother died, her emotions had romped all over the place. She suddenly seemed able to experience the emotions of others inside herself, not merely observing their expressions and stance. Something had changed or she'd started to lose her mind. She hesitated to share her concerns for fear of being dismissed or sent to an insane asylum. Or worse, mistaken for a witch. Rumors abounded as to what god-fearing men did to anyone suspected of witchery.

Shaking off her musings, she marched a few steps to the middle trunk. It was smaller and more scarred than the last. An indication of more use and thus perhaps the contents were of more importance. Made from a lighter shade of walnut, it echoed the front carved flowers and arches but in a different pattern than its mate. The flat top showed scratches and rings where something had been set on top. She traced one of the rings with a finger, pondering whether a long ago cold beverage made the dark circle.

She glanced at her brother with a flick of her hand. "Your turn."

"I get to open one, huh? Merry Christmas to me." Chuckling, he moved to lift the lid and peer inside. The scent of ink and dust wafted from the interior. "Papers. Letters and broadsides."

He lifted aside several newspapers from an assortment of towns, publication dates ranging over the last decade. Bundles of personal letters were tied with a length of ribbon. Programs from long ago plays and menus from a few taverns. Mementoes and keepsakes? She peered closer at the broadsides and papers, their generic headlines meaningless to her.

"I wonder why Ma kept them. We should look through them sometime."

"They look pretty old." He dropped the lid with a loud thud and dusted his hands. "Later."

Cassie nodded as she surveyed the room and spotted the last of the trunks across the room. The beast inside raised its head, eyes glowing the longer Cassie studied the object.

She walked across to the blond wood trunk with a domed lid and a scrolled design featuring the flying owl. She trailed her finger over the ironwork decoration and then stilled. "Give me the keys again."

"What do you need?" Giles pulled the bunch from his pocket and held them out to her.

"The door key had a similar design on it." She found the key and compared the scroll work on it to the design on the trunk. "See, it's a smaller version of this featured pattern on the lid."

"Don't you dare open that one."

Cassie shrieked and covered her mouth with her hands. Mercy materialized beside her, holding out a hand as if to stop her from lifting the lid. Cassie sensed the fear and concern wafting from the ghost and frowned. "What's in it?"

"You don't need anything in those trunks, my dear. Especially that one. Not yet." Mercy drifted closer, her eyes tight with worry.

"I doubt there's anything in them that can hurt us." Giles motioned to Mercy to step back as he advanced on the domed trunk.

"Please, Giles, don't." Mercy trembled with the agitation flowing from her.

Giles tugged on the lid but it didn't budge.

"No, don't." Mercy darted toward him, shimmering with distress.

"I need to know what you're hiding from me. From us."

He snatched the key from Cassie's grasp and soon had the trunk unlocked and opened.

He leaned over to peruse the contents as Cassie moved closer so she could peek in also. Mercy halted nearby, trembling. The beast inside Cassie purred louder, nearly vibrating her chest with its anticipation. So this is what had been calling to her all along. She spotted a hand mirror with a silver frame, some jewelry boxes made of porcelain and cedar, some old tattered books, and other keepsakes. She lifted one of the boxes to see what kind of jewels it contained. A jumble of gold chains and freshwater pearls gleamed inside the porcelain box. She stirred the contents with a finger, espying several pair of earbobs and two brooches among the mass.

Giles straightened with an old-fashioned watch in his hand.

"Careful, son." Mercy reached toward him but drifted farther from him as he continued to inspect the item.

The pocket watch featured a ring of rose cut diamonds around the clock face with roman numeral hour marks. The hands were gold with fancy arrows at the tips. The maker's name, Abraham Colomby, was signed on the face. Giles flipped over the watch to look at the back where more rose-cut diamonds surrounded an enameled portrait of a lady in a floppy hat. Cassie marveled at the elegant and obviously expensive heirloom.

"I wonder…" Giles slowly spun the winding stem. A soft ticking emanated from the watch. He met Cassie's amazed look. "It still works."

Mercy sighed with relief but continued trembling.

Cassie set the jewelry box back inside the trunk and then looked at her mother. "Why were you so worried about a watch?"

"Mama has always been worried about stuff. I've found myself recalling a lot about our life in Montgomery.

Stuff I haven't thought about in ages. In fact, I just remembered…" Giles opened the pocket watch case and then snapped it shut again. "You told me I shouldn't brag about my strength, that I should hide it. Not let others know just how strong I am. Why?"

Fear buzzed through Mercy and echoed in Cassie's chest. "I did it for your own safety."

"What? That makes no sense." Giles slid the watch into his pocket and closed the trunk lid. "What do you mean?"

"I wish Reggie were home. He'd know what to do." Mercy shimmered as she rocked side to side a foot above the floor. "You should put the watch back. Now."

"I like it and I need one." Giles lifted a brow as he stared at their mother. "Whose watch was it, anyway? Papa's?"

Mercy swallowed and crossed her arms over her heaving chest. "Not on your life."

"What are those things?" Cassie stared at her mother, willing her to tell the truth despite the spike of fear coursing from her mother into her core. "Why were they under lock and key and the other trunks not locked? I thought you said you'd locked the wedding gown up, too. But that trunk wasn't locked. Why?"

"Oh, dear. I'd hoped to avoid this." Mercy shook her head as she glanced between her children. "I never thought you'd find out. I really hoped you wouldn't. Now there's no stopping it."

"It?" Cassie stepped closer to her mother's ghost.

"What are you talking about?" Giles strode toward Mercy as if he intended to force her to reveal her secrets.

"That trunk holds family…heirlooms. Ones you will inherit…when the time is right." She chewed her lower lip for a moment. "I'm so sorry. It's all my fault."

With a cry of anguish, Mercy vanished.

Cassie searched the room for her mother's ghost but she'd left. "That's getting very old."

"Agreed." He picked up the lantern. "Let's go find food. I'm starving."

"Always. The dinner crowd should be descending upon us soon so I best go on downstairs and get to work." She chuckled mirthlessly as she followed him to the door, then paused to scan the attic one more time with a long sigh. "One question answered but so many more raised."

Chapter Twelve

The clink of tableware echoed in the dining room. Flint surveyed the many tables of hungry guests busy with their midafternoon dinner. Cassie scurried past him bearing a tray of steaming bowls, flashing him a look he couldn't interpret. Possibly annoyance, or maybe she felt overworked. Or both. Definitely not a happy face. He'd placed the ad and spread the word about needing servers but no response. He'd even served meals to several customers himself, something he rarely needed to pitch in and do. He scanned the room, pleased with the amount of business but concerned with meeting the needs of so many.

As autumn approached, he planned to switch the linens to more earthy colors. Offer more hot beverages and soups. He'd need to make sure the girls aired out the comforters and heavy blankets. Stock up on firewood to keep the guests warm and the cooking fires burning. Marshall had informed him they needed more straw for bedding down the horses and hay for feeding through the mild winter. Several of the inn's coaches needed sprucing up, fresh paint and oiled wheels. He understood Cassie's need for help as he couldn't manage the operation of the property without those who worked for him.

"Excuse me, sir."

He glanced down to see a mousy girl standing meekly at his elbow. "Yes?"

"Where might I find Mr. Flint Hamilton?"

"I'm Mr. Hamilton. What can I do for you?"

"I'm here about the waitress position." She regarded him with solemn light brown eyes beneath thick brown lashes. "My friend, Miss Haley Baker, told me you're hiring."

"I am." The girl couldn't be more than eighteen years old and quiet as the proverbial church mouse. Petite and slim, neatly attired in a simple linsey-woolsey pink dress. Brown hair wrapped in a severe bun at the back of her head. "What's your name?"

"Mandy Crawford." She slid her gaze away to peruse the busy dining room.

He didn't know any other Crawfords. "Are you from around here?"

"Not originally. I was born in Nashville, or so they tell me."

How do you not know where you were born? Suspicions floated in his mind. "You're not sure?"

She shook her head. "I'm an orphan. I was left on the orphanage doorstep as an infant. They raised me until I turned eighteen a few months ago."

"So you're on your own? No family." He sighed. Life without a family to turn to, to lean on, or argue with. A very foreign concept indeed. "That must be hard."

The thought gave him pause. His plans included moving away from family. From friends and colleagues he'd come to rely upon both socially and in his career. The slip of a girl at his side faced her entire life with only herself to rely upon. She may be stronger than he'd first presumed.

"I have friends." She stiffened and peered up at him with solemn eyes. "I'm not alone."

"Where are you staying? With those friends?" He frowned lightly, worry for her safety simmering in his chest.

"Yes, sir." She lifted her chin a touch. "They're very kind to open their home for me."

She had a place to stay and seemed in good health. Doing well despite several obstacles in her life. "Then why do you want to work waiting on tables?"

"I need a job." Her eyes sparkled with determination.

"Not everyone needs to work." He studied the rebellious set of her jaw. "Why do you?"

"Because I need to pull my own weight and not rely upon them to support me. I want to contribute, too." She straightened her shoulders as she pressed her lips together for a moment. "I'm honest and a hard worker. So will you hire me to help around here?"

"The hours are long." He skimmed her frame, head to toe and back again. "I'm not sure you're strong enough to handle the job."

"I will manage." Mandy folded her hands, weaving her fingers together. "Please, sir."

The mouse might be able to manage but would she hinder or help? The weight of the trays as well as the length of time on her feet could be more than she could handle. Her steadfast gaze held his for several breaths. Should he give her a chance?

Cassie hurried past him carrying a tray loaded with empty dishes on their way back to be cleaned and refilled. He met her quizzing look with a tilt of his head. She glanced at Mandy and then smiled at him as she sashayed past. Well, if Cassie approved, then why not?

He looked down at Mandy and smiled, infusing it with as much welcome as he could. "Yes, I think you'll do fine."

"Thank you, sir." Mandy smiled at him, a beam of light and happiness. "When do you want me to start?"

"I don't suppose you have references?" He arched a brow as he waited for her reply.

Her smile faded. "No, sir. This is the first time I've applied for work."

"That's understandable. You can start on a trial basis, then. Tomorrow morning will be soon enough." Keeping his smile in place for Mandy's comfort, he flagged down Cassie as she came back into the room with a rag to wipe down a vacated table.

"Yes?" Cassie stopped beside Flint with a wary glance at Mandy.

His happy smile drooped as he contemplated her guarded expression. "Cassie, this is Mandy Crawford. She'll start waiting tables in the morning. Will you teach her what she needs to know?"

Cassie sighed, her gaze shifting between Mandy and Flint. "Don't I have enough to do already? Why can't you train her?"

Flint blinked at her several times as his smile fell away. He struggled to absorb the animosity flowing from her. "I believe you know your job better than I do. I wouldn't presume to step in and try to teach her everything you do. Please, Cassie?"

"Sure, just add more to my workload." Cassie sighed again and pursed her lips, a worried frown weighing her brows.

"But Cassie, once she's trained, you'll be free to do other things." Why the resistance to his request? It didn't make sense to him.

She huffed a sigh. "Fine. I'll show you around so maybe you'll be ready for the breakfast crowd tomorrow."

"Thank you." Mandy offered a small smile, her frame tense. "I'd appreciate that."

"Ready?" Cassie refolded the white rag in her hands with jerky movements. "Let's get this over with."

Flint searched Cassie's sulking features, confused as to why she'd object to helping the new girl learn the ropes. Where was his easy-going girl? The helpful young lady willing to work for the common good of the inn?

"Wait just a moment, please." Mandy faced Flint with a sincere smile. "Thank you, Mr. Hamilton. You won't regret hiring me."

"I am hopeful that you're correct." He grinned at her as she nodded once and followed Cassie over to the empty table to prepare it for the supper customers in a few hours.

The two girls worked side by side as Cassie instructed Mandy on the various aspects of the job. Mandy listened attentively to Cassie's sullen explanations, occasionally asking a question for clarification. Mandy seemed like a smart young woman even if rather plain. Definitely didn't match the description of the kind of server Cassie had suggested, pretty and buxom. But the longer he studied her, the more he appreciated her calm and grace. Not a flashy beauty, but attractive nonetheless. Flint nodded to himself as he crossed to the bar to inventory the contents. Mandy might work out very well indeed but what was wrong with Cassie?

The next morning, Giles woke up out of sorts and grumpy. He'd had nightmares all night, one after another. While they differed in some aspects, the one thing they all had in common was his failure to protect his cousin from drowning. He'd only been a boy but he knew he could have saved him if Papa hadn't interfered. The memory haunted him as he finished dressing and made his way downstairs to the public dining room to hunt up some food.

The room was nearly empty so early in the day. He ambled over to a chair near the bar and sat down. Cassie hurried into the room with a tray of plates piled with flapjacks and sausages for the group of men seated two tables away. She handed out the plates like a card dealer before coming toward Giles.

"Coffee or tea?" She leaned the tray against her hip and smiled at him. "I'm assuming you want flapjacks and sausage, too."

"Tea, and you're right." He peered at her more closely, noting the hint of shadows around her eyes. "You sleep all right?"

She shrugged one shoulder. "Well enough."

"What's the matter?" He drummed his fingers on the table once and then forced his hand to lay still.

She glanced over her shoulder toward the doorway and then back to him. "Nothing I can't handle."

"I don't follow." The quick shake of her head told him her thoughts. She didn't want him to understand. "I'm not supposed to?"

She sighed. "Let's just say that after finally seeing what's in the attic, you'd think I wouldn't be so fixated on it."

"Are you?" He got the impression she was not telling him the truth. Something else hovered in her mind that she wasn't ready to share with him.

"Yeah, but I'll be all right." She lifted the tray, opened her mouth as if to say something and then closed it again. Pressing her lips together, she gave a shake of her head. "I'll be right back."

She spun around and headed for the kitchen. He watched her go until she disappeared around the corner. What wasn't she telling him? If she wanted him to know, then she'd have to say it. He couldn't guess her secrets. Hm. Perhaps his dreams had been caused by the revelation of his mother harboring secrets. Ones she felt very guilty about. Could be a connection there he hadn't fathomed in the past. He drummed his fingers on the table, contemplating what those secrets could possibly be. How could he safeguard his family if he didn't know everything he needed to do so? Like what possible threats they might face. Or past transgressions which could come back to haunt them.

A new girl walked into the room awkwardly carrying a tray with both hands. She struggled to keep it level, the bowls of porridge sliding slowly one direction and then another as she shifted her grip. Her bun sported several loose hairs poking out in all directions. A creased brow displayed her deep concentration. She finally set the tray on a table and started handing out the bowls to an older couple.

Cassie returned with his breakfast and placed it on the table with efficient swiftness. "What's your plan for today?"

"I'm not certain yet but have a few things I want to investigate." He leaned back as she poured hot tea from the pot into a cup. He pointed at the girl with his chin. "Who's that?"

Cassie glanced at the girl with a scowl. "Mandy. Flint hired her last night."

"Good, I'm glad you've got some help in here." He watched the play of emotions crossing his sister's face. "Aren't you happy he hired her?"

She shrugged. "I suppose. Once she's up to speed I won't need to play waitress all the time."

"You're good at it though." Why did she keep flicking glances at the new girl? "Are you upset about something?"

"Not really. I'd rather entertain than serve up soup." She propped her hands on her hips and again appeared to want to say something but stopped herself. "So, anyway, I'll let you eat and then see if I can help her learn how to handle that tray."

"Good idea." After the dreams of the night before, he had one main objective. He needed to find out what inspired his mother's annoying disappearing act the day before. The more he thought about her actions the stronger the urge to talk to her, pin her down on what exactly she meant. Depending entirely on whether she'd make an appearance when he requested for her to talk to him. He could hope.

"Well, enjoy your food." Cassie left him to his meal with a flick of her hand in farewell.

He tucked into the flapjacks and sausage, delighting in the hot, delicious breakfast. The spices of the savory sausage contrasted with the butter and honey on his flapjacks. Most mornings he made do with a cold roll and hard cheese before heading to the exchange for business. Life in Mobile moved at a much different pace. Far more engagement with a myriad of fellow merchants and ships captains occurred on any given day than what transpired at the Fury Falls Inn on a good day. He perused the other men and handful of women at the tables around him. Watched Cassie directing Mandy through her routine. The typical guests seemed to be simple country folk for the most part but also some more polished gentlemen and ladies as well, judging from their attire. A good mix of clientele. Flint managed the business well for a stand-in for Giles' father.

Speaking of his father, he should be on his way home soon. Flint had sent word of Mercy's death. Surely Papa would want to come back as a result. Although Reggie hadn't always acted according to how Giles thought he should. Nor as Giles would have acted in his place. He'd learned that the childhood lessons of his parents were not enough to make him feel like a man. He'd adapted his approach and attitude toward others based on how he wanted to be treated. Thus, he kept a watchful eye on the safety and security of his friends and employees. And now, of course, his family.

Taking a gulp of tea to wash down a bite of sausage, he thought again about how his father had dragged him out of the water and forced him to stay on the edge of the lake, to not help his cousin. Watching George float in the water without being able to answer the instinct compelling him to respond had been one of the most difficult moments of his life. That was a prime example of how his father acted oddly at times. Why had he held him back, prevented him from trying to help his cousin?

Maybe Mama knew the answer to the perplexing question. He pushed back from the table and strode out of the room, heading straight for the family parlor across the dogtrot porch. That was where he'd seen her last, so as good a place to start as any. He hesitated once inside and searched the room for the merest sign of Mercy. Not seeing her, he strode into the center of the large room, his patience thin as a spider's web.

"Mama! Come here." He slowly pivoted to continue to look for her. "We need to talk. Now."

He made two rotations before she materialized a few feet from him. She appeared calm, not nearly as frightened and testy as the day before.

"Thank you." He motioned for her to join him, to come closer. "I know this isn't easy for you."

"What do you want to talk about?" The slight lowering of her brows bespoke of her unease.

"Let's start with what you meant when you said it's all your fault." He studied her reaction, the slowly widening eyes that then narrowed again.

She made a vague waving away motion in the air. "Nothing really. You spooked me when you picked up that watch."

"Why? It's just a watch." He reflexively slipped a hand into his pocket to grasp the softly ticking timepiece.

"In your hands apparently." She smiled at him, drifting a little left and right for a moment. "Never mind."

"You're acting very odd." He considered the bland grin on her face. "Do you think the men who killed you wanted those things in the locked trunk?"

"No, they wouldn't know what to do with them." Her smile faded away as she stared at him. "But you need to find those men. They pose a continuing threat to Cassie and everyone. As long as they're on the loose, they may come back to try again to find the nonexistent treasure."

Adam's words echoed in Giles' mind. The man had been waiting for an opportunity to do just that. Although he was behind bars, his comrades remained unknown. His protective instincts flared into a brushfire. He had a definite purpose for his next few days. Find those men.

"I will find them, Mama. But I have another question."

"I'm listening."

"Why did Papa stop me from helping my cousin all those years ago?"

Mercy shook her head slowly. "You'll need to ask Reggie. I can't tell you. I'm not strong enough."

"But you know, don't you." He heard it in her voice, the reality of one of the secrets she kept close. "I remember so much about that day, but I never knew his reasoning."

"You're strong, Giles. Stronger than you know in more ways than one." She studied him silently for several ticks of the mantel clock. "You've always been protective of others. It's in your nature."

His strength remained one aspect of his life of which he was proud. He used it to help others, not hurt them. Unless he had to. "Then answer my question so I can be prepared to protect Cassie to the best of my ability."

She shimmered where she floated several feet from Giles. "I can tell you that you have always been and will always be a guardian. Don't ask me more than that."

"If that's true, then I'm even more confused as to why Papa did what he did." He raked a hand through his hair as he thought again about that long ago day. "I was strong enough to save George."

Mercy nodded sadly. "We knew that. Your father did

what we thought was best for you and the family. But now, Giles, I charge you with keeping Cassie close and safe. She's key to everything. With my death, I can no longer protect her like you must."

Giles frowned deeply at her comment. "You're making me more confused."

She sighed harshly and shimmered in place. "I'm sorry. I don't want to be the one to tell you what you want to know. Wait for your father. Please."

"What am I to protect Cassie from? Those men?"

"To begin. Keep your eyes and ears open." Mercy started dematerializing, fading into a shadow. "Keep John Baker away from her, too. Guard her with your life."

Then she disappeared entirely, her command echoing in the sudden stillness.

"Baker? What's he got to do with this?" He dropped down onto a nearby chair, mulling all she'd told him and fuming about what she refused to share. His priority was clear. He had to find those men. To do so, he needed to go talk to Adam Jacobs and force him to reveal who they were. Then he'd track them down like the murderous animals they were and hand them over to the sheriff.

The rest of his mother's directive invoked grave concerns in his chest and his heart. He'd forgotten while he'd been separated from her by so many miles and years. But Cassie was a friendly, caring young woman who worked hard to help others. She'd never intentionally hurt anyone. So the big question was, who wanted to harm her?

Chapter Thirteen

Silence did not sound encouraging. Flint strode around the side of the inn to check on the men's progress in digging the new well, Beau and Pickles trotting alongside. The men had picked the spot likely to offer the greatest water table access, out beyond the laundry shack. The site would prove more convenient for the laundress as well, since it was closer to the shack than the previous fouled well on the other side of the outhouse. As he passed the privy he sniffed. They'd have to move it soon, but not yet. First, the well. The closer he drew to the new well site the more upset he became.

The two giant slaves John Baker had sent indeed could accomplish the task in short order. If they worked instead of lounging about on the ground. The larger of the two, Tobe, regarded him with wary eyes. Anthony, or Ant'ny as they called him, had his eyes closed, his hat pushed forward to shade his face while he lay on his back. His ire rose at the lazy slugs.

"What are you doing lollygagging about like that?" He stopped beside the two dark-skinned men sitting in the shade of nearby trees. The dogs kept going, nosing their way past the laundry shack and around the end of the inn.

"You need to get this job done and soon."

"We's taking a lil break is all." Tobe rested his large hands on his kneecaps, sitting cross-legged on the ground studying Flint with a half-smile. "Like marster Baker told us."

Ant'ny opened his eyes and shifted up to rest on his elbows, his long, powerful legs stretched out in front of him. "Yes, sir, he sure told us to not get too hot and then not be able to finish. We be making a good size hole in this here heat."

Flint glanced over at the beginnings of the five-foot-diameter hole that they'd need to dig in order to reach the water table. An empty wheelbarrow stood to one side. Several pick axes, short-handled shovels, and buckets littered the ground. A stack of planks waited to shore up the walls of the well. The depth of the hole remained an open question, entirely dependent on how low the water table resided. That open question of depth meant the length of time it would take to finish the well also remained an undefined quantity.

He scowled at the men, his fists on his hips. "I don't care if it's hot. What do you expect? It's August. Now get on your feet and get back to work."

The two men didn't move. Flint crossed his arms over his chest and scowled at them. They weren't his to order about but they'd been loaned to him to dig the well. Presumably faster with their superior strength. Yet there they sat, disobeying his demand. Frustration swelled inside, heating his chest. He was no driver to whip them into action. He couldn't do that. He swallowed the bile in his throat at the thought. Zander's tales of how terribly he'd been treated before Giles stepped in to free him swirled in his mind. Lashing and burns as punishment for not working fast enough. No, he couldn't force them onto their feet. But what would motivate them to resume their digging?

"We get back to it in a min't." Tobe picked up his hat by the crown from where it rested beside his huge thigh on the grass. "Don't you worry none."

Ant'ny sat up and brushed his pants off with scarred and dirty hands. Stared up at Flint without saying a word.

Flint dropped his arms to his sides as he noticed Cassie on the back porch. She hesitated at the top of the steps and then quickly descended to the ground. Great, just what he didn't need. Her censure regarding the mere presence of the mutinous slaves on the property. In addition to the confusing animosity of the other day when he'd hired Mandy. Her attitude changed from accepting the girl to obvious resentment when he'd asked Cassie to train her. He didn't fathom what sparked such resistance. He tensed as she approached. She carried a large empty basket in one hand, swinging it lightly as she strolled over to join him.

"What's the matter? You look upset." She peered at him and then glanced at the two men with a smile.

"I am." He speared Tobe with his glare. "I don't feel like this well will ever be done, especially when these two are sitting around taking breaks."

She frowned, the downward pull of her brows marring her pretty features. "They're entitled to take a break now and again. I'm sure it's hard work they're doing."

"That's their job, though." He shook his head at her. "Don't be making excuses for them."

She dared to defend the two lazy son-of-a-guns? She objected to slavery, as did he, but at the same time these men were placed here to accomplish a task. A much needed task. Until they finished the acknowledged hard labor the inn couldn't operate efficiently and comfortably for everyone. He must make them understand the importance of finishing the work. But how could he with Cassie interfering? He bristled, preparing his reasoned arguments, when Cassie tossed her long braid over her shoulder.

"I don't need to." She aimed a sweet smile at the pair of sweaty men grinning back at her. "I'm sure they will be happy to help us out of our difficulty. After all, they surely know how hard it is to haul filled water buckets from the river all the way down to the kitchen and such. Don't you?"

"Yes'm, I can 'magine." Ant'ny bobbed his head with his smile widening.

Flint stood amazed at how she wove a spell around the two men, changing their defensive attitude into an amenable pair hanging on her every syllable.

"So it would be greatly appreciated by everyone here at the Fury Falls Inn to have the well finished as quickly as you can. Big, strong men like you will make short work of it, I'd think." She swung the basket around in front of her pale yellow flowered dress. "If you wouldn't mind?"

Flint studied her expression and marveled at the dulcet tones of her voice. He looked at the two men, surprise sweeping through him as they practically jumped to their feet. Energy pulsated from them with every movement. With such activity, they may finish the job that very afternoon. How did she manage to inspire them so easily? He needed to learn her technique for future reference. Quite a valuable talent.

"We's getting right on it, miss." Tobe jammed his hat firmly in place and motioned to Ant'ny. "Get in dat hole, boy."

"I's coming." Ant'ny shuffled over to the hole and peered over the edge. "A long way to go, I bet."

"We'll rig up that chair lift thing to lower you down." Tobe glanced at Cassie with a grin as he positioned the empty wheelbarrow near the hole. "Go on with ya, miss. We'll have this'n here well dug in the shake of a lamb's tail."

"Thank you. Both of you." Cassie returned the smile and then met Flint's gaze. "What?"

He motioned to the two men busily climbing over the lip

and employing a pick and shovel, steadily filling the wheelbarrow with soil and rocks. "You're remarkable."

"All it takes is respect and kindness." She clasped her basket with both hands.

"And a pretty woman's smile." He grinned gently at her. "I'm glad to know you, Cassie."

Her smile wilted for a flash before she smiled softly. "I'm pleased to know you, as well."

Her tone conveyed a gentler nature than she'd worn when he'd hired the new waitress. Perhaps he could inquire as to how she felt toward him and ascertain what might have caused her distress. He swallowed his reluctance and pressed on.

"Have you forgiven me for whatever I did to upset you the other evening?" He held his breath, anxious for her forgiveness despite his confusion. "I had the impression I'd done something wrong?"

"In a way, I suppose." She squared her shoulders and drew in a long breath, searching his eyes as she released a sigh. "You were flirting with that new girl. I-I didn't like it."

"No, I wasn't."

"It sure looked like it to me." She folded her arms over her ample bosom. "All batting of lashes and smiling so big at her."

"I was trying to make her feel comfortable." He replayed his actions in his mind and then suddenly froze to peer closer at her. "Oh, no. Do you think she thought I was flirting with her?"

She flung a hand out to brush aside his comment. "She is such a clueless lass I doubt it. But I noticed."

"Oh, I understand now. You were jealous?" He blinked several times in surprise. "Of that little mouse?"

"Mouse?" She chuckled as her eyes twinkled. "I guess you could call her that since she's such a quiet thing and all. So you're not interested in her?"

He raised both brows as he took her upper arms in his hands to draw her closer. "Not one tiny bit." He pressed a kiss to her lips and then eased back.

Emotions flickered across her face as she gazed at him for a long moment. He hoped she believed him and would set things right between them. If only they could proceed forward in their relationship rather than two steps forward and three steps back. The on again, off again nature made his head and his heart ache.

"All right then. You're forgiven." Spinning around, she tossed a grin at him as she went about her business.

She strolled toward her garden at the far end of the clearing, her steps light and graceful. She'd been jealous of that slip of a girl which could only mean he had hope of a future with Cassie. If she didn't care for him, then his smiling at the other girl wouldn't have bothered her. She liked him certainly. But did she like him enough?

Just after noon, Giles found Zander enjoying the shade of the front porch of the inn, picking on his banjo. The melancholy tune seemed appropriate after all the excitement of the morning. Giles adjusted the other chair then sank down onto its hard surface and listened to his friend's playing. A sweating pitcher of lemonade sat on the table, several cups and a plate of iced teacakes surrounding it. The dogs lazed at the far end of the porch. Beau and Pickles, the brown and black Labs, dozing while Cocoa, the Cocker spaniel, and Red, the Golden, kept an eye on the comings and goings of the customers. Giles poured himself a glass of the cold sweet-tart beverage and lifted a cake to his mouth.

His mama had claimed he was strong in more ways than one. Then called him a guardian. Those words replayed over and over in his mind as he chewed the sweet treat. Something about the way she spoke imbued them with importance.

He'd always taken his strength as natural, but maybe he could do more than normal men. In fact, he seemed even stronger now than a mere month before. His muscular arms hadn't changed in size, nor his powerful thighs. Yet he could tell a difference in the ease with which he moved. The incident with the Baker's coach and Matt's pinning replayed in his mind. How was it possible he'd had the strength to lift the vehicle not merely enough to release Matt's leg but several feet?

He relaxed back in the chair, head against the wall while crossing his booted ankles and closing his eyes. He couldn't solve the mysterious change but he could make time to think through his plan for going after the men. The gentle tune lulled him into a soothing trance as he let his mind roam the possibilities. No man had ever bested Giles in a hand-to-hand contest. Not that he'd faced many adversaries, given his size and temper. He'd take Zander with him, no question. With Zander's equally large frame and intense glare, combined with the black man's anger from his past mistreatment, they'd get results. Zander as a freeman didn't take kindly to others insulting or threatening him. Together they were indomitable and dangerous.

Opening his eyes, he studied his closest friend as he bent over the instrument, strumming and picking the strings as he sang a lilting air. The man did justice to the instrument. His hands and fingers flew over the strings at times, caressed them at others. His deep bass voice supported the tune, balancing the tones into a beautiful harmony. He finished the song, meeting Giles' steady regard with a question in his eyes.

"I need your help, Zan."

"I'm listening." Zander started plucking softly on the banjo as he waited for Giles to respond.

"My mother is worried for Cassie's safety but she didn't tell me what the threat might be." Giles folded his arms over his stomach. "I need you to keep an eye open for signs of trouble."

Zander nodded slowly as he played. "I'll do that."

"And I want you to go with me to the jail later to get Jacobs to tell me who his friends are. I need to find them and soon."

"Are they part of the trouble?"

"Yeah."

The rapid three-beat of horses' hooves drew Giles' gaze to the lane leading up to the inn. Flint cantered up the carriage drive toward the stable, his buckskin paint gelding lathered from the ride into town. He reined to a halt and dismounted in one smooth motion. Marshall emerged from the barn to talk with Flint as he removed the saddle bag from behind the saddle, before the lad led the horse inside. Flint crossed the busy carriageway toward the inn. He trotted up the few steps and then paused when he spotted Zander and Giles.

"Enjoying the shade?" Flint slung the saddle bag over his shoulder.

"It's a scorcher today. Want something to drink?"

"No time. I'm running behind as it is." Flint eyed the sweating pitcher for a moment and then returned his gaze to Giles. "You won't believe what I discovered on the ride into town."

"What's that?" The urgency in Flint's voice put Giles on alert.

"A body beside the road. I informed the sheriff when I got to town."

"Who was it?" Giles tensed.

Flint shook his head with a rueful shrug. "They'd been stabbed several times. Sheriff Neal sent Deputy Parker out to look into the matter."

Zander stopped picking at the strings of his banjo. "Was it nearby?"

"Not too far away, maybe three miles from here." Flint rubbed his jaw. "I don't like it."

"Another murder in the area isn't a good thing." Giles lifted his glass and took a swig.

"I'm going to set out a guard at night. Make sure nobody sneaks in and causes mischief." Flint gazed at Giles with serious eyes. "We need to protect our own."

"Yes." Giles gestured to the bag. "Anything interesting in the mail?"

Flint clutched the leather strap as his brows dipped briefly. "Mostly bills and such for the inn. There's a letter for Cassie from her father, too."

Giles shifted to sit up straight, pulling his feet under the chair. "I hope Papa is on his way."

Flint shook his head, pressing his lips tight. "He's not planning to return until the end of October."

"Damn it." Giles slapped the armrest and shook his head. "Of all the…"

His father yet again didn't disappoint in acting for his own interests over that of the family. The past seemed to be repeating as far as his father's refusal to step up and do the right thing. Forcing Giles to wait, sit on his heels and do nothing. This time, though, he had no intention of letting events unfold as they might. He intended to bend events to his will. No more playing the waiting game. Seething, Giles glanced at Zander and then back to Flint.

"I understand. I hadn't expected to be here this long either." Flint repositioned the bag on his shoulder. "He said he'll come back as soon as things are settled there. Maybe he has more to tell Cassie than that."

"He's so far away. He'll have a difficult journey when he does venture home."

"Wait. There's another letter of interest." Flint fished in the saddlebag and pulled out a bundle of letters, flipping through until he found the one he wanted. "Here."

The postmark read Montgomery. Addressed to Mercy. "I wonder who it's from." He turned it over, reluctant to pry by opening the folded paper. Likely it was from one of his aunts. Indistinct and faded memories of them floated through his mind. Mainly of the mysterious hostility they'd aimed at his mother. Both of his parents, really. What had happened to spark such heated exchanges and cold shoulders?

"I figure you're the oldest of her children, so it's appropriate to give it to you." Flint shrugged. "Do with it what you will."

"Yeah." He shoved the missive into his inside vest pocket as Sheridan strode around the corner of the building, dusting his hands on his slacks. "Hey, Sheridan, where you been?"

"Just visiting the privy, if you must know." Sheridan chuckled as he climbed the steps to the porch, glancing between the gathered men. "What's going on?"

"We were talking about a murder near here and then wondering when Reggie may come home and pondering the kind of trip he's facing." Flint dropped the saddle bag to hold between his hands.

"A murder?" Shock opened Sheridan's eyes wide. "Where?"

"Several miles away but close enough that we'll need to take turns standing guard at night." Flint's tone had a thread of steel running through it. "We're not going to let anything happen here again."

"Right. About Mr. Fairhope, I hope he's careful on his trip. Carriages aren't all that safe. We've heard tell of many folks injured, some killed, as a result of one overturning." Sheridan slipped his hands into his pockets. "I was nearly killed in an accident myself years ago."

"Looks like you survived fine." Giles grinned at him. "You lived to tell about it."

"Almost didn't though." Sheridan leaned against a column and regarded each of them. "But then I wouldn't be here if it weren't for that accident. That's how I met Mr. Fairhope."

"What happened?" Flint let the bag hit the floor as he peered at Sheridan.

"He came along just after we'd rolled down an embankment. Saved my life." Sheridan's gaze turned inward, reliving the event. "My leg had been trapped under the roof but he was able to lift the coach enough I could drag myself out. I was so grateful to him I told him if he wanted, I'd work for him the rest of my life."

"And here you are." Flint gestured to Sheridan, a grin on his face.

"Mr. Fairhope saved me again by buying me and then setting me free." Sheridan's gaze sharpened as he looked at Zander. "Like his son has done for you and your brother. I can't never repay Mr. Fairhope for his generosity, which is why I've stayed put."

Sheridan's gaze rested on Zander for several moments before sliding to meet Giles' regard. "Your papa is a decent man, Giles. He may not be perfect, but he's got a good heart."

"I'll keep that in mind." Even if he didn't always agree with the sentiment. At least, his papa had apparently treated others well. Something to consider as he waited for him to finally make an appearance.

Zander stilled, the banjo yet again falling silent.

"What is it?" Giles squinted at the inward look his friend wore.

"When I was still a boy, I heard my papa died in an overturned coach. That was after Matt and I got sold to that evil plantation owner in Louisiana so who knows if it's true." Zander rested his arm on the banjo. "Then again, he might have made it up so we'd not go looking for family."

"He who? The man who whipped you for no good reason?" Giles bristled recalling the treatment of Zander and Matt at the hands of the plantation owner. "I wouldn't put it past that no good rat."

"It makes no difference whether he told the truth or not. I ain't never gonna see my parents again." Zander resumed picking out a somber tune on the banjo, head lowered over the strings.

"You're both part of my family, Zan. I'm closer to you than my own brothers." Sad but true fact of Giles' family. They'd scattered apart when their parents chose to move to northern Alabama. "Heck, this is the first time I've seen my sister in many years. At least you've had Matt with you."

Zander lifted his head and aimed sad eyes at Giles. "Yeah, I guess we're both orphans just in different ways."

"Family is more than blood relatives. We can choose to expand our family to include our friends. The people who really want to be with you." Flint hefted the saddle bag back onto his shoulder. "While this has been an enlightening conversation, gentlemen, I'm afraid I have work to do."

"Yes, so do I. Zander and I are going to visit Jacobs." Giles stood and stretched his back as Flint nodded sharply at him.

"Do you know where the jail is located?" Flint paused in turning toward the doorway.

"I'd guess on the town square like most places." Along with the pillory and whipping post as visual deterrents to the residents as those who had been charged with a crime were punished. "Right?"

"Up until a few years ago you'd be right." Flint huffed a chuckle. "But the ground proved too low and flooded when it rained, so they built a new one at the corner of Clinton and Greene. You can't miss it."

Giles swept a glance at Zander and then back to Flint. "Good. We need to have a little talk with Jacobs because I really want to meet that man's friends. Soon."

Chapter Fourteen

The ride into Huntsville gave Giles time to think. To imagine all the ways he'd compel the inmate to tell him the names of his accomplices. He cantered easily beside Zander down the hard-packed Huntsville Road. Barely glancing at the extensive forest stretching as far as he could see. Slowly the trees gave way to houses and streets as they entered the outskirts of town. They rode up Clinton Street past the impressive Baptist church and stopped in front of the new jail at the corner of Greene. Leaving their mounts at the hitching rail, Giles stormed up the stone steps, ready to confront the man responsible for his mother's death. Zander followed a few steps behind him.

Once inside the stone and brick building, Giles peered around the nice sized office with a large wood desk facing the door. A blotter and calendar with days crossed off in red sat in the middle. To one side were a couple of pens along with several pairs of handcuffs. Giles scanned the room, past the man at the desk and on to several cells at the rear half of the building, complete with heavy metal bars on the doors and small windows. Adam Jacobs glared at him from one cell, hunched over on the hard cot shoved against the outside wall.

The hefty officer rose from his chair behind the desk. "Can I help you?"

Giles estimated the man's threat level. No doubt about it, he could take the man if he got in the way. Although obviously strong, his shorter stature gave Giles the advantage, and his weight would slow him down enough to make it easy to grapple him into submission. Should the need arise.

"I'm here to talk to Jacobs." Giles glared at the man in the cell.

"I'm Deputy Barney Parker. Talk to me first." He braced his feet apart and crossed his muscular arms over his chest. "What do you want with him?"

"Deputy? You're the jailer, too?" He couldn't say what was in his heart to a lawman.

The desire, no *need* to rip into the bastard who'd threatened and harmed his family. His mama lost her life to that criminal. If Giles dared to speak words along those lines, though, the deputy would most certainly object and try to thwart his mission. Then he'd put himself in harm's way and Giles didn't want to hurt a man of the law.

"No, the Jailer, Daniel Rather, had to attend other business today." Barney studied him with caution in his regard. "Now, what business do you have with the prisoner?"

Giles inspected the deputy more closely. A challenge in his dark eyes. Attitude and brawn combined. "That man was in cahoots with the man who killed my mother."

"And you are?" Barney raised his brows as he waited for Giles to respond.

"Giles Fairhope."

"Ah, I see." Barney tossed a glance over his shoulder at Adam. "What do you expect to happen next?"

"I need to speak to the rogue." Giles crossed his arms over his massive chest. "No one is going to stop me. That's what I expect."

"Well, I can't let you beat on him." Barney feigned an apology. "You can talk to him, see what he'll say. As long as you keep your distance, you hear me?"

Giles glanced over to where Zander stood near the door. Standing by in case Giles needed help. He lifted his chin in a silent communication to be ready. Zander nodded once.

"I hear you, deputy." With a jerk of his head, Giles strode past the deputy and approached the cell. He glared at the killer. "I think you know you're not going anywhere anytime soon, don't you?"

Adam nodded, silent and wary.

"Were you behind the fouling of the Inn's well?" Giles glared at him as the man glowered back.

"Why would I skunk the well?" Adam smirked.

"You did, didn't you?" Giles studied the slight tremble across Adam's shoulders. Why would he want to interfere with the water supply? Poor Teddy had to lug buckets from much farther away as a result. Hm. "You wanted to make Teddy come to where you spied on the inn so you could nab him. That's why."

Adam showed his teeth when he grinned at him. "He's my son. You had no right to keep him away from me."

"That's a matter for debate. Not that you actually care about his well-being." Giles crossed his arms and raised his chin. "Let me ask you this. Have you told the authorities who your pals are that helped you kill my mother?"

Adam shook his head rapidly. "I didn't kill nobody."

Giles took two steps toward the barred door. He wanted to reach through the bars and throttle the rogue but he'd promised the deputy. "Then tell me."

Adam flinched backward, gripping the edge of the cot. "What's in it for me? You gonna let me go if I do?"

"Not my call. But I'll let you live. How's that for an incentive?"

"You can't touch me." Adam dared to smirk at him again.

He'd reached his limit. Giles grabbed hold of the bars and shook them, mortar dust cascading from the walls where the bars were secured. All the encouragement he needed to shake them harder, force them to give way and allow him access to choke a confession out of him. "Wanna bet?"

Barney hurried to wrestle Giles away from the door, grabbing at his arms with little effect. "That's enough. Calm down or you'll have to leave."

Adam chortled as he taunted an enraged Giles from behind Barney. Giles dodged past the deputy and attacked the bars again, rattling them and praying they'd give way. He shook the bars with clenched hands. Metal screeched with each jerk of his hands. He'd choke the names from the man's bloody throat.

"Stand down." Barney grappled him from behind and dragged him half a step backward. "Hey, you, help me."

Giles heard Zander grunt before his muscular hands grabbed hold of him. The additional restraints made his anger flare brighter. He twisted and wrenched free with all his might. Barney fell back against the desk and then flopped to the floor with a groan. Giles shoved Zander off him, the big black man bouncing against the wall and sliding to the floor. He glared at Barney and Zander in turn. Rage sizzled through his veins, hot and fast. Barney groaned again, putting a hand to his head. Zander stared at him with wide eyes. Giles blinked as he realized what he'd done. He'd hurt his dearest friend as well as a man of the law. Exactly what he'd vowed he'd never do. What the hell was wrong with him? He forced himself to quiet, breathing hard from the exertion.

Barney slowly struggled to his feet and then held out his hands as if trying to calm a frightened horse. "Steady now. I'm not your enemy, thank goodness. Damn, man, you're strong. Sure wish I hadn't volunteered to give Rather the day off."

"Sorry, I don't know what came over me." He grimaced and hurried to give Zander a hand and help him to his feet. "I'm sorry."

Zander gulped as he stared at Giles. "When did you get so strong, man?"

He looked down at his hands, feeling the strength coursing through his veins. "I don't know. I've never done anything like that before."

Barney chuckled drily as he leaned against the desk. "It's a good thing you don't need to beat it out of him. I don't think he'd survive. If you'd told me what you wanted to know I could have told you that we think we know who those men are."

Now the deputy had Giles' full attention. "You do?"

Barney lowered his hands to press on the desk as he nodded. "After asking around, we learned this guy has been seen with Joe Madison and Greg Chalmers, some other low-life white trash from up in the foothills."

Adam looked away at the mention of the other men, then slid a frightened and guilty glance back at Giles who huffed a mirthless laugh. "Joe. Yep, that's got to be them. Where do I find them?"

Barney's eyebrow slowly slid into an arch. "You?"

"Yes, sir. Make me a deputy."

"Will you promise me one thing?"

"What's that?" Giles glanced at Zander and then back to the deputy.

"Bring them in alive when you find them." Barney lifted two sets of handcuffs off the desk and held them out to Giles. "Please?"

"I'll do my best." First, he'd gather up Flint and Matt and then along with Zander go find the thugs. He accepted the clinking cuffs and tilted his head to one side. "But I can't promise what condition they'll be in."

Impatience simmered inside as Giles and Zander dismounted back at the inn. A duly deputized man, he wanted to head out immediately and hunt down the two killers. The day spun toward evening. No time to waste. But he needed more men with him, which was the only reason he'd returned to the Fury Falls Inn. He swiftly tied the reins to the hitching rail and brushed his hands on his jeans.

"Let me track down Flint while you get your brother." He pivoted and headed toward the porch steps.

"It's kind of late to go today, don't you think?" Zander tied his horse to the rail and then fell into step with Giles. "It can wait another day."

He frowned at the suggestion of delaying, every fiber of his being quivering with the longing to remount and ride. "I don't think so. We've got enough daylight for a while yet."

"You're the boss."

Giles stopped on the porch to stare at his friend. "With each passing day it's going to be harder to locate those men."

"More so in the dark in unfamiliar territory." Zander crossed his arms. "But we know who they are so we'll find them. Never fear."

"I'm anxious to get them off the streets." Giles turned away from his friend to stride inside the inn.

Cassie bustled into the entrance hall from the kitchen. "Hey, Giles, how'd it go with Adam Jacobs?" She sauntered over to stand by Giles, a smeared apron covering her pale green dress.

"I have the names of the two men." He glanced from her surprised expression to Zander's sullen frown. "Deputy Parker suggested we search up in the foothills."

"Do you know of any caves round abouts?" Zander slid his hands into his pockets.

"I have heard some of the patrons talk about the abundance of caves in this region." She pointed to the dining room. "You might ask some of those men. They may even know the men you're looking for."

Any short cuts to finding the villains were worth taking. Giles shifted his weight, preparing to stride over to talk to the men. "That's a good idea."

"I'll get Matt and tell him what's going on but I sincerely doubt anyone will agree to go now." Zander ambled away in search of his brother.

Obviously his friend didn't agree with the urgency flowing through Giles. He turned to his sister. "Do you know where Flint is?"

"No, I haven't seen him for a while." She gestured to the closed kitchen door. "I've been busy helping Sheridan."

Damn, he needed Flint's knowledge of the area to guide them to possible hiding places in the hills. He'd have to hunt him up. He started to brush past Cassie then remembered. "Did Flint give you a letter from Papa?"

"Yes, he was just checking in with me to see how I'm doing after…you know." She shrugged and glanced away. "But he's not coming home any sooner. Said there's no need to with you and Flint here."

Sounded like his old man, thinking of himself more than anyone else. "Well, I'm only here for a short time. Flint will be here until Papa gets home, though."

"I know, but I need to speak to Pa in person." She met his gaze with a sad smile. "I have so many questions only he can answer. Very many about the new members of the family. Or at least new to us. And I think he should be here. He should pay his respects to his wife. I even hinted in my last letter that Ma wanted to talk to him, but he didn't seem to understand my meaning."

"I understand and I know you're strong and will manage fine." Giles embraced her briefly and then carefully set her away from him. "You're a good woman, Cassie. Always looking out for people."

Even as a young girl she'd been eager to help their mother around the house and in the garden. He'd been old enough to understand how fortunate the family had been to be so close-knit. Despite living near a big city, they'd been mostly self-sufficient. Raising their fruits and vegetables, and hunting and trapping wild game to provide meat. Cassie learned early how to skin and dress a rabbit or squirrel to make stews and soups. Mercy had educated her on how to grow an abundance of vegetables and beans as well as how to make and mend their clothes. Only after he'd failed to save his cousin did the family break apart. A chill swept his broad shoulders.

"What's wrong?" Cassie peered at him with a slight frown dipping her brows.

He stared at her as the realization filtered through his memories, coloring their significance in a harsh light. "It's all my fault."

"What?"

He'd wanted to dive in and save his cousin because he knew he was strong enough to even though he was still young himself. He'd always been stronger than his friends. Papa had held him back, saying it was too late and not the right time for him to demonstrate his prodigious strength. He hadn't understood, had fought the firm hand on his shoulder but couldn't wrest himself free in time. Before his cousin stilled in the water, sinking out of sight. Only then had Aunt Hope raced up and dived in to pull the body to shore.

Aunt Hope had been furious with Papa, shouting and stomping about before slapping him across the face. Reggie didn't fight her, but everything changed that day. Aunt Hope banned them from attending the funeral. Mama never allowed Giles and his brothers to see their cousins again. As the years passed, Reggie informed the boys that as soon as they reached the proper age they were to leave home and fend for themselves elsewhere.

He aimed his shocked gaze at Cassie, the harsh recollections tumbling through his mind. "The breaking up of our family."

"How could that be?"

Memories and feelings flashed through him. Sudden realizations he'd never contemplated before. "Papa was ashamed of me and therefore wouldn't let me even try to help our cousin." He stared at her as the memories flooded his mind. The hurt and guilt associated with that afternoon. He wrapped his arms around his waist as grief washed through him, threatening to double him over. He stayed upright with an effort, not wanting to appear weak before his sister. "I let George die. It's my fault he's dead."

"I can't believe that, Giles." She laid a hand on his forearm. "You didn't kill him."

"I could have saved him." He balled his hand into a fist. "I should have tried harder. Then I wouldn't have killed our family, too."

"After George died, Ma and Pa acted very differently." She squeezed his arm and then stilled, searching his eyes. "Maybe you're right."

"I am." He jerked away from her gentle touch. "Maybe finding Mama's killers can help bring our family back together. Our aunts… Oh." The letter. Pulling it out of his vest pocket, he stared at it.

"What's that?" She rocked onto her toes to inspect the paper in his hands.

"A letter for Mama." He met her curious gaze. "Should I open it?"

"Who's it from?" She leaned closer to read the handwriting upside down.

"I don't know. It's from Montgomery, so family?" Grandparents or aunts? Cousins perhaps? He held the letter away from him, reluctant to do what he knew he must.

"Then you should open it." Cassie motioned to the letter. "Go on. It may be important."

"I hope Mama doesn't mind, given the circumstances." Opening the pages with cautious movements, he read it out loud.

August 5, 1821
Montgomery, AL

Dear Mercy,

You are likely surprised to hear from me after our last contentious parting. Faith and I are well and continuing to pursue our interests and hope you will find it in your soul to join us as Father desired before his untimely death. We will forgive your transgressions of the past, as terrible as they were, if you'll do as he wanted and move back home so we may be united as never before. Your destiny as well as ours demands your return.

Please write me soon with your answer. It's our only hope.
Sincerely,
Hope Hawkins

"Gramercy, what does that mean?" Cassie stared at him with wide eyes.

"No idea." He gingerly folded the letter and handed it to her. "But now you can write to her like we'd discussed earlier and give her the bad news."

"That Ma can't save them?" She huffed a chuckle as she slid the letter into her skirt pocket. "I doubt Ma would have gone back anyway. She rarely talked about her family."

"Neither of our parents spoke about their families." Odd to suddenly realize his father never mentioned his side of the family to him. "I wonder if they didn't like their families."

"Maybe. Ma was good at keeping secrets. I guess Pa was, too."

"Secret relatives aside, I know what I need to do."

"What's that?"

"I need to find those men. They're dangerous." He dragged his fingers through his hair. "I'll find them and make them pay for what they did to our mother. You have my word."

"I've always looked up to you. But knowing you and Pa let our cousin die…"

He braced for her disdain and disappointment as she hesitated. He wouldn't blame her for not trusting him to protect her. He'd tried to be the best man he knew how to be, but he couldn't erase the reality. He'd pushed away the memories, the doubt and guilt for years. Somehow being with Cassie awakened everything he'd suppressed. Forced him to face the facts of his failure and the resulting disaster for the close-knit family they'd once been.

"Now you hate me?" He didn't fault her if she did. He didn't much like himself.

"I don't know what I'm feeling." She chewed on her bottom lip. "Other than sad. I've got to go think about all of this. I'll see you later."

"You're sure you don't want to talk?" He'd prefer to not, but the sorrow on her face hurt him as well.

"No, not right now." She strolled out of the inn and down the front steps, turning left at the bottom.

After he could no longer see her, he released a pent-up breath on a long sigh. He may never be able to make up to her for what he'd done, but he'd try.

Chapter Fifteen

S niffling, Cassie shifted on the bench, grateful for the shadows of the gazebo. Through the tears blurring her vision, she observed guests arriving and departing in the fading sunlight as usual. Again her world had upended after shocking revelations. She'd needed air. Quiet in which to consider her life. She'd escaped her brother's heart-wrenching confession in order to think through the events since the terrible day when their cousin died. She'd been so young she was unaware of what actually occurred. She only knew their pa had fought with their aunt and she couldn't play with her cousins.

Then as her beloved brothers left one by one, she'd felt utterly abandoned by them. She remembered when Pa had harped on them to start their own lives, to go make their reputation and whatever fortune they could manage. But to leave home nonetheless. They'd gone with hard words exchanged and never looked back. Never came home. Until Giles arrived after her ma died. She could only hope the others would follow but she'd not received any word from them.

She dabbed at her eyes, and then closed them. Leaned her head back against the wall of the gazebo. She tried to imagine what her life would have been like if her cousin hadn't died. If she'd been permitted to play with her cousins. If she'd known her aunts and uncles and grandparents. Her life would have included so many more family members, so many more happy memories. All the opportunities to interact with her extended family had been stolen from her. All because Giles hadn't saved their cousin?

She couldn't control the past, nor change the way it had unfurled. She could do something about her future. Staring unseeing at the bustling carriageway, she decided to take matters into her own hands. She liked Flint and she wanted to see whether they did indeed share feelings leading to love. No longer would she wait to have a conversation with her pa since he didn't seem to care whether she needed him or not.

"Hey, Cassie, what's the matter?" Boots sounded on the steps.

She opened her eyes to find Flint standing closer than she'd expected, studying her with a worried expression. She must look a fright after crying so long. Probably sported puffy red eyes. No wonder he seemed concerned.

"Go away." She shooed him away with a hand.

Ignoring her gesture, he moved closer, sitting beside her on the bench. "I can't do that when you're obviously distressed. Why are you crying?"

"Giles told me something shocking." She dabbed at her eyes with a handkerchief.

"He upset you? I'm sorry."

She sniffled again. "I just can't believe it."

"What did he say?" Flint leaned his elbows on his knees and looked askance at her.

The blame Giles had placed on his actions echoed in her mind. The sound of guilt in his voice while admitting to killing their cousin through his inaction increased the flow of tears down her cheeks. Why had their father stopped him from trying? Why hadn't their father *done* something, for that matter? Both of them conspired to let the boy die. They should both be held accountable for the death. Not just Giles, both of them. But the very idea of her father and brother permitting the drowning by not trying to intervene quaked her heart.

"There, there, sweetheart, it can't be all that bad." He draped an arm around her shoulders and pulled her head to his shoulder. "I'm here."

She succumbed to his tender invitation and let herself sob within his compassionate embrace for several minutes. A caring friend to share her sorrow and grief. Finally, she sniffed loudly in an attempt to stop the tears as she pushed away, sitting up straight to blow her nose.

"Do you want to talk about it?" He lowered his arm to rest in his lap. "What Giles told you?"

Should she share the revelation with him? He might react badly to learn the sad fact about her brother and father. But he should probably know who he worked for and with.

"I'm upset because what he told me is so terrible." She drew in a breath and let it out on a shaky sigh. "It seems that Giles blames himself for the death of our cousin, George Hawkins, years ago. Which he believes led to the breaking up of our family."

"Whoa, that's a lot of blame to carry." Flint narrowed his eyes as he contemplated her.

"I don't think it's all on him, though. Our pa had a hand in it, too." She dabbed at her eyes and then met Flint's concerned gaze. "Pa didn't let Giles help nor did he help George."

"He let him die?" Flint sat up straight, bracing his palms on his legs. "Why?"

"I don't know the answer but I do know after that day our family slowly broke into pieces. My parents chased away my brothers." She wadded the handkerchief in her hands. "After my grandmother died, Pa made them leave and decided to move here, far away from the rest of the family. We didn't even go to her funeral. As a result, we haven't seen any of my parents' family since George died."

"And Giles claims he caused all of that?" Flint gripped his knees, the veins standing out on the back of his hands. "Seems rather a harsh view of the matter. Surely there's more to the story."

"Most likely. I know we have family, but it's been forever since we've seen them." She blinked away the remnants of her tears. "Aunt Hope wrote to Ma and wanted her to move back to Montgomery."

"Was that the letter I gave to Giles the other day?" Flint's voice carried a note of concern as he clasped his hands between his knees.

"It was weird how she seemed to blame Ma for doing some terrible things in the past." She glanced at him, tears trickling down her cheeks again. "My family is so broken. But how can I trust him to do the right thing, the honorable thing, knowing all this?"

Flint pulled her into his embrace, settling her head on his shoulder again. "I think he's learned from the experience how to be the good man he is at heart. Give him a chance. Don't be dismayed by his past actions. Remember he was only a boy himself at the time."

She bristled at his tone. He had no right to tell her how to act or feel. She sensed Flint's happiness and more at being close with her. Too close. She sat upright and stared at him.

"I don't want to do this right now."

"I was only trying to help." He held his hands away from her as his inner delight changed to uncertainty.

Agitated at her own wavering, she stood and paced away from him, then turned to scowl at him. "Don't take advantage of me like that, Flint. I know you care, as do I, but it's not the right time. Not when I'm so upset about my brother."

Flint stood and propped his hands on his hips. "You're being fickle."

Fickle? She'd show him fickle. "I may have needed someone to talk to, but I don't need you touching me for your own aims."

"My aims? What are you talking about?" Anger and disbelief echoed in his voice as he frowned.

"I know how you feel about me, and I know that we agreed to try it out. But not now." She folded her arms around her waist. "I'm feeling confused and overwhelmed."

"You're right about it being confusing when you go hot and cold on me all the time." He stared at her for the span of three deep breaths as his annoyance flowed across the small space. "Fine. Have it your way."

He spun around and ran down the couple of steps to the yard and marched away. She started to go after him, to try to explain, but it was better to let the matter drop. After all, she had no idea what to say to him. She didn't trust herself to not either explode in anger or melt down into tears. As he disappeared from view, her tears started again. She did want to be with him, but she was very worried about what other family secrets waited to be exposed. Her emotions jumped around unpredictably which she'd never experienced before. Not until recently. What had changed inside her to bring about such an incomprehensible swing in her feelings?

Ever since her ma had died she'd been troubled and far too aware of how others were feeling. Perhaps she was grieving in some odd way she'd never encountered before. That must be what was wrong with her. Grief affected everyone in different ways. She'd just discovered a new, weird, even scary way of working through the sorrow and, yes, the guilt surrounding her mother's death. Now all she had to do was figure out a way to get a grip on herself.

Fuzzy images of the past swept slowly through her brain as Cassie climbed the stairs, tawny Cocoa at her side. She'd been what…five years old when George drowned. Turning the corner at the top of the stairs, she scurried past her parents' bedroom and into her own. A blast of heat took her breath. Gramercy, she forgot to open her window. Leaving the door ajar, she rushed across her room. She dropped her aunt's mussed letter on the desk and then heaved the window up to urge what little breeze there may be to come inside. She spun away from the window, her gaze landing on the mysterious request. Cocoa padded up to sit in front of her, panting with hopeful eyes.

"What do you want?"

Cocoa wagged her tail and inched closer.

"Silly dog." Cassie bent down to pet the soft tan-and-white hair. "I can't spend all day loving on you. You should take a nap or something while I write to Aunt Hope."

The Cocker yipped twice before shaking her long hair and moving away to curl up on the oval rag rug beside the bed. The dog seemed to grin at Cassie for a moment and then put her head on her crossed front paws.

"Sometimes I think you understand exactly what I say." Smiling at the whimsical idea, Cassie strode to her desk and pulled out the chair. "Now what should I say to her."

Unfolding the letter, she scanned its contents. Ma definitely couldn't go back home as requested. Nor would she have wanted to. Frowning, Cassie searched her memory for scraps from the past about her mother's family. About life before her grandmamma died which seemed to be the final strain that broke them apart.

After her cousin drowned, her parents forbade them to

even play with their other cousins. Aunt Hope never set foot in their house again and she barely remembered what Aunt Charity looked like. Grandmamma had tried to bridge the divided sisters but every effort failed. She would come to the house and tell them what the others were doing, how they were doing, encourage Mercy to visit Hope and Charity. Ma had cut her off with an abrupt, "You know why I can't." She never explained the reason within Cassie's hearing.

Picking a sheet of stationery from the stack in a drawer, she tapped her pencil on the page. What to write to the aunt she never really knew?

Aim for chatty? Or serious tone? She was writing about her mother's death, so the latter. Perhaps explain everything leading up to the murder, including Cassie's stupid slip in the dining room. Her guilt over her mother's death. Giles coming to try to find the killers and how much she'd missed him. How sorry she was to not have the opportunity to grow up knowing her two aunts and all the rest of the family. How awful she felt about her mother and father keeping them apart. The pain of learning of an entire branch of the family kept secret from her. Ask her aunt if other life-changing secrets lurked in the shadows waiting to pounce. She experienced immense pain associated with all the loss of time with her extended family.

Cocoa whined. Cassie blinked, a tear sliding down her cheek, and glanced at the dog. Head lifted, Cocoa's eyes studied her.

"I'm all right, girl. Just a little sad." She swiped away the dampness on her skin as Cocoa lowered her head but kept her gaze on her. On a sigh, Cassie picked up her pen. Best to keep it simple and to the point. Then see what kind of response she received before offering more personal information to an aunt with whom her mother hadn't wanted to engage in discourse.

August 11, 1821
Fury Falls Inn, north of Huntsville, AL

Dear Aunt Hope,

I'm in receipt of your recent letter to my mother. You may be wondering why she is not responding herself. I regret to inform you that Mercy passed away last month, the result of a heinous murder right in her very bedchamber. She was buried in the family cemetery behind the inn.

I hope you enjoy fine health.

Yours truly,

Cassandra Fairhope

Chapter Sixteen

The small posse reined to a halt downhill from the mouth of a cave. Giles swung from the saddle and then looped the reins over a nearby branch. The dark maw above stood silent, waiting. Flint joined him, the brothers close behind. Giles had instructed Flint to stay with him since he might recognize the men they sought. Otherwise, he'd have preferred to have Zander at his side. He motioned for quiet and then led the way up the slope, his boots slipping on loose stones along the narrow path. He grimaced at the rattling noise the stones made rolling downhill. So much for quiet.

Hunched down, he placed each foot with care as he neared the entrance, gun drawn. The others knew what to do from checking ten other caves in a similar fashion over the course of the day. Zander had been wise to make Giles wait until the next morning to begin the hunt, though he'd be loath to admit as much to him. Flint eased up beside Giles, his flintlock pistol in hand. Giles glanced at his tired stance, sweaty shirt, and hat. They were all hot after a long day of riding through the hills searching for and checking out caves. Hopefully, they'd find their quarry before long so they could rest knowing they'd succeeded in their mission.

High time the dangerous pair found themselves under the tender care of the sheriff.

"Come on." Giles stepped into the medium-sized cave, hesitating a moment to let his eyes adjust.

A banked campfire sent whiffs of smoke into the air. Boot prints matted the dirt floor. A scarred table and two short stools, one overturned, stood against the back wall. Chicken bones and bread crumbs lay scattered across the table. Two bedrolls waited near the fire.

"Looks like we found the place but not the men." Giles holstered his pistol with a sigh of frustration.

He scanned the cave again, searching for some form of proof they were indeed in the right place, closing in on the villains. Proof the men occupying the cave had a hand in his mother's death. A surge of revenge swelled his chest. He tamped it down with an effort. He'd vowed to bring the men to justice. Promised the deputy to at least try to bring them in alive. His breathing quickened with anticipation. Just how hard he'd try remained to be seen.

His eyes swept the area until they landed on a curious drawing on the wall above the small table. He strode closer, shock dawning inside with each step.

Matt intercepted him. "What's the matter?"

Giles pointed to the wall. "That symbol. I saw it in my mother's attic."

Flint joined the men staring at the wall, looking at Giles askance. "What symbol?"

"You don't see that owl right there? Clear as day?" Giles frowned at Flint.

"It's a blank wall, my friend." Flint chuckled. "You sure the heat didn't get to you?"

Giles gaped at the flying owl symbol for a moment and then closed his mouth. The owl image in such a remote place had to link the men to the robbery and killing. Something seemed odd about the appearance of the attacking owl in so many places. His guard went up the longer he considered the risks related to the singular design. He didn't believe in coincidences therefore something more lurked beneath the obvious. His mama's concerns echoed in his chest, tightening the muscles and making it hard to draw a deep breath. He'd keep his eyes wide open and his other senses alert until he found the two rogues.

Almost imperceptibly, the image faded away until only a blank wall met his astonished eyes. Now he was seeing things. He blinked and then spun away from the wall to meet the curious gazes of the rest of the posse.

He swallowed the knot in his throat, afraid he'd started to lose his mind. "Well, nonetheless, we've found their hiding place."

"Now all we need is to find those villains." Flint put his gun away, perusing the camp with a frown. "They'll come back. We merely need to wait for them."

"Let's move our horses and keep watch." Giles motioned to the others to vacate the cave, leading them back outside and down the hill.

After securing the horses out of sight, they took up a position where they could see the approach to the cave but were screened from view by underbrush. How long they'd be forced to watch and wait was an open question. Giles hoped the men returned soon but who knew what mischief they may be up to in the region.

Giles looked at Zander leaning against a tree trunk with his arms crossed. "Comfortable?"

Zander smirked at him. "Sure."

"Stay vigilant, my friend. Once we catch these guys we can head for Mobile."

"You're leaving so soon?" Flint sounded surprised and confused combined. "I thought you'd stay longer."

"I have to get back to my business. Besides, once I've

taken these rascals off the street, I'll have done what I came to do. Find Mama's killers."

Matt shifted on a fallen log nearby, one foot on top of the rough bark of the trunk. "You mentioned something about needing to protect your sister. Is catching these guys all we need to do to ensure her safety?"

His sister's health and well-being seemed perfectly fine to him. Why his mother worried so about her, he couldn't fathom. Once the killers were in custody, she'd be safe as anyone living in the wilds. She had everything she needed. Flint to keep an eye on her after he left. He trusted the other man to support and protect her in his stead. After all, the man had proven he could shoot straight and he cared for her enough to ensure she wouldn't face any dangers alone. She also had Sheridan to look out for her. Besides, he didn't want to linger around his mother and her demands much longer.

"All I know is that ever since I've been here I've had to relive some terrible memories. Cassie is fine. And Mama has been even worse than I remembered and won't speak to me. It's time to go home."

"At least you *can* talk to your mother." Zander pushed away from the trunk. "I don't even know if mine is alive."

Giles stared at him for several beats of his heart. His friend had a point. Which was worse? Not knowing, or finding out your mother had been murdered? "Yeah, but mine's a ghost."

"So you say. I haven't seen her." Zander punched Giles in the upper arm with his fist.

"Ow." Giles jerked away from his friend. "What's that for?"

"Making sure you are real and not a ghost." Zander chuckled, eyes twinkling.

"Very funny." Giles rubbed his arm with one hand. "I'm not the only one who sees her. Right, Flint?"

"Right." Flint peered at Zander and then at Matt. "So neither of you has seen Mercy's ghost?"

The brothers shook their heads.

Giles frowned at Flint. "So what does that mean?"

Flint puzzled for a minute and then his frown lifted. "Maybe only people who knew her when she was alive can see her?"

"That's interesting." Giles folded his arms over his chest as he regarded Matt and Zander and then met Flint's sparkling eyes. "And good news."

Flint pressed his lips together for a moment. "Why?"

Zander snapped his fingers as a grin spread on his mouth. "Because most of your customers would never know if she's in the room. Good for business."

"But she knew a lot of them and those people would surely tell others." Flint shook his head as hope faded out of his eyes. "She has to stay out of the inn for us to have a shot."

Matt stood up and peered down the trail. "Speaking of a shot…"

Giles pivoted to look toward the narrow, winding approach to the cave. Two rough-looking men, dressed in brown trousers and loose hunting shirts, rode toward the campsite on brown horses. The man in front acted as if he was in charge, scanning the area as they drew closer. The other rode slightly behind with blond hair poking out from under his floppy brimmed hat. Both were armed with pistols at hand. They rode to a small clearing near the cave and dismounted, hobbling the horses but leaving them saddled. Obviously, prepared for a quick getaway should the need arise.

"Let them get inside and then we'll take them by surprise." He met each nod of agreement with one of his own.

The scoundrels gathered their weapons and saddle bags and then climbed the slope to their hideaway. Giles drummed his fingers on the tree he hid behind, staying put with an extreme effort, waiting for them to feel safe inside. Relax and settle, perhaps even doze awhile. Let their guard down, feeling safely hidden. He forced himself to hold his position for several more minutes. Until finally the sun started to head for the horizon. Time to wrap up this business.

"Let's go." He pulled his gun and rushed toward the cave.

Footsteps behind him confirmed the others followed close. He climbed stealthily up the slight hill, avoiding any annoying stones, and halted out of sight of the entrance. Glancing back he received nods from each man. They were ready and had a plan of action. Time to make it happen. He hurried inside.

The villains lounged about, one at the table, the other by the fire. They startled at his sudden appearance, scrabbling for their weapons.

"Put your hands up if you want to live." Giles aimed his pistol at the closest man stumbling to his feet. "Stop right there."

"Who the hell are you?"

"That depends." Giles snickered at the two men. "Tell me your names."

The man aimed angry brown eyes at Giles. "Why should I?"

Giles cocked the pistol and kept it trained on the man's forehead. "Because I said so."

Flint sidled up beside Giles, aiming his gun at the other man. "He's got green eyes."

Giles pointed his chin at the second man. "What's your name?"

"If he ain't going to tell you, then I ain't either."

Giles glanced to his friend with a wink. "Zander, would you mind helping these men remember their manners?"

"Sure thing, boss." Zander strode toward the blond man with long, powerful steps.

Zander's greater height and wide shoulders dwarfed those of the blond. The man's mouth fell open and his eyes widened the closer the big man threatened. He raised his hands higher and shook his head.

"Ain't no need to get violent." He took an involuntary step backward as Zander kept coming. "My name's Joe Madison. Now call off your dog."

"Watch what you call my friend, you hear me?" Giles took several steps toward the man, adding his own threat to that of Zander's. "Nobody talks to my friends like that."

The man swallowed hard and jerked his head in a brief nod. Giles stared at him for another minute for good measure.

"All right, Zander, that's enough." Giles glared at the other man quaking in his boots. "Then you must be Greg Chalmers, right?"

"What you want?" Greg started to lower his hands but Giles lifted his chin and he raised them again. "We ain't done nothin'."

"Now you're lying to me and I don't like liars." Giles mockingly shook his head at the two men. The guy had no idea how much danger he faced. Acted as if Giles couldn't snap his legs in two with one swift movement. Or his neck. "So?"

"I ain't tellin' you nuthin'." Joe frowned and cast a glance at Zander's bulk. "What you want with us?"

"I'll tell you what we want." Flint edged closer to Greg's stiff frame, his flintlock steady on the scoundrel's chest. "You're coming with us to pay a visit to Sheriff Neal and Deputy Parker. They have a nice, cozy jail cell waiting for you two."

"Matt and Zander here will handcuff you." Giles nodded at the brothers, who lunged toward the culprits, pulling metal cuffs jangling from their pockets. "Then we'll take a ride."

Greg let out a holler as he leapt back from Matt's grasping hands. "I ain't going with you nowhere." He twisted and dodged toward the edge of the cave, knocking Flint's gun to the ground as he pushed past him.

"Grab him!" Flint scrambled to retrieve his pistol from under the table.

Zander latched onto Joe with his massive hands, securing Joe's hands without further incident. Matt raced after Greg, tackling him to the stony ground outside of the cave. Giles ran out in time to help Matt wrestle Greg into submission and cuff him, clenching his jaw in an effort to refrain from making good on his earlier idea. Once Matt secured the handcuffs around Greg's wrists, Giles snatched his hat out of the dirt and brushed off his trousers.

"For that, you don't get to ride to town." Giles glared at the pair of subdued men. His veins buzzed with a need to hit something, or someone. Damn promise. He squashed the tempting urge. "You march."

In a short amount of time they traveled toward jail, Giles riding ahead while Zander and Flint made sure their prisoners set a brisk pace, and Matt followed with their spare horses in tow. Having tracked down and apprehended the murderers, he rode with a new sense of confidence and satisfaction in a job well done. He'd ensured his sister no longer would be under threat from those men. His job was done. He could go back to his normal way of life just like he'd planned.

The dining room was quiet for a stormy afternoon. Cassie hummed to herself as she waited on a family and two groups of workmen. Knowing her ma's killers waited for justice while relaxing in their cell lifted her mood. She wanted to dance and sing but work must come first.

Mandy hurried past her carrying a stack of empty bowls, heading for the kitchen. She'd proven to be a fine waitress over the last few days she'd worked at the inn. Neat, polite, friendly. Despite her somewhat plain appearance, the customers had taken to her quiet efficiency and gentle smile. The girl did her job and kept to herself, leaving work to hurry home without lingering to chat or even eat a meal. Just as well to Cassie's mind.

Flint toiled behind the bar, taking stock of what liquors needed replenishing and preparing the garnishes for the fancy cocktails he'd started offering. Matt had suggested to Sheridan a few new menu items as well, his former work as an esteemed cook shining through. Another step toward bettering the inn's draw for current and future customers. She delivered the family's plates of apple cake then paused to see what else she needed to do. Everyone seemed satisfied for the moment, no waving hands or expectant faces. A fine time to take advantage of the lull to play her newest pieces.

Cassie propped the empty tray against the wall before walking to the square piano angled in the corner so the pianist faced the guests. Ever since her pa had bartered with a young piano maker, James Stewart, the elegant instrument had graced the inn's dining room. Although she'd been too young to attract his attention, she'd fantasized what it might be like. Handsome Mr. Stewart unfortunately decided not to stay in the area but moved to Boston to find a partner to build pianos of similar fine and renowned quality on a larger scale. The distinctive grain of the flame mahogany tempted her fingertips. She caressed the glossy wood before lifting the keyboard lid up and back to lay flat. Flexing her fingers over the black and white keys, she sifted through the tunes in her head. Choosing her favorite "Brown-eyed Belle," she sang as she played the lively ballad.

Giles strode into the dining room as if drawn by her voice, taking a seat at the bar. The whimsical thought brought a smile. He'd left his ebony hair loose to brush his shoulders. Flint poured an ale and set it before him, a clump of foam flowing slowly down the outside of the tankard. Seeing the two men side by side let her compare them in a way she hadn't before. Her brother's broad shoulders and chest tapered down to a narrow waist. The fabric of his jeans stretched over powerful thighs as he sat on the tall stool. His hazel eyes judged the situation and the people around him with the most casual glance.

By contrast, Flint stood a couple inches taller but with a lush blend of auburn and golden hair. Although taller, he was slimmer and didn't carry himself with an inherent threatening posture. His kindness and gentle nature revealed itself in the twinkling of his green eyes and the deference he presented to everyone around him. He acted as if he wanted to serve others, not direct their actions. He accepted and counseled rather than pushed his own interests upon others. Her heart swelled with pride for the man and of course something more.

The guests stopped talking to listen to her sing, grinning and tapping their fingers on the table in time with the beat. Pleased with their happy reaction to her performance, she moved on to another lively song. A small amount of pride filled her and warmed her cheeks at their acceptance and encouragement of her efforts. Halfway through, the Bakers arrived and Flint showed them to a table on the other side of the room from the piano.

Surprisingly, Haley was with her parents. The young woman stared at Cassie, wilting the smile on Cassie's lips even though her fingers danced on the keys. Haley's lavender dress featured the empire waist currently in vogue. Her brown hair glinted with red in the sausage curls bouncing around her shoulders with each step she took. Her tight smile indicated either she didn't feel well or hadn't wanted to emerge from the safety of home to venture to the inn.

Cassie kept her fingers on the keys and a smile on her face as she sang. Soon the tune restored her good humor and she carried on as before. Flint bent to speak to John Baker for a moment and then nodded in response. He motioned for her to join them. Suppressing an inner sigh, she finished the tune with a flourish and stood as the guests applauded. She curtseyed to the small crowd, then snatched up the tray and hurried to see what Flint needed.

"Good afternoon, Mr. and Mrs. Baker, Haley." She sensed a strong curiosity from the girl. She peered closer at Haley as her stoic expression softened into an easy smile. "How are you faring on this rainy day?"

"You have a lovely voice, Miss Fairhope." John smiled at her with pleasure shining in his eyes. "The people were captivated with your singing."

"Thank you. I wanted to cheer them up on this gloomy day." She linked her fingers together as she surveyed their neighbors, noting hunger as well as an underlying concern pulsing from Tabitha and Haley. "I'm sure you're here for dinner. Sheridan has conjured up some delicious spicy gumbo."

"I've never heard of that dish." Tabitha sat primly, her hands hidden in her lap. "What is in it?"

Cassie chuckled as she shrugged lightly. "All kinds of things. I know I saw him put chicken, some sausage, and peppers into the cauldron. I don't know what else but it smells heavenly."

"Intriguing. I'd like to try it." Tabitha studied Cassie for a second and then glanced at Haley. "What about you, dearest?"

Haley shook her head. "What other offerings do you have?"

Surprised at the vehemence in Haley's tone as well as the look from Tabitha, Cassie hesitated to reply. "I'll have to see what's left from yesterday's menu. Mr. Baker?"

"I'm game to try this…gumbo, too." He threw a disapproving look at his daughter. "My daughter has particular tastes."

"Father, you know I don't like peppers." Haley crossed her arms over her chest, pouting prettily at her father.

"It's impolite to be finicky, dearest." Tabitha laid a hand on her daughter's arm, tugging until Haley uncrossed them and put her hands in her lap.

Conflicting emotions battered against her chest. Cassie flinched inwardly at the rebuke but did her best to keep her features schooled into a welcoming expression. As if she hadn't felt the embarrassment flowing from the other girl. Or the seething inside of her calm parents.

Giles rose from the stool he'd occupied at the bar and sauntered over to join the group. "I had the pleasure of meeting these fine folks on my travels to the inn, but not this lovely lady. Would you introduce us?"

"Of course." Flint quickly made the proper introductions.

Giles bowed slightly as Flint introduced Haley to him. He slid his gaze over to her parents and nodded a greeting, his eyes guarded as he looked at her father. But his eyes strayed more than once to Haley. The girl did not return the same level of interest, however. At least not outwardly. Cassie hid a smile at the contradiction.

Then she pressed her lips together in consternation. Giles felt humiliated by Haley's rebuff. How could she know what he was feeling? What anyone was feeling? For weeks now she'd experienced others' emotions. How long exactly? Longer than a few weeks, actually. She searched her memories until the moment clarified in her mind. Her ma's death. The new weird form of grieving seemed to be changing her more than she'd first realized.

"Are you all right?" Flint touched her shoulder and then dropped his hand back to his side. "You look a little pale."

"Um…I think…" She shrugged off the worry and

confusion. She'd have to think about all of it later. After she finished her chores and could escape to her room. "I'm fine."

"Are you sure, dear?" Tabitha peered at her, her hands balled into fists on the edge of the table. "Flint is right that you don't look quite yourself."

The older woman's steady, searching regard unnerved her. Not only did she appear worried but Tabitha also oozed a current of unease that wrapped around Cassie's heart and squeezed. Shaken, Cassie looked away from her.

She drew in a deep breath and forced a smile onto her lips. "I assure you I feel fine. But thank you both for your concern."

"If you're quite certain?" Tabitha's open expression and sense of relief drew Cassie's attention.

"I am. Now what I can do for you folks?" She cast her glance around the table and then to her brother.

Giles cleared his throat and lifted a brow. "Will you sing some more?"

She sensed her brother wanted her to walk away but why? "I need to get them some food first since Mandy's apparently disappeared for the moment." Cassie indicated the Bakers with a tilt of her head and a quizzical smile. "Unless you want to do so?"

Giles shrugged, his intent gaze sliding first to John and then on to Haley and back to Cassie. "I can do that."

So not only did he feel some concern with John but he really was interested in the other girl. Cassie handed over the tray. "Fine. Just behave yourself."

He motioned with his head for her to go to the piano before he turned and headed for the kitchen. She hesitated to abandon the Bakers but his concern simmered in her gut.

"I hear the well is finished?" John lifted his sherry cobbler cocktail, one of Flint's newest creations, and examined the citrusy blend before tentatively sipping.

"Yes, just this morning we've been able to draw clean water from it." Flint lifted a brow at John. "What do you think?"

John tasted the drink again and nodded. "Refreshing. The combination of sherry and pineapple juice is pleasing to the palate."

"Flint's been experimenting." Cassie winked at the bartender, letting her feelings for him shine in her eyes.

"Just trying to improve the offerings on the menu." Flint sarcastically half bowed to her, his smile acknowledging her silent message. "Why don't you go play something?"

"If you'd like." She tilted her head with a grin.

"Something sweet and meaningful, please." John raised his glass to her in a silent salute.

"Very well." Cassie walked back to the piano and took her place.

Mandy sashayed into the dining room, a tray of steaming porcelain bowls balanced between her hands. She smiled at Cassie and then hurried over to a group of three housemaids from up Winchester Road. Cassie nodded a greeting to them, glad they'd made a point of coming back for another meal after their first one a week or so previously. Having improved the offerings and thus the reputation of the inn, the fact that customers first sought them out and then returned provided further evidence of Flint's capabilities. Pa should be glad he'd hired Flint to manage things.

She flexed her fingers briefly and then played one of her favorite hymns, "Amazing Grace," singing with as much love and emotion as she could infuse into the song. The diners again stopped talking to listen, becoming somber and thoughtful. Her singing was well received even though she'd never had any training. She simply loved to sing and entertain. Zander came into the dining room and stopped to listen. Everyone enjoyed the impromptu concert. Except one person who experienced deep fear. Frowning slightly, she searched for the source of the fear, skimming her gaze over the people gathered. Until she met Tabitha Baker's stricken expression from across the room.

Cassie blinked several times, stunned by the other woman's reaction. What triggered such a response? Tabitha composed her features, smoothing the worry lines from her forehead, as she jerked her head to address her husband. She said something to him, pressing a hand to her stomach, and then they hurriedly rose from the table and departed in a flurry of motion. Tabitha threw her a warning look as her husband escorted her from the room, Haley behind them with a confused look on her face.

Flint went after them but returned in a few moments scowling. He speared Cassie with a look of disbelief. Giles entered the dining room carrying a tray of steaming plates, stopping when he spotted the empty table. She finished the song and rose to subdued applause smattering about the room, and then scurried over to Flint.

"What on earth happened?" Cassie stared at Flint's concerned expression before meeting Giles' perplexed one. "Why did they leave?"

"Mrs. Baker said she wasn't feeling well." Flint met Cassie's gaze. "Such a sudden onset of stomach discomfort. She hadn't even eaten anything yet."

More than an upset stomach based on what Cassie had sensed from both her emotions and her countenance. "Was it my choice of hymn? Did she object to it?"

Giles held the tray between his hands. "I can't imagine they'd take exception to your songs."

Cassie regarded her brother for several moments as she attempted to see how others were feeling. She had a faint sense of a typical range of emotions from her uncertain probe but under everything she had a vague notion of something amiss. Disquiet simmered beneath the surface. She couldn't pinpoint what caused the sensation but it lingered like the whiff of a bad odor. Perhaps Tabitha had sensed it as well and her body reacted to the undercurrent by upsetting her stomach.

"Since they've gone, I guess I'll take this back to the kitchen." Relief flowed from Giles as he hefted the tray.

Flint splayed his hands. "I don't understand what that was all about."

"Maybe Mrs. Baker didn't want to try Sheridan's gumbo after all." Giles chuckled but then sobered when his gaze landed on Cassie. "What's wrong?"

"I just feel like…I can't shake the feeling that something bad is coming." She hugged herself as she peered into Giles' eyes. "I don't know what, but something…"

Giles laughed before turning to walk away, saying over his shoulder, "Nothing is going to happen, Cassie. The bad guys are caught and you're safe from harm. Everything is fine now. You'll see."

Flint watched Giles disappear into the kitchen after backing through the door and letting it swing shut behind him. Then he met Cassie's concerned gaze. "I hope he's right. Now that the murderers are in jail, they no longer pose a threat to anyone."

"I know. You're right." She shrugged, pushing away the feeling as best she could with the movement. "It's probably just my overactive imagination. Forget it."

Chapter Seventeen

Confused and antsy, Giles wandered into the family parlor and sat down on his favorite chair near the fireplace. He needed to say goodbye properly to his mother before he mounted up and rode away. The time had arrived for him to depart. He let his gaze drift around the room. The doll's house seemed odd in the formal gathering place. The other furnishings and furniture were as familiar as the back of his hand. It was comforting, truth be told. But he'd promised Zander and Matt they'd be heading back to Mobile soon. He'd shuttered his business, risking its demise in his absence, to make the journey home.

He paused the direction of his thoughts. Home? When had he started thinking of the inn as home? Perhaps being with Cassie had prompted the feeling. Seeing her daily seemed so natural and right. If the family hadn't cleaved into parts then their relationship would have stayed close. He'd know her far better than he did. Despite his desire for a tightknit family, it was time. He had to leave. Had to return to his business. He rubbed his smarting eyes with his fingers. Why did it feel like he was running away then?

"Mama? Can we talk?" He stood and paced the room, searching for her.

He hoped she'd show but he also remained reluctant to confront her. He wished she'd be more open and honest with him as to what she was afraid to share with him. What she played close to her proverbial vest. Something obviously tormented her. A double-edged sword. If it were good, she wouldn't be so hesitant. Whatever she held close had to be bad. Perhaps very bad indeed.

After only a few moments she materialized by the fireplace as before, floating a couple of feet from the floor. "Hello, son."

"Thank you." He tried to smile up at where she hovered but it felt forced and awkward. "I'd like to speak with you."

"What's on your mind?" Mercy inched down, closer to the floor, calm and relaxed, a decided change from previous visits.

"I'm not sure how to begin." He had much he wanted to say but struggled to find the right words.

Speech-making wasn't something he did often or well. He'd rather talk one-on-one than to a group. As for talking about his feelings, he avoided ever doing so. He pretended he didn't have any most of the time, ignoring as best he could the reality. Which all made this conversation far more challenging and difficult for him.

"First, I've come to say a proper goodbye." He stood a few feet away from her, arms at his sides. "Second, I'd like to thank you for raising my sister into such a fine young woman."

"It's my job as a mother to raise my daughter well. But I appreciate your comment." She drifted closer, shaking her head as her brow furrowed. "As for saying a proper goodbye, I understand. I do. You have your own life you want to go back and live. But, Giles, you absolutely cannot leave. Your work is not done."

"I did what I came to do. Found your killers and brought them to justice." He shifted his weight to his other foot. "What more do you want?"

"You're still needed here." She pointed at him with her forefinger. "You promised to protect Cassandra."

"From what exactly?" He leaned forward slightly. "You'll need to be more specific if you want me to believe you."

Mercy stared at him for several seconds, worry flickering in her eyes. "If I tell you, will you promise to at least try to understand why I haven't before?"

"I'll do my best, Mama." He braced for whatever terrible news she prepared to reveal. "Tell me the truth."

"Very well but, please, don't be mad." She moved to sit on a chair and motioned for him to do the same. "You'd better sit down."

"You're worrying me." He strode to the chair he'd vacated earlier and crossed his arms over his chest. "Fine. I'm sitting."

"You'd asked me about the day George died..." She hesitated, tapping the tips of her ghostly fingers together as she studied him. "That day changed everything."

"I know that much." He leaned forward, propping his elbows on his knees. "But what really happened?"

She contemplated him for several moments, dragging out the suspense until Giles wanted to shake it out of her. Not that it would do any good to act on such an impulse with a ghost. His fingers, as powerful as they were, would go right through her. He shuddered at the image the thought evoked in his mind. He arched his brows to prod her to reveal whatever news she hesitated to share.

Mercy pressed her lips together for a second. "You nearly gave away our secret which would have threatened the very existence of our family."

"What secret?" Surprised confusion crashed through his chest. "What did I do?"

How could he have possibly let loose a secret he didn't know he was keeping?

"Your heart was in the right place, son. Wanting to save that boy. But your pa had to stop you from revealing your…ability."

He frowned at her, not understanding. "What ability are you talking about?"

"Your superhuman strength." She smiled wryly at him. "You should have discovered it by now, I'd think."

"Superhuman?" His frown deepened as she nodded slowly.

"Yes, Giles. You've always been stronger than others, haven't you?"

"Yes." He recalled the fight at the jail and how easily he threw off the other two strong men. Lifting the Bakers' coach with ease. Causing Cassie pain when he grabbed her arms. "But now it's different."

"Yes, it would be." She lowered her hands, smoothing her skirt automatically as she gazed at him. "It was only a matter of time."

"Explain what you mean." Irritated by her reluctance to say what she needed to, he examined the complacent expression on her face.

She aimed a rueful smile at him. "My binding spell was broken when I was killed."

"Your spell?" He blinked several times, struggling to comprehend the meaning of her words. "You're a witch?"

"My sisters are, too." She clasped her hands together, interlocking the fingers. "You should know the whole truth."

"There's more." He leaned back in the chair, gripping the armrests. "How much worse could it possibly be?"

"Depends on whether you can accept what I'm saying." Fear tinged her voice, making it quaver as she spoke. "Your father and his family are also witches and wizards."

"Both sides of the family." He shook his head slowly, fighting to understand the far-reaching ramifications of the huge secret.

Not only had his father suppressed any knowledge about the existence of his brothers and sisters, but he'd foregone sharing that they were all magical. His very father a wizard. Secrets piled upon secrets. The weight of the revelations threatened to bury him in confusion and mistrust.

"Don't look at me like that, son. We didn't mean to deceive you." Mercy shook her head slowly but kept a small smile on her lips. "We'd decided to inhibit your ability along with those of your brothers and sister to protect all of you."

He searched her eyes to make sure she spoke the truth. Saw her steady regard and honesty. He drew in a long breath. Could he accept what she revealed? "Protect us from what exactly?"

"First from my father and now my sisters. They're dark witches and had threatened to use all of your skills for their purposes. Reggie and I wouldn't allow such an awful thing to happen."

"What do you mean?" Colors of witches and of magick. Parents hiding the true natures of their children. Family hidden in the shadows of time and distance. Deception swirled through his mind like fog on a fall morning, obscuring and shifting the truth.

"Father wished for me to be like Hope and Faith, join our powers to create a dark trinity of power." She moistened her lips as her eyes darkened. "But I couldn't go that way. I'm a white witch like your father's family. That's one of the reasons I married him."

His head spun with questions and disquiet. "So what happened with your father?"

"He kept pushing me to convert, to be united with my sisters. As the years passed and my powers grew stronger, he became more and more insistent. After my mother died in an…accident, the shield she'd been all my life, protecting me from his dark aims, vanished. The entire family was in danger from my father and sisters."

"So you fled?" He stared at her as all the pain and torment he'd experienced for years because of his parents' actions flashed through his mind. "And chased us all away."

She flinched but nodded. "Yes, for your own good."

Over Mercy's head, he saw Cassie slip into the parlor, a finger to her lips. He returned his attention to his mother. "Why keep Cassie with you? Why not push her out of the nest as well?"

"A single girl on her own would have been easy prey for men. She didn't know about her own powers nor how to use them." She clutched her hands together. "I wouldn't take that risk."

"Why not marry her off and be done?"

"She wasn't ready. Still isn't." She frowned at him and shook her head. "Don't let her marry Flint. I know she has feelings for him. She'll be stuck like I was living in a public place instead of her own home."

"That was Papa's decision, to move here and set up this inn."

"We agreed on doing so. Only to save our family from mine." She met his gaze with a shrug. "I'm sorry to have to tell you like this. I'd hoped he'd come home and handle everything. I knew when I died it was only a matter of time before you'd each find out about your abilities."

"What's mine, Ma?" Cassie strode farther into the room, drawing her mother's attention with the sound of her leather shoes on the floor boards.

"Cassie…how long have you been eavesdropping?" Mercy sighed and stood, pivoting in the air to face her daughter.

"Not long enough. We all have special abilities? Is that what you were saying?" She folded her arms under her breasts. "What's mine?"

"If you think about it, I believe you already know." Mercy tilted her head with her smile growing on her lips.

"Don't play games with me." Cassie scowled at her mother's ghost. "I'm not in the mood."

"You're sensing the way your brother is feeling right now, aren't you?" Mercy shimmered as she shifted from side to side. "And you've sensed others' emotions, too."

Cassie blinked, her eyes widening. "How'd you know?"

Mercy drifted toward the fireplace, stopping by the opposite chair. "You're an empath, with a very unique ability you don't realize you have."

"What on earth is an empath?" Cassie's eyes widened as she waited for her mother's explanation.

"It's a remarkable gift for a young witch to possess." Mercy rested her hands on the back of the chair. "You can sense the emotions of others."

"That's why my emotions have been all over the place? I'm actually feeling what others feel?"

Giles' mouth fell open. "You can?"

Cassie nodded once and then looked at Mama. "Is that what you meant?"

"Yes. That and even more than that. You can influence how others feel with your singing." Mercy smiled at her. "It's a marvelous and powerful gift when used properly. But be careful until you have mastered the nuances or you'll cause damage you may not be able to repair."

Giles stood as Cassie glanced at him. Now he understood the guests' reaction to Cassie's impromptu concert earlier in the day. His own response of hurrying into the dining room to hear more of her singing. Zander as well. As if lured by the sound.

"So, Giles, what's yours?" Cassie pinned him with her surprised eyes.

"Strength." Though he obviously didn't have the strength to resist her siren song. He'd have to guard against that as well.

"Figures." Cassie rolled her eyes at him.

Mercy pinned her gaze on Cassie. "He's destined to be your Guardian."

"Why do I need a Guardian?" Cassie looked at Giles then her mother.

Mercy peered at Giles, her expression serious. "Because now that your powers are free from my binding spell, you're all in grave danger."

Later that afternoon, Giles wandered out of the inn, heading toward the gazebo to meet Zander and Matt for a private conversation. He dreaded raising the subject but they deserved the chance to decide for themselves. He had to be honest with them and tell them about his newfound abilities. As he descended the front steps, he could make out their silhouettes relaxing in the shade, each on separate benches. He steeled his spine and hoped they'd understand why he'd promised his mother to stay.

"Mr. Fairhope, may I have a word?" Haley Baker hurried up to him, appearing out of nowhere. "In private."

Her perfume reached his nose, hints of orange and cinnamon and cloves tingled his senses. He would like to speak with her for as long as she'd let him. "Of course."

She walked a few paces away from the front of the inn. "I need to apologize for our abrupt departure the other evening."

"I was sorry to hear your mother was not feeling well. How is she doing?"

Haley clasped her hands together and peered at him. "She was not ill. What I'm about to tell you must be between us. Do you promise?"

A flash of concern warmed his chest. "Of course. What is the matter?"

"Someone is targeting people who appear to be magickal." Her beautiful eyes filled with unshed tears.

"I can't say who but my mother and I suspect your sister may be at risk."

"Cassandra? Why would you say that?" How did the woman know his sister was an empath when they'd just learned the truth of their nature themselves? Fear shot through him as he wrestled his features into a calm he didn't feel.

"Trust me, Mr. Fairhope. We have, shall we say, a sensitivity to those who practice magic. Such as yourself."

"Me?" Shock ricocheted through him at her words. "How do you know this?"

She glanced furtively around and then met his gaze. "As you are her Guardian, I come to you to forewarn you of the danger to your sister. Please, I pray you'll keep her here at home and do not let her venture out. It's not safe."

He narrowed his eyes at her, struggling to fathom how she'd come by her intimate knowledge of his role. "I do not know how you know all of this."

She lifted the corners of her mouth in a reluctant smile. "That's not important. I've said what I came to say. Farewell and be safe."

She whirled around, her long skirts billowing, as she hurried away to a chaise standing nearby. The beautiful woman climbed quickly into the vehicle, lifted the traces to urge the single horse into a trot, and rattled away down the carriageway. He stood there, dumbly blinking in astonishment. Could she also be a witch? Is that how she knew so much? His pulse raced in his ears while he reviewed all she'd said. One thing was perfectly clear: his mama had been correct in insisting he remain at the inn to protect his sister. Drawing in a deep breath, he pivoted and marched toward the gazebo and his waiting friends.

"There you are." Zander gestured to the remaining empty bench. "I thought you weren't going to show."

"Despite asking us to meet you here." Matt crossed his ankles, reclining back on the metal bench.

"I'm sorry I'm late." Giles flopped onto the hard bench with a grunt. He'd promised not to share what Haley had said, so chose not to even mention the conversation.

"So what's the matter?" Zander leaned forward to rest his elbows on his knees.

"It's hard for me to say this to you both." Giles hesitated to spit out the real reason for the meeting.

"Come on, man, it's not like you to be so mysterious." Zander regarded him in silence for a long moment. "Just say it."

He struggled to choose the right words to convey the depth of his hope they'd remain with him despite his magical family and the resulting threats. The brothers may well want nothing to do with wizards and witches and family secrets and in-fighting.

"Well, it's like this. I've promised my mother to stay here to protect my sister from whatever dangers are lurking." He hated to say the next words but he must, though he didn't want the result he feared most. "So I guess you'll both want to head back to Mobile and get back to work."

Zander blinked at him, his half smile fading away. "You sending us away?"

Hell, no. Not by choice. "I thought you'd want to go."

Matt straightened in his seat, pulling his feet under the bench in one fluid movement. "Do you want us to leave? Is that what you're saying?"

Giles swallowed his protests. "It's up to you two. You need to decide what's right for you, not for me. I've made my choice. Now you have to make yours."

He sat back, crossing his arms over his chest. Hoped they'd agree to stay but knew in his heart they'd leave. He wouldn't beg. He'd miss them terribly. The idea of parting left him feeling bereft despite the fact they sat staring at him in disbelief.

"What about your business? It can't go on without you." Matt studied him with shuttered eyes.

"I know." Giles raked his fingers through his hair and sighed. He'd worked hard to build his business and it hurt to let it go. "I'll contact the guy who has been after me to sell to him. Whether I really want to or not."

Zander peered closer at him, searching his expression for several moments. "What aren't you telling us? There's something more."

Giles swallowed hard, the dreaded moment upon him. "I don't know how to tell you what my mother finally revealed to me."

Matt braced his hands on his knees. "Just say it. We'll not judge you."

"Easy to say before you know the truth of the matter." Giles raked his fingers through his loose hair and then sighed. "Turns out my family…we're all witches and wizards of one kind or another. Some good, some bad."

He pushed back in his seat, physically and mentally preparing for them to jump up and race away. The two men he'd depended on for years. His friends and compatriots. Swallowing the sudden lump in his throat, he watched the flashing emotions playing across their features.

"You're a wizard? Holy smokes." Zander leapt to his feet, a frown on his face, and paced the confines of the gazebo, glancing repeatedly away and back to Giles. He halted near the steps and faced him straight on. "What kind of wizard are you?"

Matt stared at him, his mouth hanging open for a moment. "You do magic? Spells and potions?"

"No, I'm the Guardian." Couldn't blame the man for worrying about just what kind of wizard he might be. "I have superhuman strength, which shouldn't be a surprise to either of you."

"That explains the day at the jail." Zander nodded, his eyes crinkling at the corners. "I'd never seen you do that before."

"It surprised me, too." Giles wiped his sweaty palms down the jeans covering his powerful thighs. "Mama said I'm destined to be the Guardian of my sister so I must stay to fulfill my obligations."

"What kind of obligations was she talking about?" Matt placed his feet flat on the floor and studied Giles.

"Apparently, her sisters wanted to form a trinity of black magic witches with Mercy to combine their powers." Giles drummed his fingers on the bench seat. "With Mercy unavailable for obvious reasons, she thinks they'll come after Cassie to form a wicked trio."

"I can't imagine Miss Cassie being an evil witch. Not with her caring personality." Zander shook his head slowly as he crossed back to the bench and sat down.

"She's not a dark witch. She's an empathic white witch with the ability to use her singing to influence others." Giles folded his arms loosely over his stomach. "But I need to ensure my aunts do not force her into something she doesn't want. So I have to remain to do my job. But you guys do not have to put yourselves in danger."

"That's why you're suggesting we go on back south." Matt nodded slowly as a grin eased onto his lips. "So you don't feel guilty keeping us here?"

"This is not about me. I'm just looking out for your best interests like I always have."

"You have. That's true." Zander leaned back and crossed his arms, a brow quirked high. "But I'm not leaving you to defend that girl by yourself. No way."

"Are you sure?"

"Yes, sir, I am." Zander glanced to his brother. "What about you? Leaving or staying?"

"I see no reason for me to go back if you're going to stay." Matt grinned wider at Zander. "I don't want to miss the fun."

Relief flooded his chest. Both planned to stay. Hallelujah. "Are you sure?"

"Now that that's decided, we'll need a place to live if we're going to be moving here for good." Matt settled back on the bench again. "Should we go look for a plot of land?"

"Then we can build a cottage." Zander rubbed his strong hands together. "Just need to find the right spot."

"No, I want to stay close for now." Giles relaxed in his seat, glad his friends dismissed his idea without any hesitation. Accepted his remarkable news without a hint of disdain or fright as he'd feared on his way to the private discourse. "We need to keep an eye out for anything unexpected."

"Like that flying owl drawing you said you saw in the cave?" Zander tapped a finger on his upper arm. "Nobody else saw it but you."

"That was indeed unusual. It was there and then it wasn't." Perhaps his role as Guardian enabled him to see the symbol as a means of knowing he'd found a threat. That was the only explanation he could conjure. "I don't know what it means exactly, but I intend to find out."

"How you going to do that?" Matt briefly gripped his knees and then rested his hands on his thighs. "I mean, who can tell you the answer?"

"Good question." Giles pursed his lips. "I'll start with Mama and if she doesn't know, then I'll write to Papa and see what he has to say about all of this."

"What if they don't tell you the truth?" Zander squinted at him and chewed on his lip. "They've kept that secret all your life."

"That cat is out of the bag." Giles stood, gazing down on the two men. "I'll get an answer out of either Mama or Papa one way or another. Just wait and see."

Chapter Eighteen

From her position on the front porch, Cassie could see the three men hobnobbing in the gazebo. She had settled on one of the chairs by the small table, a mug of small beer at her elbow. As each guest arrived, she smiled a greeting while trying to sense their emotions. Knowing she could read others' feelings gave her a new way to gauge the mood of the clientele. But could she control her gift? Probe less or more?

Cocoa and Beau jogged across the carriage drive and up onto the porch, insisting on her petting them. The soft hair beneath her fingers belied the hard-working dogs. They spent their days guarding the property and went out hunting with the men when needed. She enjoyed their company, stroking their heads one at a time. Cocoa's limpid eyes remained on Cassie as she fondled her silky ear. Jealous, Beau butted his head under Cassie's hand, transferring her attention to him.

"Silly cur." She patted his head and then glimpsed an elderly couple hobbling their way toward the steps. Fresh targets for practicing on. She gave each head a final pat. "Be off with you."

She settled back in her seat to concentrate on the gray-haired man and ash blond woman as they approached arm in arm. His somber coat and trousers as well as his black beaver top hat suggested he'd been to a funeral. Her long black skirts and dark gray blouse with a matching bonnet confirmed the impression. Their carriage driver clucked to the pair of flashy palominos, and the light vehicle rattled toward the area beside the stable to wait. The dogs trailed after the carriage to use their noses to inspect its wheels. Cassie stared at the woman's gentle expression, reached out with her mind to sense her feelings. Strained to read them but the more she tried the less she sensed.

Shifting her gaze to study the careworn features of the man, she opened her mind and heart and tried again. The couple started up the steps, spotted Cassie and nodded in greeting. Cassie smiled in return, breaking off her attempt with an inner huff of frustration. She didn't understand what she'd done wrong. When she hadn't been trying, she felt everyone's emotions. The couple went on into the inn, the sound of Flint's welcoming greeting drifting out to her ears.

Flint's voice carried manly tones of warmth in its depths. His gentle smile of greeting and twinkling eyes moved into her mind's eye, tugging her lips up into a similar expression. He had found a home in her heart whether she cared to admit it to him or herself. She could push him away physically but only so far emotionally. She'd fallen for his calm, his strength of character, and his willing acceptance of others. She intended to inform him of her decision to allow him to court her.

Suddenly, she sensed a jumble of worry and relief mixed with determination and happiness. She squinted as she perused the area, seeking the source of the emotions. The three friends ambled toward the porch. Giles's straight-forward strides spoke of his concern and determination.

Zander's swagger and Matt's purposeful pace demonstrated the happiness and relief they emoted her way. Now, why could she sense their emotions but not when she'd attempted to probe the couple?

"Hey, sis. Why are you sitting out here?" Giles stopped at the top of the steps as the other two went on inside.

She glanced around to ensure they were alone. "Practicing."

He narrowed his eyes and raised a finger of warning. "Be very careful. You don't want anyone to know about our gifts."

"I know." She took a sip of her beer and set the mug down. "But I need to learn how to control it. It's not easy. I've been trying."

"I'll be inside if you need me." He touched his forehead with a finger. "Don't try too hard and reveal our secret." With that, he left her alone.

She was very glad Giles had come when she'd asked. She loved having time with him. Rebuilding their relationship one day at a time. He'd managed to unveil the deep secrets her mother had harbored so they could face whatever dangers lay ahead. Together. Brother and sister along with their amazing new abilities. She had yet to hear from her other brothers, but looked for a letter from them every time Flint brought the mail. How surprised they would be to learn of whatever their abilities might be. Should be interesting to find out. If they respond. If they come to the inn. Many questions yet to be answered.

Mulling over her efforts, his words echoed in her brain. Don't try too hard and reveal her ability. That was the problem. Cassie blinked at her sudden realization. She'd been trying too hard.

Perhaps she'd pushed the waves of emotion away by working to read them. If she opened herself and let the waves roll in, then she didn't have to make an effort to receive the message. Maybe. She tapped a finger on the side of the mug, impatient for another practice target. Before long, she'd have to abandon the effort and go help Sheridan fix the supper menu. Not that she minded working in the kitchen, but she must learn to control her power. If only so she didn't inadvertently harm someone. She'd never forgive herself if she did.

The rumble and rattle of an approaching coach-and-four drew her attention. Good. Maybe an entire family would pour out of it so she'd have multiple targets. Excitement built in her chest as it neared. She clenched her hands together in her lap, fighting to remain calm.

The coach rolled to a stop in front of the inn, the horses stamping and tossing their heads as the liveried footman jumped down and opened the side door. The crest on the door shot disappointment into her heart. The Bakers' coach. Well, it wouldn't be a large group but it was an opportunity. How many would emerge into the dusky light? Two or three? She held her breath, craning her neck as a man's suit and then head appeared in the doorway. Just one man. Discontent squashed the excitement as John Baker hurried out of the coach, tamping his top hat on his head as he strode toward the porch.

One target was better than none. Struggling to ignore her own emotions, she gazed on the familiar features of their neighbor. John visited frequently to enjoy Sheridan's cooking, usually for afternoon dinner or an early evening supper. Flint attempted to not resent his visits but he knew the reason for the man's regular appearances. To check up on him to report to her father as to how well he managed the property. How difficult it must be for Flint to treat him with respect and courtesy knowing the man judged him the entire time. She'd experienced the same form of resentment with her ma's constant supervision and criticism.

She reached out with her mind to the man of business. This time Cassie didn't force the effort but waited for his emotional waves to come to her. At first she didn't sense anything but hunger and thirst propelling him inside. She studied his somber expression and detected a faint annoyance and dismay simmering inside the plantation owner. Maybe he found reporting to her pa irritating. As he put a foot on the bottom step, he happened to look her way and wary appraisal swept through her core. Was she sensing his concern or merely interpreting it from the slight frown before he smiled at her?

"Miss Fairhope, I didn't see you there." He removed his hat to hold at his side. "How do you fare on this fine evening?"

"I'm fine, thank you. And you?"

"Fine, fine." He restored his hat to his head. "Do you know where Flint might be?"

So his concern had something to do with Flint. Not much of a surprise there. Yet she sensed his wariness toward her despite acting normally. Interesting. "I believe he's in the dining room."

He tapped the brim of his hat with a finger. "It was nice to see you. I hope you'll sing while I have my supper."

Hope and pleasure replaced the suspicion as he waited for her response. He really did want her to sing, then. "Of course. I'll be in shortly."

"I shall look forward to it. If you'll excuse me." He flashed a grin and then strode into the inn and out of sight.

The man behaved normally but underlying his outward actions was a layer of doubt and concern. Which could be stemming from the matter he needed to discuss with Flint. No, she hadn't felt the wariness before he realized her presence on the porch. Then the suspicion erupted inside of him. She bit her lower lip, replaying the stream of impressions through her mind. And realized his suspicion had been aimed in her direction.

The pile of offers winked at him from the desk. Flint sipped from his morning mug of hot coffee and then set the mug beside the letters. The managers at three different elegant hotels in three very different locales awaited his reply. He hadn't expected such an eager response from his queries. Nor so soon. Which should he respond to in the affirmative? Which to decline? He'd wrestled with the decision for days and still had come no closer to settling on one over the others. Each represented a unique and tempting prospect.

An opportunity to run the day-to-day operations of the prestigious Emory Hotel in Boston lay on top of the pile. Not because of priority, just the most recent one received. The manager's letter inviting him to visit at his earliest convenience included a fancy brochure boasting of the hotel's accommodations. He perused the crisp folded paper, featuring a sketch of the massive, impressive building on the front with more details about what guests could expect inside. The extensive and high-brow menu of fine meats, cheeses, wines and liquor, as well as fancy desserts. Elaborate breakfast buffets, not simple bowls of porridge or hoecakes and bacon like Sheridan offered. No. The Emory served up waffles with fruit compote on top. Perhaps he should look into having a set of waffle iron plates made for the inn before he departed. If Sheridan would agree to adding another new item to the menu. While Flint could easily overrule any objections the man might raise, he'd much prefer his agreement on the matter. He'd rather not incite a conflict with the cook. Or should he say 'cooks' since Matt had taken to helping out more and more with his natural abilities in the kitchen. He laid the brochure on the desk and lifted the linen stationery and skimmed the letter. A reply had been requested but he didn't know what to tell the manager.

He shoved the pair of papers aside and stared at the next letter. Not quite as large as the Emory, the Maynard Inn of Philadelphia sought a competent innkeeper to assist with building their clientele and improving the guests' experience. Essentially what Flint strived to do with the Fury Falls Inn but on a larger scale in a major city. He'd be living and working in one of the most revered cities in America, filled with the important history of founding the country. The temptation to accept surged through him. His fascination with the beginnings of the country couldn't be fully assuaged while living in Huntsville and definitely not while in the wilderness surrounding the growing town. Imagine seeing the famous Liberty Bell and the President's House where George Washington had lived. Walk the same streets as Ben Franklin and James Madison. Chills swept down his spine. What he wouldn't give.

He reread the letter and then picked up his quill pen. Should he accept? Could he? He flicked the feather against his cheek. While the Philly offer proved tempting indeed, he hesitated. Glanced at the last paper on the desk. Another intriguing offer he must consider carefully before he wrote to any of the interested managers. He put the pen down and picked up the letter.

He held the creamy stationery lightly in his fingers as he pored over the surprising offer presented in clear and flowing penmanship. The owner and manager of the famous Robert Xavier Hotel in New York wanted to find not just a manager, but a partner. Someone who would become a joint owner of the property. The hotel itself enjoyed a stellar reputation and serviced an international clientele. Dignitaries and envoys from other countries frequented their accommodations and dining rooms. Xavier had been immensely impressed with Flint's initiative and creativity with his approach to managing the Fury Falls Inn. He'd narrowed his search down to three candidates, Flint shockingly one of them.

Every invitation flattered his ego. Any one of the three offers suited his plan to perfection. His aim of moving up in the hostelry industry in a meaningful and lucrative way. He dropped the page on the desk and sat back in the chair. Imagined himself assisting the Emory hotel manager, greeting important guests and finding unique ways of bettering the accoutrements of the hostelry. Envisioned himself working at the fabulous Maynard in close proximity to all of the history he craved to experience. But the Xavier offer tempted him the most. Co-owner of such a luxurious and respected establishment appealed to his ideas of who he aspired to become.

He pulled a sheet of stationery out of the cubby on the desk and lifted his pen. Held the tip over the blank page. He'd gain much from each opportunity. He needed to decide which one afforded him the chance for the greatest satisfaction. He brushed the feather across his cheek. Dipped the tip into the ink pot and wiped off the bead of ink, delaying putting pen to paper. Delaying committing until he decided which felt right.

He lifted his coffee with the other hand and took a gulp. Outside his window, Cassie sauntered by in a freshly pressed pale blue dress and straw hat, singing as she went. She carried her empty flower basket in one hand, swinging it gaily with each stride. Heading out for fresh flowers to perfume the air within the inn and welcome their guests. Slowly, he lowered the mug to the desk as her sweet voice grew more distant.

He put the quill down, staring out the window for several seconds. No wonder he couldn't decide. Cassie. How could he leave when Giles believed her to be in some kind of danger from unknown sources? Her brother had elected to move in permanently in order to protect her. His friends as well chose to remain as backup. Flint couldn't in good conscience abandon Cassie with her life in jeopardy.

If he were totally honest with himself, the idea of never seeing her chilled his soul. Living and working hundreds of miles apart from her beautiful face did not appeal. Somehow a deeper part of him had recognized the reality of his feelings he'd hidden from view. Tamped down beneath his ambition. But his true feelings finally surfaced.

Dreams change. He finally had a clear vision for his future. He'd write to each manager and decline and then continue working as before, but with a renewed sense of purpose. He yanked open the desk drawer, scrabbled the letters into a haphazard mess and shoved them inside. Nobody need ever know about the lure of the offers.

Chapter Nineteen

The morning sun warmed her back as she puttered about her garden the next day. Cassie hummed a ditty while she inspected the results of her labor. Plump red and yellow tomatoes, firm green cucumbers, and her white potatoes all ready to harvest. She pulled a basket off the stack she'd carried out from the work shed, dropped it to the ground, and started gently tugging the tomatoes from the vines.

Knowing she had special abilities made her anxious to learn more about using them. What could she do with her voice? What had she been doing without knowing? Could she control people or only influence them? What about animals? Questions swirled through her thoughts as she plucked tomatoes and put them into the basket.

"Morning, Cassandra." Sheridan stepped into her garden and leaned against the fence.

"Good morning." She tossed him a smile as she continued her work. "What brings you out here?"

"I needed some air between rushes." He sounded weary as he perused the rear of the inn, staring at the activity of the stable boys working and the guests relaxing on the porch with a cup of coffee. "Beautiful day to be working outside."

"Before it gets too hot." She wiped her hands on her gardening smock. "I try to avoid gardening in the afternoons during the summer."

"Many folks don't get to choose when they work." Sheridan continued to look around the yard and up at the foothills, anywhere but at her. "Even if they be sick or tired."

A slight frown creased his forehead. She sensed his reluctance to say more but underneath his hesitation was sadness and grief. She pressed her lips together as she studied his expression. He was referring to slaves and his own past. She moved to stand in front of him, peering up at his dark eyes when he finally lowered his gaze to meet hers.

"I understand. I wish it were different. I wish I could wave a magic wand and make slavery end. But I can't." She laid her fingers on his crossed arms. "One day it will end. It has to."

"Maybe, but not until white men don't profit from the system." He glanced at her hand on his arm. "Not everyone sees black folk as people like you and your family do. To them others, we're not human beings."

"I don't know how they can't see you as a person, a man." She gently squeezed his muscular arm and then lifted her hand.

"I don't pretend to know their way of thinking. I just know I don't agree with their views. Breaking up families for their own gain just ain't right."

She wondered if her pa had found Sheridan's wife or sons but refrained from mentioning her efforts to try to reunite the family. Or at least to know if they were alive or dead. She'd start with that and then see what more could be done. Perhaps her pa could do like he did for Sheridan and pay for Pansy and the boys and then set them free. If they could be found.

"Good thing you work here then." She tried to put a

lighter note into her voice to see if she could maybe lighten his mood. "I am glad you've stayed. I don't know what we'd do without you."

"You'd get by, especially now that your brother is here." Sheridan's frown disappeared as he looked at her. "Giles has brought some happiness to you."

"I've missed him, so yes, I'm glad he's home and going to stick around." She picked another basket off the pile and carried it to the row of cucumbers. "We'd been close before he moved away despite the difference in our ages. I didn't know he blamed himself for the family breaking up like it did."

Perhaps her mother's death might serve to reunite at least part of the family. What could her brothers do? Were they aware of a change in themselves? When would they notice? More questions surrounding her mother's revelation. She longed to see the look on their faces when they discovered their special abilities. Mayhap they already had found new capabilities, unexplained and surprising. She smiled at the imagined reaction to the discoveries they might experience. Sliding a paring knife from her apron pocket, she sliced through the stems and laid the cucumbers into the basket.

"Why did he blame himself?" Sheridan draped one arm over a fence post.

"He didn't fully understand what had happened back when we were younger. I could have told him not to feel guilty about it since he was but a youngster when our cousin died. It couldn't have been entirely his fault. Any more than it's your fault that you're not with yours."

"I had no say in what happened to Pansy, George, and James, but it was my fault in a sense." He gripped the top of the post with one large hand. "I miss them every day."

"What happened to them?" She searched his eyes, seeking understanding.

"I used to have quite a temper." He pressed his lips together, staring at her but looking inward. "I learned to control it after that day."

"What did you do?" She felt his guilt wash through him like a tsunami.

"I hit the man in the face and he fought back."

"What man?"

"The man who owned me. He demanded I do something I refused to do."

"Oh, Sheridan." The look in his eyes warned her not to ask what he'd refused to do. His guard was up. She sensed the distress and sorrow he carried as a result of his impetuous action. "How did he respond?"

"He punished me by selling my wife and kids but kept me so he could continue to torment me." His dark eyes glittered with unshed tears.

She sensed the depth of his sadness pulling him down into an abyss of despair. Worry and fear surrounding their fates. The unknowns about their health and safety. She'd never experienced such a dark feeling and had to claw her way back out of his emotions to stabilize her own. Hot tears coursed down her cheeks as guilt swept through her since she could escape the darkness but her friend could not.

"Why are you crying, Cassie?" He pulled a red handkerchief from his pocket and handed it to her. "You've got your family coming together. You should be happy."

She swiped at her cheeks and sniffled. Swallowed the lump in her throat and handed him the handkerchief. "I wasn't aware of how painful being separated from your wife and sons is for you. I'm so, so sorry."

"Thank you. I wish there was something I could do."

Smiling softly, he shoved the rag into his pocket. "You're my friend and you help me in the kitchen. That's something."

"I wish I could do more." She wrapped her arms around her waist and aimed a frown at him. "You deserve to be happy, too."

"I'm fine. You needn't worry about me." He turned to leave, striding to the gate. "I've got to start dinner. See you later?"

"I'll be there in a little while to help."

He acknowledged her words with a wave as he strode away. She looked down at the half-filled basket of cucumbers and sighed. Her feelings of guilt surrounding her mother's death paled in comparison to the pain Sheridan endured. Even Giles' actions didn't equal or surpass how her friend felt daily regarding the fate of his family. Not knowing gnawed his insides into a bloody pulp. Colored his every thought and action. He'd changed into a much meeker person as a direct result of his hot temper and how it had impacted those he loved. He didn't send his family away like her parents had but they still ended up forced apart.

Being his friend and helper would have to serve for now, but someday she'd find a way to remedy the situation. She couldn't let him suffer forever.

Later that afternoon, Cassie sat by her doll's house in the parlor. She'd sewn some rugs to put down on the floors, made from a worn out favorite blouse and apron. Placing them in the rooms, she hummed a merry tune. Over time she'd furnish her little house as she'd once imagined. Even though marriage may remain a dream for now, she still held fond ideas for her future home. She could dip into the money stashed in her room to buy some of the furniture. Some she might be able to make. Could she? She tilted her head as she considered the types of beds and chairs and tables she'd want to use. Maybe she'd try harder to make some cash so she could buy more refined miniature furniture with padded seats and finished wood. She could make little needlepointed seat covers, maybe with flowers on them. Where might she find doll's house furniture for sale? Maybe the general store in town would carry such whimsical items among their extensive offerings. Or maybe a carpenter could help her out.

The door opened and Flint strode into the room, a stack of papers in one hand. He hesitated when he spotted her sitting on the floor. "Am I interrupting?"

She laid the last dark green rug in the formal parlor and shifted to stand. "Not at all."

He dropped the papers onto a nearby table and held out a hand. She accepted his help to get to her feet, aware of his indrawn breath when she accidentally bumped into him. She met his surprised and hopeful expression with an apologetic shrug. Sensed the wave of desire and pleasure as it swept through him, tingling her fingers. An answering wave flowed up her arm and coursed through her entire body. He clasped her hand, steadying her as he searched her eyes for a moment.

She stared at his hand holding hers, her heart beating in her ears. She should pull her hand free, break off the electric contact. Only she couldn't find a shred of desire to do so. She swallowed and forced her eyes to meet his gaze. "You can let go now."

"What if I don't want to?" His eyes twinkled as he waited for her to answer his challenge.

She moistened suddenly dry lips with a swipe of her tongue. His gaze dropped to her mouth then back to meet hers. Her thudding heart picked up speed. "Then hold onto it a while longer."

He pulled her a hair closer to him, his gaze flicking between her eyes and her lips. "I want to kiss you, Cassie. May I?"

She drew in a sharp breath, not in surprise but in anticipation. His simmering desire for her proved impossible to resist. Indeed, she wanted him to kiss her as much as he wanted to. Amazing how clear her emotions were as she regarded him. Such a powerful combination defeated her silly arguments for waiting to be with him until her pa came home. She needed to ease the tension building inside with the immediate prospect of sampling his kiss again. "Yes."

"Are you sure?" He peered into her eyes, hope mingling with desire.

She grinned as she pushed up onto her toes to press her lips to his. He responded by sliding his arms around her torso to hold her close as he returned the kiss. Their lips met for several exhilarating moments.

"Stop that at once!"

Cassie jerked backward onto her heels and spun to face an angry ghost, one hand pressed to her chest. "Ma, you scared me."

Mercy had both hands on her hips in her classic angry mother pose. She glared at Flint. "I've warned you to stay away from her. And this is how you honor my request?"

"Demand is more like it." Flint stood slightly behind Cassie, legs braced apart as he met the agitated spirit. "You shouldn't be spying on us. It's rude."

Mercy floated close to him and shook her finger in his face. "I may be dead but I can still stop this thing between you two."

Cassie shook her head at her mother. "It was just a kiss, Ma. Nothing more."

"'Just a kiss' she says." Mercy's rage flickered around her as she turned her glare to her daughter. "You wanton creature. I raised you better than to act in such a slatternly way."

Anger flushed heat into Cassie's cheeks. "I don't think you get to have a say any longer. Not after all the secrets you've kept from me. I'll make my own decisions as to how I behave." She flashed a smile at Flint and then addressed her mother. "And who I'll allow to court me."

"You little hussy. You should be ashamed." Mercy trembled as she drifted a few feet away from her.

"Stop calling me names. It's beneath you. Just go back to wherever you hide most of the time." Cassie crossed her arms over her heaving chest. "I don't want talk to you right now."

"Well, I never—"

"Go!" Cassie flung her arm out, pointing toward the door. She huffed at her foolishness. Like her mother used doors anymore. She dropped her arm back to grab hold of her waist. "Just be gone."

"We're not finished with this so don't think we are." Mercy shimmered and then vanished without another word.

Cassie looked at Flint with a long sigh, releasing the dregs of anger at her mother's hurtful words. She met his worried gaze. "What?"

"Two things." He help up two fingers. "First, did you mean what you said about courting you?"

"Yes. If you still want to." She pulled one of his fingers down. "Do you?"

"I do indeed." He clasped her shoulders to draw her closer and then kissed her lightly on the mouth. "So we're a couple now, right? You're mine?"

"I'd like that very much." She searched his shining eyes while her lips tingled from his kiss. She'd made her choice and anticipated a long span of time to get to know him even better. "What's the other thing?"

"What did you mean by secrets?"

"Oh, that." So much had transpired in a short period of time she'd forgotten to tell him her news. "Ma kept some pretty big ones all these years. Several, in fact."

"Are you going to tell me?"

"Do you really want to know?" Sharing the surprising revelations with Flint seemed like the right thing to do, especially after the searing kiss they'd shared. Since she agreed to be in a relationship with him, he deserved to know the truth. To understand the kind of woman, or witch, she was.

"I wouldn't have asked if I didn't." He squeezed her upper arms and bent his head to peer into her eyes. "You can tell me anything."

She slowly scanned the room, looking to see if her mother lingered in some corner. "Well, if you really want to know... First, I come from a family of witches and wizards."

"Witches and wizards?" His eyes widened as he searched her eyes, his grip on her arms tightening.

"And... I'm an empath and a siren, apparently." His expression slid into shock and disbelief tinged with wariness. "My reaction exactly."

"A siren?" He gripped her arms tighter though not enough to hurt. "What do you mean?"

"I can sense you're confused and even a bit afraid of me right now." She stepped closer and he flinched back. "See? But you don't need to be afraid of me. I won't hurt you. I like you. More than a little, in fact."

"And the siren part?" He eased the pressure of his fingers on her flesh.

"When I sing, how I'm feeling flows out to affect others. At least that's what I think happens." She sensed his fear lessen which put her more at ease as well. "I don't know if I can control that or how to do so, exactly. Not yet."

"Then you could hurt someone without knowing it." His brow furrowed. "You need to be careful."

"I am trying to be cautious both in how and when I use my newfound abilities. Never fear."

"What other secrets did she keep?"

"Not just her, but my pa as well recently told me in a letter about his brothers and sisters in Georgia. All of whom he's never spoken about before."

"That's incredible. Why wouldn't he have told you about his family?"

"Good question. But that aside…" She arched a brow at him with a smile forming on her lips. "Why did you come to find me?"

"With all the commotion, I nearly forgot. You've a letter." He crossed to the table and retrieved the stack of newspapers and mail. He flipped through the short stack until he found the right one. "Looks like it's from one of your brothers."

"Good." She quickly opened the letter, scanning the contents.

August 9, 1821
Washington, Territory of Columbia

Dear Cassie,

I was surprised to receive your brief note. I wrestled with my response to your request to come to Alabama. My job here as aide to Senator Thompson is demanding on my time and attention. While I'd intended to refuse your request, he told me that I should take the time to travel in order to fulfill my familial obligations. Therefore, I have made the appropriate arrangements and will be following this letter in a day or two.

Your obedient servant, etc.

Abram Fairhope

"Well, he's coming." She grinned at Flint, pleased with Abram's imminent arrival.

"Not willingly." Flint pointed at the letter in Cassie's hand. "Under orders, apparently."

"I'm glad his boss insisted." She read the letter again as joy filled her heart and soul. "He's coming."

"You didn't mention he works as an aide to a senator. I wonder if he knows Percy Graham." Flint pointed to the letter in her hand. "That could be a grand connection for the inn."

"I don't know but you'll be able to ask him in a few days." She shrugged lightly as happiness flooded her heart. It had been so long since she'd seen Abram. He most likely had changed over the years, but how much?

"If he does, he may be able to help prepare for the esteemed man's arrival so we can provide him with specialized offerings of food and drink as well as linens and entertainment. Whatever it will take to ensure his comfort and pleasure." Flint grinned, his eyes twinkling. "I can't wait to meet Abram even if he's rather put out about making the trip."

"That's just his way." She waved the paper with gusto, excitement like lightning flashing through her. "He's on his way. I can't wait to see him after all these years."

"Wait until he finds out about your powers." Flint shook his head as he peered at her, his smile widening. "I imagine he'll be quite taken aback to learn of his family's history."

"And Giles' powers, too." She bobbed her head.

He blinked at her from wide eyes. "Does that mean all of your brothers have some special powers?"

"I do believe so. We won't know for certain until they come. If the others are coming." At least two of her brothers would once again have the chance to be brothers. She could only imagine what it must have been like for the four boys to never see each other for years. They'd been so close before. Hopefully, her other two brothers, Daniel and Silas, would write to her soon and inform her of their plans, whatever they may be. "I have to tell Giles that Abram will be here soon."

"What kind of ability does Giles have?" Flint gathered the rest of the papers with a rustle and tap.

"His immense strength makes him the family's Guardian." She folded the letter and tucked it into her skirt pocket. "We shall see what Abram's is when he gets here in a few days."

"I'm not sure I want to know." He firmed his lips as he regarded her for several seconds in silence. "Things may get very interesting around here."

"In what way?" His lips twitched as she perused his features, her gaze finally landing on his tempting mouth.

"With so many unknowns surrounding your family and your special talents, it's rather hard to predict." He watched her as she eased toward him, the pupils of his eyes dilating with each step she took.

"I believe you're right." She smirked up at him when she finally halted inches from his chest. "Let's start the discovery of interesting times with another kiss."

Flint scanned the parlor in a quick sweep. Then he smiled at her as he pulled her into a strong embrace and lowered his mouth to hers. "Happy to oblige, sweetheart."

Chapter Twenty

"Giles, there you are."

He'd needed some alone time, to sit quietly and let his mind wander instead of worrying about anything. The quiet parlor had proven empty so he'd settled onto the couch by the front window. So much for privacy. He glanced up from the magazine announcing the latest innovations in weaponry to address his mother's distraught ghost. "What's the matter?"

"Flint Hamilton was kissing Cassandra!" Mercy propped her fists on her ghostly hips, a frown drawing down her brows. "I won't have it."

"She's a grown woman and knows her own mind." Giles resumed perusing the features of the pistols in the publication. "You needn't worry."

"She's a girl and she doesn't understand what she's doing." Mercy moved closer with a nearly imperceptible swish of her long, light-blue skirts. "You promised to protect her and he's a threat, I tell you."

He sighed and laid aside the magazine he'd finally found time to read. "No, he's not. I've spoken to him about Cassie and her feelings. He's a gentleman, Mama, he won't overstep where she doesn't want him to. So if he was kissing her, then she must have wanted it."

Mercy huffed and crossed her arms. "I don't want him touching her."

"It's not your decision any longer." He studied her for several beats and then rose to his feet. "I do have a question for you, though."

Mercy's frown deepened. "I doubt I have any answers."

"Let's find out, shall we?" He crossed his arms to mirror her posture. "On one of the keys is an owl symbol. Do you remember it?"

She rolled her eyes at him with a smirk on her mouth. "Of course. They're my keys."

"Is there a reason for the symbol on the key?" He inspected every nuance to her shifting features, the flash of suspicion followed by chariness and then defiance.

"Why do you ask?" She drifted a foot or two away.

"I have my reasons. Please answer me." Using his manners might score him enough points to win her cooperation. She'd tensed with his first question, he could only imagine how she would react to his more pointed ones.

She drew in a longer breath, held it for a span of heart beats, and then let it out slowly. "It's from the Fairhope family crest, if you must know."

He nodded, thinking fast as to how to ask the more burning question in his heart. "So Papa gave you the key?"

"No, his sister Scarlet fashioned it for me. Sent it along with the lock hardware from Georgia when we moved here."

"His sister?" Giles shifted his weight to rest on one leg, striving to appear casual and at ease despite his pounding heart and sweaty palms. "Why would she do that?"

"She knows how much I value my privacy and the family heirlooms. It was her gift to me." Mercy's tone dripped with reluctance. She dropped her crossed arms to clasp her hands in front of her chest. "What is this about, son? You're scaring me."

"Why am I scaring you?" He could see concern etched on her face as she briefly chewed her bottom lip. "I just want to know if there's a meaning to the symbol."

Mercy visibly relaxed at his comment. "I've told you. It's from the family crest and represents protection of their own."

"How does an owl demonstrate that?" He rubbed a hand over his sore forehead, all the mystery and secrecy stirring the beginning of a headache.

"An owl is a guardian, much like you. For centuries, it's been revered as the guardian of the dead." Mercy smiled limply at him. "Like me, I guess."

"But you wanted me to guard Cassie who's living." He pressed his temple to ease the throbbing. "You want me to do both?"

"No, just protect your sister." Mercy shrugged and drifted closer. "The other thing owls are known for is their wisdom. You have much wisdom to share with her, especially about men and the dangers they pose to innocent girls."

"I'm not feeling so wise at the moment." He let his fingers fall from rubbing his head. "One more thing."

"Yes?" Mercy shimmered, as if preparing to disappear before he could even ask the question.

"I saw the flying owl symbol in the cave where those villains had been hiding out." His comment set his mother's ghost to trembling. She wrapped her arms about her waist, hugging tightly.

"Oh…" Mercy's image began to dissolve.

"No, don't go, Mama." He reached out a hand toward her, as if he could grab hold and keep her in the room. "Why could I see it and nobody else?"

She swallowed hard, her eyes darting away and back to stare at him. "I-I can't explain that."

"Can't, or won't?" He stepped toward the shimmering ghost.

"I'm going a little insane trying to understand what it means. Tell me what you know."

"I only know that such an event can only happen to a Guardian." She faded as she spoke, slowly vanishing before his eyes. "Your father can explain more when he comes home."

"Wait! Papa knows?" He leapt toward where his mother's ghost had appeared. "I need to know."

But she was gone.

A day later, Giles picked out a tune on his guitar, sitting on the front porch watching the comings and goings on a steamy midweek afternoon. He had much to contemplate, to figure out how best to proceed when the path forward remained obscured with uncertainty. He stopped in mid-strum when he spotted Deputy Barney Parker galloping up the carriageway. Setting aside the instrument, he hurried down the steps to meet him as he halted and dismounted.

"What's wrong?" Giles slipped his thumbs into his pockets.

"Trouble." Barney looped the reins of his sweaty bay horse to the rail and followed Giles back onto the porch and the shade.

"Have a seat and tell me what kind of trouble you mean."

Barney took off his hat and rubbed a sleeved arm over his sweaty brow. "Flint needs to hear this, too."

"He's inside."

"We need to find him, if you don't mind."

"Not at all. This way." Giles led Barney into the dining room, hesitating at the open door to scan the room for Flint. "Over there with Mr. Baker and his daughter."

"Let's go." Barney motioned toward the group seated at a table by a window on the far side of the room. "They need to be warned as well."

Giles shot him an inquiring look and then quickened his pace. Cassie waited on a family at a table by the fireplace. Giles invited her to join him with a lift and tilt of his head. She finished placing the plates on the table before making her way toward the Bakers' table. Haley cast him a small smile as he drew closer. A fine young lady from all appearances. One he'd like to become better acquainted with now that he'd decided to stay in the Huntsville area. He tipped his hat to her and kept walking.

He stopped by Flint's elbow and cleared his throat, drawing Flint's attention. "Hey, Barney needs to talk to you." Giles gestured to the deputy. "Seems important."

"What is it?" Flint peered at the large man beside Giles.

"You all need to take some extra precautions. I've been investigating a rash of deaths, possibly murders, in this region." Barney slid his gaze over the people seated around the table. "Lock your doors at night and know where your friends and family members are."

Cassie stared at Barney, her fingers clutching the tray in her hands. "More killings? Why?"

The deputy grimaced as he regarded her for a moment. "I'm working on that."

"Any clue as to who might be doing this heinous act?" Every protective instinct Giles possessed stood at attention, waiting for any hint to guide him in what he needed to do to defend his family and friends as well as the guests at the inn.

"Not yet. All I know is that the people who've been killed all seemed to be reclusive and very private, according to their neighbors."

"How were they discovered if they're so reclusive?" John squinted at Barney, one hand resting beside the knife on the table in front of him. "They wouldn't have many visitors, would they?"

Cassie tensed beside Giles. He frowned at her and then followed the direction of her gaze to land on John. What had she sensed?

"You're right, sir. A neighbor stumbled upon the body in most instances. Like the one Flint discovered a while back." Barney rested his hand on the pistol at his hip. "Lying a ways from the road leading to their house, like they'd been surprised on the way home."

Giles looked at Haley sitting quietly, somberly listening to the discussion, her eyes shuttered and dark. He recalled her warning. Was there a connection? He met Barney's serious gaze. "Thanks for the word of caution. We'll take appropriate actions to ensure nobody here is harmed."

John relaxed in his seat, dropping his hand to rest on his thigh. "I shouldn't think you'd have anything to worry about here. What with all the people coming and going all the time, I mean."

"I, for one, don't feel safe." Cassie aimed wide eyes at Giles, a hand pressed to the base of her throat. "We've already had one murder."

A chill settled on his shoulders at the fear shining in his sister's eyes. He laid a hand on her shoulder. "I won't let anything happen to you."

"Bad things happen to good people." Haley shifted in her seat and then shrugged. "It's the way of the world."

"Don't be so cynical, my dear." John tapped a finger on the table. "It's unbecoming."

"Haley's right, though." Giles regarded the young woman as he considered ways to safeguard the property. Not just the inn. The entire county lay under threat of an attack at any time. He glanced at John. "You should maybe go on home and take precautions. You wouldn't want anything to happen to your daughter on the road."

John shrugged dismissively. "I don't believe these are random killings. As I have no enemies, I think we'll be fine."

Giles rounded on the man. "Don't be so cavalier with your lovely daughter's life, sir."

John reared back in his seat, palms flat on the table top. "How dare you?"

A flash of annoyance ripped through his chest. "How dare you act as if her well-being centered on your reputation."

"My standing in the community is high enough to—"

"To get you killed. Damn it, man, don't you see? Anyone could be targeted. Right, deputy?"

Barney nodded grimly. "Until we know what or who is behind these deaths, you're right."

"I still say I have nothing to fear, and neither does my family, since we have no enemies." John pushed back his chair and stood, dropping his napkin on the table. "And watch your language in front of my daughter, sir."

Giles grimaced at him and then half bowed to Haley. "My apologies."

She nodded with her lips pursed, struggling apparently to not make matters worse by smiling or laughing at his discomfiture. He appreciated her efforts with a slight nod and then turned his attention back to the disturbing conversation.

"Mercy Fairhope hadn't any enemies either and she's dead." Barney shifted his weight to the other leg and pinned his gaze on John. "I advise you to take care with your family and property."

Flint crossed his arms over his chest. "I think it's safe to say everyone needs to be aware. Keep your eyes open and report anything out of the ordinary."

Haley laid her napkin on the table and also stood. She smiled softly at Giles, an echo of her previous conversation with him reflected in her eyes. "Thank you for your concern. I trust my father will ensure my safety as well as that of my mother and everyone on the plantation."

The lilt of her melodic voice enthralled his senses, effectively calming his anxiety on her behalf. "I wish you well, miss. I'd hate to see harm come to your gentle person."

"That's sweet of you." Her smile widened as she sidled closer to her father. "We should be on our way."

His heart fell at the thought of her leaving, taking her enchanting features out of his sight. He suppressed an unexpected desire to escort her home with a sigh. "Travel safely."

"I'm sure we'll see you again in a few days." Her eyes sparkled with humor. "Never fear, sir, we shall most definitely meet again."

John studied Giles for several moments, one eyebrow slowly lifting. "I suggest *you* stay close to home, understood?"

Giles glanced at Haley's laughing eyes and then back to John's challenge. The man understood more than Giles had given him credit for. Giles had indeed started to contemplate excuses for journeying to the neighboring plantation to ensure the pretty girl remained safely at home. "Yes, sir."

John picked up his top hat from the table and tamped it onto his head. "Very well. Good day to you all."

Haley followed her father out of the dining room, the gentle sway of her hips beneath the fine fabric of her dress captivating. Giles swallowed hard. Smitten, that's what he was.

Cassie swatted him with her hand. "What are you doing? Flirting with Haley Baker?"

Her knowing eyes laughed at his infatuation with the girl. "Of course not."

"'Of course not,' he says." Flint chuckled and started clearing the vacated table. "Why don't I believe you…?"

"Because you've a keen sense of truth." Barney donned his hat with a grin on his lips. "I've got to go, too. Be careful."

"I'll make sure of it." Giles squared his wide shoulders. "I'm not going anywhere. Neither are Zander and Matt."

"Between all of us, the inn and everyone on the property will be safe and secure." Flint stacked the plates, the ring of porcelain punctuating his words.

"I sure hope so." Cassie held out the tray for Flint to deposit the dirty dishes. "I don't know what Ma's afraid of but it wasn't a rash of mysterious killings. Now we've got more trouble than we bargained for."

Giles rested his fists on his hips, scanning the other guests in the dining room continuing with their conversations, all while unaware of the danger lurking in the shadows. "You don't need to worry, Cassie. Everything is under control."

She paused, half turned away ready to carry the tray into the kitchen. "For now. But we don't know what is coming, or when it will arrive." Without another word, she carried the tray across the room.

She was right. But he was ready for whatever or whoever threatened to harm a hair on her pretty little head.

Chapter Twenty-one

Later that afternoon, a sturdy wagon pulled by a team of dapple gray draft horses lumbered to a halt in front of the inn. The noise alerted Giles to a stranger arriving. He hurried to the front porch to see a man hop lithely down from the driver's seat. Flint soon appeared beside Giles, wiping his hands on a towel as he squinted into the bright sunlight bathing the vehicle and animals. Pickles and Red sniffed around the wheels while Cocoa greeted the lead horse with a touch of noses. Giles chuckled at the sight then turned his attention to the visitor. The brawny man strode to the bottom of the steps and pushed his wide-brimmed hat back on his head.

"Good afternoon. Do you know where I can find a Mr. Flint Hamilton?"

Flint flipped the towel over his shoulder. "I'm Flint Hamilton. How can I help you?"

"Name's Sloan, the stone mason. I've got the headstone you ordered." He gestured to the wagon where his horses twitched and shook their manes to shoo flies from their sensitive skin. "Where do you want it?"

"Round back is the cemetery. How heavy is it?" Flint stepped down to the carriageway.

Giles lingered on the porch, reluctant to descend and view the carved stone. Doing so would make it all very real in a way he'd been able to avoid. Until now.

Sloan tossed back a gray tarp in the bed of the wagon. "A couple strong men could carry it. Or if you have a wheelbarrow that'll work too."

From where Giles hesitated, he could barely see the edge of a dark gray marble stone in the wagon bed. The sun glinted off the polished surface. Standing in the shadows seemed downright cowardly. Swallowing the knot in his throat, he sauntered down the steps to peer over the side of the wagon.

"I'll get the barrow. Just a minute." Flint barely glanced at Giles before he dogtrotted toward the barn.

Alone with the mason, Giles squared his shoulders. He could do this. He walked around to the end of the wagon to read the inscription.

Mercy
Wife of
Reginald Fairhope
Born Dec 25, 1781
Died July 14, 1821
Aged 39 Y's, 6 Mo. & 19 D.

Short and simple. Then why did his heart ache? "Looks right to me."

Sloan pulled his hat brim down and glanced at Giles. "Did you write it?"

Giles gripped the side of the wagon, pretending to inspect the quality of the carving of the letters. Held on to keep his composure in the face of the grim reminder of his mother's death. "She is my mother."

Sloan lowered his brows. "Is? She's still alive and you bought her a headstone?"

Giles shook his head and stepped back from looking into the wagon. "She was murdered last month. Buried out back in the cemetery, the only grave."

"My condolences on your loss, son." Sloan removed his hat and held it in both hands in front of his chest. "That's a terrible way to lose your mother."

"Thank you. You've done a fine job on that stone." Even if it made him queasy to look at the glossy memorial of his mother's life and death.

Sloan patted his hat back into place on his brown hair and clambered into the bed of the wagon. "I appreciate that. It's important to show respect and reverence to our loved ones."

Flint trundled the wheelbarrow from the side of the stable over to the rear of the wagon. Giles climbed into the wagon and helped Sloan use the tarp beneath the heavy stone to slide the slab closer to the edge of the tailgate. Flint positioned the barrow to receive the load.

"Hang on, we'll help you." Zander jogged over to one side while Matt went to the other.

Having their help felt as natural as rain. They seemed to know when they were needed and appeared out of nowhere, ready to pitch in and get whatever job done. Yet again, Giles was glad they chose to stay with him.

Zander guided the stone toward the wheelbarrow. When the stone touched the front of the barrow, the weight of it nearly toppled it over. Flint struggled to right the barrow with Matt's strong hands steadying it. Between the four of them, they wrestled the stone carefully into the wheelbarrow. Giles and Sloan jumped out of the wagon.

"Thanks, guys. That was heavier than I thought it would be." Giles grinned at the group of sweating men, all staring obstinately at the recalcitrant stone. Reluctance settled on their shoulders. The stone turned out to be much heavier than anticipated, so they needed a moment to recover from the exertion. He didn't blame them but he didn't require a break before transporting it to the cemetery. "Let me move it around back."

Flint wiped his brow with one arm, a slow smirk spreading on his lips. "Fine with me."

"I'll get a shovel and meet you there." Zander waited for Giles to nod his agreement and then headed for the tool shed, his long strides quickly traversing the distance to the small building beside the barn.

"What do you want us to do?" Matt dusted his hands off and then slipped them into his pockets.

Sloan closed the tailgate with a loud thud. "I'm done here, so I'll wish you a good day." He tipped his hat and moved to climb up to the driver's seat.

"Thank you, sir." Flint saluted the man and then turned to Giles. "You don't need help with installing that, do you?"

Need? No. But the idea of being at his mother's grave rattled his nerves. He'd managed to talk with her by convincing himself she wasn't really dead. Something he couldn't do while digging in the dirt where she was buried. "I wouldn't mind your help if you have time."

Flint studied him for a long moment and then nodded once. "We can do that. Right, Matt?"

"Sure." Matt started walking toward the side of the inn.

"Thanks, Flint. I appreciate it." Giles grasped the handles and trundled the wheelbarrow in the same path Matt chose. He followed him around the end and to the back of the building, across the grassy yard to the closed cemetery gate. Matt waited at one side of the barrier. Giles rolled the stone closer and closer until finally he set the wheelbarrow down with a grunt in front of the gate.

"That's impressive." Flint gestured at the stone resting in the small vehicle. "That stone is downright heavy and you made it look easy."

Giles stared at the closed gate and swallowed. "Let's get this over with."

Matt crossed to the gate and opened the latch. Giles grabbed the handles and rolled the stone inside the fenced area, settling the stone near the head of the mound of dirt marking the gravesite. Flint and Zander joined him and Matt.

"What now?" Flint rested his palms on his hips.

Giles regarded Zander and the shovel propped on his shoulder. "We need a hole somewhat larger than the base of the headstone." He held out a hand to take the shovel but Zander shook his head.

"I'll do it." Zander stuck the shovel into the ground and started digging.

Relief eased the tension in Giles' entire back. Digging so near where his mother's body lay in the ground held no appeal. The rustle of a woman's skirts set his pulse racing. He looked around, afraid he'd see his mother's ghost. But it was only Cassie. He let out a pent up breath. She sauntered closer to stand beside him, laying a hand on his crossed arms. The touch comforted him as they stood side by side to witness the steps necessary for the installation of the headstone with the inscription they'd devised together.

"That should suit." Zander propped his hands on the shovel handle.

"I believe so. It'll take all of us to wrangle that stone in place." Giles smiled at his sister before he unfolded his arms, Cassie's hand falling away.

He moved to grip one corner of the rectangular headstone. The other men shuffled around to take up positions on opposite sides. "Grab a corner and we'll lift on three."

Cassie moved out of the way, standing at the foot of the grave with her fingers interlocked in front of her skirts. "Careful."

"Ready?" Giles skimmed the others' nods. "One... two...three."

The air filled with grunts and scuffling feet as they carried it the few feet to place one end in the hole. Giles kept a hand on the wobbling marker while Matt snatched up the discarded shovel to start filling in the dirt to stabilize the slab.

Cassie gasped. "Wait! It's backwards."

"What?" Giles bent over to check and sure enough they'd inserted it with the inscription facing away from the grave. "Damn."

Matt sighed and started scooping the loose dirt away.

Giles nodded at Zander. "All right, help me turn it around."

"Once was bad enough." Zander huffed a mirthless chuckle but took hold of the marble.

They lifted and turned the stone and then plunked it back down. Matt filled the hole with dirt while Flint stomped down the soil to secure the stone in its upright position. As Giles held the stone steady, he glanced over at Cassie and froze.

Behind her, his mother stood, a soft smile on her lips. When Mercy noticed his attention on her, she nodded. He swallowed his initial surprise and grinned back at her, slowly realizing he was glad she approved of the new marker even if having her ghost at the grave made him distinctly uneasy. Now if only she'd rest in peace… What would it take for her to be able to do so?

The need for his guardianship over his sister surely played a part in her restlessness. If his mama knew what the precise danger to Cassie might be, she'd not even hinted at it when she'd revealed their special abilities. Or had she? Her comments regarding her father and sisters being dark witches suddenly linked with Hope's letter wanting to do what their father had desired. Which was what? How big of a threat those hopes and desires might prove to the family worried him.

"How's that?" Matt held the shovel in one hand as he peered at Giles.

Giles shook off his ponderings and attempted to wiggle the stone but it held firm. "That'll do."

When he looked back at Cassie, she stood solemnly gazing at him. But she was alone. He looked around but saw no sign of his mother.

"You all right?" Zander lifted a brow at him.

"Yes." He met Zander's questioning gaze and shrugged. The stone was set. His mother seemed pleased. "I guess we're done here."

Several days later, Cassie hummed to herself while she used a fine brush and oils to create some miniature portraits to hang on the walls in her doll's house. The parlor windows and door were all open to allow any hint of a breeze to waft inside. From her seat by the fireplace, the sounds of a normal day reached her ears. The occasional moo of a cow, the rattle of a wagon pulled by rhythmic pounding hooves, the chirp of the birds. The scents of manure from the pig pen, lye from the laundry, and of the hot sun baking the wooden structures tickled her nose. Booted steps on the porch alerted her to someone approaching. She paused, waiting to see if the person planned to interrupt her painting.

"There you are." Flint surged into the room, bringing life and energy in with him. He carried a stack of mail in one hand. "You've a letter."

"Lovely. I enjoy getting mail." Let it be from one of her brothers. Any of them. She set aside the paint brush and held out her hand to accept the letter he offered. "Thanks."

He bent to kiss her briefly and she accepted his attention with joy. She perused the outer markings of the letter with anxiety in her core. Gramercy. "It's from my aunt. I want Giles to be here when I read it."

"I just passed him on the porch, heading for the stable. Hold on a minute." Flint spun around, dropped the stack on the casual table between two chairs, and hurried out of the room.

Cassie inspected the paper in her hands. How had her aunts received the news of their sister's demise? She turned over the letter, inspecting it for any other markings or notations but discovered none.

"In here." Flint returned with Giles in tow. "Found him."

Giles pulled off his hat and dropped it on the seat of a chair. "What did you need?"

She waved the letter in the air. "I wanted you here when I open this. I'm nervous about how our aunts may have reacted to the news of their sister's murder."

"Do you want me to stay?" Flint picked up the mail from the table. "I can go on about my business if you don't need me."

Whatever the letter contained, it would likely impact all of them, one way or another. "Yes, please, stay. This may be important for you to know, too."

"Very well." Flint laid the stack back on the table and then sat down on a chair. "I'm ready when you are."

Giles moved his hat to hang on the back of the other chair, then sat down. "Go on. Open it."

She stared at the folded paper for several moments. Then carefully broke the seal on the back and smoothed out the single page on her lap. She looked at Flint, glad he'd stayed to provide emotional support. Then she glanced to her brother and his stalwart expression. She lifted the page with tense fingers.

Monday, August 13, 1821
Montgomery, Alabama

My dear Cassandra,

I'm in receipt of your recent letter with such sad news. Charity and I were very upset to learn of our sister's death. We have decided it's in your best interest for us to pay you a visit in the near future. We want to see for ourselves the situation you have found yourself in. Family must join forces at a time like this, so once we have made the appropriate arrangements here, we shall journey to you. I will write again once we have a plan in place.

In the meantime, I want to express my heartfelt desire to reconnect as family after such a long time apart. I'm certain Mercy wouldn't object to our coming together under these extreme hardships.

I'll write more soon.

Sincerely,

Hope Hawkins

"No, I do not approve." Mercy materialized at Cassie's elbow. "Not at all."

With a small shriek of surprise, Cassie jolted back in her seat. "Don't do that, Ma."

Mercy paced to the fireplace and spun around to glare at the offending letter. "I didn't mean to alarm you. But you cannot let that witch anywhere near here."

Giles leaned forward to peer at Mercy. "Why?"

Cassie scowled at her ma. Again with the fear and animosity toward her sisters. "Yes, why?"

Mercy paused in her agitated pacing. "You do not want to be associated with my sisters. No good will come of it."

"Because they're dark witches?" Cassie waved a hand as if shooing flies. "That doesn't explain what you're afraid of."

"I know them. They want you, Cassie." She chewed her lower ghostly lip for a moment.

A cold wave of shock washed through her gut. "Me? Why?"

"Because they can't have me." Mercy pinned her with a terrified gaze, eyes squinched with fear and furrows between her brows. "They need a third witch to join with them to accomplish their dark purposes. They need you to increase their power to its greatest heights."

"That's what you're afraid of." Cassie sat up straight, glaring at her mother. "You think I'm a dark witch like them? You really do not know me, do you?"

Flint inhaled sharply from his silent perch. Cassie had never seen him look so uncomfortable with a conversation. Giles also seemed wary and alert. Her mother was plain terrified by the idea of her sisters visiting.

"I know you are still very young and inexperienced. You don't know yourself yet. My dear, you just learned you're a witch. If you let them come, they will take advantage of that naiveté. They'll strive to make you over into the kind of witch that serves their aims." Mercy drifted closer to Cassie, her expression serious and scared. "You may not have any choice."

Flint stood and strode to stand behind Cassie's chair. "I won't let them force her into anything she doesn't want to do. You have my word."

Mercy rolled her eyes at him as she crossed her arms. "You? I know how useful you are to my daughter. You're not."

Flint huffed in frustration.

Giles pushed to his feet and walked over to address Mercy directly. "I'm her Guardian. I give you my word to protect her from any threat. Flint as well as Zander and Matt have all agreed. And Abram is on his way."

"Abram is coming?" Mercy's eyebrows rose in perfect arches over her suddenly smiling eyes. "When?"

"I expect any day now." Cassie folded the letter and laid

it on the small table at her side. "When he gets here, you'll need to tell him all about his ability, whatever it is, and about all of the family you and Pa never told us about."

Mercy's smile wilted away as she sank closer to the floor. "Everything?"

"Of course." Certainty rang in his voice. Giles stood and strode over to lean on the mantel as he perused the others in the room. "He'll need to know in order to be prepared to help us defend Cassie."

Cassie looked from one to the other, sensing the fear, the concern, the terror as well as the love shared between them. Knowing how everyone actually felt gave her an advantage. She had yet to fully grasp the ways she might use the knowledge but she'd slowly been refining her ability to tune in and tune out from others' emotions. Erecting an emotional barrier of her own to protect her composure and comportment. She snuck a peek at Flint, standing behind her. Flint rested his hands on her shoulders, and she put one hand on his.

"We're a family, Mercy." Flint squeezed Cassie's shoulders and kissed the top of her head. "All of us here at the inn. You need to trust us to do what's right for everyone."

"He's right, Mama." Giles stepped closer to Mercy. "Together we can face anything. And if the rest of my brothers come like Cassie has asked, then there will be more of us to protect the entire family."

Ma regarded Giles with a worried regard, then frowned at Flint, and finally dropped her concerned gaze to meet Cassie's tentative smile. "I'm afraid you all do not know what might happen if Hope and Charity do come here. Please do not permit them to do so."

"We can't stop them from making the journey if they wish to come." Cassie stood up to face her mother eye to eye. "But you can tell us what we need to do so we can prepare."

Ma searched her eyes with her own fearful ones. "I don't know. Not exactly."

"You're afraid but you don't what they're capable of?" Giles raked his fingers through his hair and released a sigh of frustration. "Maybe it's just your imagination then."

"No. It's not." Ma shook her head vehemently. "Their powers now are likely far more powerful than when I last witnessed their abilities. They were dangerous then. Believe me."

Flint moved to stand beside Cassie, slipping his arm around her waist. "We will be ready as best we can."

Cassie darted a trusting glance at his handsome face. "We're family and stronger together."

"Exactly what my sisters believe. But not for the good of mankind." Mercy shuddered and shimmered and then vanished.

Flint pulled Cassie closer against his side as Giles pivoted to peer at them. "What do you think?"

"I'm glad you summoned me, sister." Giles pressed his shoulders back and down. "Sounds like we're in for quite a time."

"Indeed, we may be. But we have each other to rely upon and figure out how to protect ourselves. Together, we'll be fine." She smiled at her brother and then Flint. Reached up and kissed his lips, happy to be with him, surrounded by his strength and love, before returning her regard to her brother. Having the two men standing with her made facing the unknown possible. With luck her other brothers would arrive shortly. She grinned at Giles. "Just wait until Abram finds out what he's been missing."

The End

Thanks so much for reading *Under Lock and Key*! The adventure is just beginning, so stay tuned for more to come in this six-book series.

To find out about new releases and upcoming appearances, please sign up for my newsletter via my website at www.bettybolte.com. I send out a monthly newsletter with book news to share with my readers, upcoming events and signings, and even a few favorite recipes, puzzles, and other doings!

I'd love to hear from you! Feel free to send me an email at betty@bettybolte.com, find me on Facebook at www.facebook.com/AuthorBettyBolte, follow me on BookBub, or connect with me on Twitter @BettyBolte.

You can always find an updated list of the titles in this series, as well as all of my other books on my website, at www.bettybolte.com/books/.

Thanks again for reading!

www.ingramcontent.com/pod-product-compliance
Lightning Source LLC
Chambersburg PA
CBHW021118110726
47900CB00007B/2237